There was a time

when the only way

to uphold justice

was to break

the law.

KEVIN COSTNER

— IS —

ROBIN HOOD
PRINCE OF THIEVES

WARNER BROS. PRESENTS

A JAMES G. ROBINSON PRESENTATION A MORGAN CREEK PRODUCTION A KEVIN REYNOLDS FILM

KEVIN COSTNER

"ROBIN HOOD: PRINCE OF THIEVES"

MORGAN FREEMAN   CHRISTIAN SLATER

ALAN RICKMAN AND MARY ELIZABETH MASTRANTONIO

MUSIC BY MICHAEL KAMEN   CO-PRODUCER MICHAEL J. KAGAN

EXECUTIVE PRODUCERS JAMES G. ROBINSON AND DAVID NICKSAY & GARY BARBER

STORY BY PEN DENSHAM   SCREENPLAY BY PEN DENSHAM & JOHN WATSON

PRODUCED BY JOHN WATSON, PEN DENSHAM AND RICHARD B. LEWIS

DIRECTED KEVIN REYNOLDS

D1464341

KEVIN COSTNER
— IS —

ROBIN HOOD
PRINCE OF THIEVES

A NOVEL BY SIMON GREEN
BASED ON THE STORY BY PEN DENSHAM
AND THE SCREENPLAY BY PEN DENSHAM
& JOHN WATSON

FANTAIL

FANTAIL BOOKS

Published by the Penguin Group
Penguin Books Ltd, 27 Wrights Lane, London W8 5TZ, England
Penguin Books USA Inc., 375 Hudson Street, New York, New York 10014, USA
Penguin Books Australia Ltd, Ringwood, Victoria, Australia
Penguin Books Canada Ltd, 10 Alcorn Avenue, Toronto, Ontario, Canada M4V 3B2
Penguin Books (NZ) Ltd, 182–190 Wairau Road, Auckland 10, New Zealand

Penguin Books Ltd, Registered Offices: Harmondsworth, Middlesex, England

First published in the USA by Berkley Books, New York 1991
First published in Great Britain by Fantail Books 1991
3 5 7 9 10 8 6 4 2

Filmset in Monophoto Times New Roman

Made and printed in Great Britain by Clays Ltd, St Ives PLC

1
JERUSALEM

Darkness fell across the desert like a hawk upon its prey, and the sinking sun splashed blood across the clouds. Shadows lengthened as light fled the land, and night closed in around Jerusalem. The crimson sun glared down on the sprawling, mud-walled city like an unblinking malevolent eye, a reminder, if one was needed, that God saw everything, even in the darkest night.

An ancient, withered figure clothed in black studied the sun from an open-mouthed minaret, and raised his voice in the howling, haunting Moslem call to prayer. All through the city, lights burned fitfully against the coming of the dark, and people surged through the narrow streets like ants in a disturbed nest. Day was done, night had come; but for some the true darkness was just beginning.

Jerusalem, in the Year of Our Lord 1194, the third year of the Third Crusade. An Arab city. A bad place to be a Christian. A worse place to be a Christian prisoner.

In the dungeons under the city, it was always night. Prisoners spent the endless hours locked up in cramped, tiny

1

cells without even the comfort of a lamp or candle. The guards carried torches on their infrequent visits, but since all too often their appearance meant a journey to the Interrogator or the Executioner, men learned to fear the light, and huddled back in the shadows whenever light filled the corridor outside their cells. Only one part of the dungeons knew light on a regular basis—the torture chamber of the Interrogator.

The torture chamber was a humid, oppressive place, with a low roof soot-blackened by the huge iron furnace that dominated the far end of the room. Long iron spikes and barbed steel hooks and blades protruded from its glowing crimson maw, ever ready for use. The room was stiflingly hot, and water ran down the pitted stone walls in sudden, darting streams. A few of the prisoners chained to the wall by the door tried to lap at the water in their thirst, but it was unbearably bitter. Just another torture, more subtle than most. Rats scuttled across the floor, and the prisoners awaiting the Interrogator's attention watched them with avid, hungry eyes. The rats kept their distance for the most part, but occasionally one would dart in to gnaw at a foot or an ankle that hadn't moved in a while.

The prisoners sat listlessly together on the bare stone floor, heads bowed as much as the looped chain round their necks would allow. Sweat ran freely down their faces, as much from fear as from the heat. They sat in silence, the time for pleas or bargains long past. Whatever they eventually said would be decided by the Interrogator. No one would come to help. No one cared what happened to them. They were scum, the lowest of the low. Cutthroats and petty criminals, politicians with powerful enemies, or perhaps just someone who happened to be in the wrong place at the wrong time, or worshipped the wrong god. All were equal now, in the eyes of the Interrogator.

Among the twenty or so dark faces, two paler faces gleamed dully in the flickering light. White men, infidels, the most hated and despised of all. Their clothes were rags, and their skin showed the filth and abuse of long imprisonment, but something in the way they held themselves set them apart from their fellow prisoners. Something that in another place and time might almost have been nobility.

Robin of Locksley and Peter Dubois had come to the East on a glorious quest, to reclaim the Holy Lands for Christendom. They lost their ideals on the endless bloody battlegrounds, where there was precious little honor or chivalry to be found, and damn all glory for the quick or the dead. And finally their luck ran out, as it had for so many others, and they were taken prisoner. Seventy-four Englishmen had been captured that day, and were dragged in chains through the streets of Jerusalem. The populace jeered and laughed, poked them with sticks and daggers, and threw stones at them. By the time they reached the dungeons under Jerusalem, seven men had died. In the hellish weeks and months that followed, the dwindling number of survivors often wondered if those seven men had been the lucky ones.

Five years passed and the Englishmen died, one by one. They died from beatings and torture and starvation, or simply through neglect. A few lost all hope and faith in the never-ending dark, and took their own lives. Robin of Locksley and Peter Dubois did not die. They bent beneath the pain and despair, but did not break. And as steel grows stronger through the tempering heat and blows, so they grew harder and more stubborn, and watched and waited for a chance to escape. Or if not that, a chance to take revenge for what had been done to them, and their friends.

Robin of Locksley was tall and wiry, held together with long strings of muscle and a grim intensity that pulled his face into a lowering scowl. He might have been handsome once, but gnawing hunger kept his features painfully gaunt, and any softness in his face or eyes had vanished long ago. He sat quietly, ignoring the heat and discomfort, his eyes following the Interrogator's every move. There was always the chance the man would grow careless or overconfident, and come just that one step too close. And then Robin would wrap his chains around the Interrogator's throat, put his knee in the man's back, and do what he had dreamed of for so many days and nights. The guards would kill him, of course, but it would be worth it.

It would never happen. The Interrogator was too professional, too experienced to make such a foolish mistake. Robin sighed silently, closed his eyes, and saw England: the wide open fields and sprawling acres of woodland. Sometimes it seemed to him that England was only a dream, and he had always been here, in the heat and the dark and the endless suffering. But despite everything, he would not give up his memories of England. They gave him strength, and the will to go on. As long as England was out there, somewhere, free and beautiful and untainted by blood and death, he could go on.

Peter coughed harshly beside him, and Robin looked at him worriedly. Beneath the dirt and rags, Peter Dubois was little more than skin and bone, held together only by hatred for his captors and a stubborn refusal to die. Peter had been a giant of a man in his day, a warrior and adventurer who fought and laughed and loved with equal bravado. There was little of that man left in the living skeleton at Robin's side, but sometimes his ghost moved briefly in Peter's eyes.

Robin looked away, anger and despair churning within him, and his gaze fell upon a broad-shouldered Moor chained to the wall opposite him. His muscular frame suggested he hadn't been a prisoner long, and his eyes

4

burned with a fierce stoicism that impressed Robin despite himself. He tried to sit up a little straighter, and met the Moor's eyes with his own level gaze. Neither of them spoke. There was nothing to say. What had brought them here no longer mattered, and they both knew what the future held.

Light flared up briefly against the gloom as one of the Interrogator's assistants opened the furnace door a little to pull out a glowing steel blade. The red-hot metal steamed gently in the humid air, and Robin's flesh crawled at the sight of it. The assistant spat on the blade and watched absorbed as the spittle hissed and danced on the heated metal. The Interrogator had two assistants, but Robin could never tell them apart. They were both short, squat, heavily-muscled men with constant broad grins and eager eyes. They moved for the most part with a ponderous inevitability that was subtly intimidating, and took no notice of threats or pleas or bargains.

The one at the furnace thrust the glowing blade back into the coals and smiled widely at the watching prisoners. He looked them over slowly, taking his time, and Robin fought not to shrink back as the man's gaze dwelled on him for a moment. Finally the assistant gestured at a scrawny, rat-faced prisoner farther down the line, and the other assistant strode unhurriedly over to unlock the prisoner's manacles and drag him out of line. The rat-faced Arab shrieked and jabbered at the assistant as he dragged him effortlessly over to a sturdy wooden block before the furnace, his voice rising in a frantic wail as his pleas went unheeded. Robin looked at the wooden block, spattered with old, dark bloodstains, and swallowed dryly. Men without number had lost their hands or their heads on that block. Some of them had been Robin's friends.

The Interrogator stared impassively down at the rat-faced

5

prisoner as the two assistants tied a cord around his wrist and stretched his arm across the block. The prisoner continued to rant and howl, twisting helplessly against the hands that held him, and then he pointed suddenly back at the other prisoners. The Interrogator turned to follow the pointing hand, and Robin's heart jumped painfully in his chest as the cold gaze fell upon him, and Peter. Robin's breathing grew short and hurried, but he made himself stare calmly back at the Interrogator. They had taken away his pride and his dignity, but he still had his courage and his honor.

Seen up close, the Interrogator was even bigger than Robin had remembered, and far more intimidating. He was well over six feet in height, and looked to be almost as wide. His huge muscles gleamed with so much sweat they looked as though they'd been oiled, and he moved with the slow, sure arrogance that only comes from total authority. In this chamber his word was law, and men lived or died or screamed at his command. His face was dark and fierce, but his eyes were what caught Robin's attention. They were cold, unfeeling, uncaring—the eyes of a man who could do anything, anything at all, because mercy and compassion were no part of his nature. He would do terrible, necessary things without once hesitating or questioning his orders, because all that mattered to him was getting the job done as quickly and efficiently as possible. He loomed over Robin and Peter, and his gaze moved slowly from one to the other and back again. When he finally spoke, his voice was flat and emotionless.

"He says you stole his bread."

"That's a lie," said Peter quickly. He meant it to come out defiantly, but his tired, wavering voice was only pathetic. "I caught him stealing our bread, and made him return it. That's all."

Behind the Interrogator, the rat-faced prisoner burst into fresh pleas and accusations, but the Interrogator silenced him with a few short words, without once looking away from Peter. After a long moment, he turned away unhurriedly and nodded to his assistants.

"Cut off the infidel's hand," he said calmly, and moved back to the wooden block.

One of the assistants pulled the rat-faced prisoner away from the block, while the other moved over to unlock Peter's manacles. Rust flaked off the heavy shackles at Peter's wrists and ankles as the assistant threw the chains aside and pulled Peter to his feet. He swayed unsteadily on his bony, trembling legs and stared dumbly at the Interrogator. He was so weak he could barely walk unaided, but he still tried to struggle as the assistant forced him to kneel beside the wooden block and stretched his bare arm across it.

"No!" said Robin sharply, and there was enough authority in his voice to bring everyone's attention back to him. The Interrogator turned his dark, unwavering gaze on Robin, but he took a deep breath and held his head high. "Release him. I took the bread."

"That's not true!" Peter twisted against the assistant's hands to look back at Robin. "You know that's not true."

Robin smiled at him sourly. "They're not interested in the truth. You're too weak, Peter. I can't let them hurt you. You wouldn't live through it."

The Interrogator looked at them both, and then nodded slowly. "How very noble. As you wish, infidel." He turned to his assistants. "Cut off this one's hand as well. But first . . ."

He indicated the rat-faced prisoner, and Peter was thrust carelessly to one side so that the Arab could take his place at the wooden block. He howled and screeched, fighting and kicking every inch of the way, but in a matter of moments he was kneeling beside the block again, his bare arm stretched across the bloodstained wood. Sweat ran down his face, and he whimpered as they tightened the cord around his wrist again. The Interrogator stood before him, a red-hot scimitar held carelessly in one huge hand. All the breath went out of the rat-faced prisoner as the glowing blade hovered above his arm, and he stared piteously up at the Interrogator.

"Be strong," said the Interrogator. "Show the infidels the courage of Allah."

The prisoner screwed up his face, his hand clenching and unclenching spasmodically. The only sounds in the chamber were the quiet crackling of coals in the furnace, and the massed breathing of the watching prisoners. The scimitar flashed down, biting deeply into the wood, and the severed hand jumped forward on the block. The prisoner fainted. The assistants dragged him off to one side and treated the bleeding stump with hot pitch to seal it. The Interrogator flipped the severed hand neatly into a nearby basket with the tip of his scimitar.

One of the assistants came over and unlocked Robin's chains. Raw white skin showed where the heavy irons had held him for so long, and Robin looked at it almost wonderingly. It had been a long time since the rest of his skin had been that white. The assistant hauled him to his feet, but Robin threw off his hands and walked over to the wooden block unaided. He knelt unhurriedly beside the bloodstained block and defiantly stretched his arm across it, glaring coldly up at the Interrogator. One of the assistants wrapped the thong around Robin's wrist and pulled it tight. Robin gritted his teeth at the sudden pain, but didn't let it show in his face. The Interrogator studied him dispassionately, the red-hot scimitar held loosely in one huge hand. He lifted it with cruel slowness and held it over Robin's bare arm. The heat from the blade singed the hairs on his arm. Robin lifted his eyes from the glowing blade to meet the Interrogator's cold, merciless eyes, and smiled suddenly—a wild and wolfish snarl that had nothing of humor in it.

"This is English courage," he said softly, dangerously.

The Interrogator raised the scimitar and brought it sweeping down. Robin braced himself and yanked backward suddenly, pulling the assistant holding his arm forward across the block. The Arab screamed shrilly as the red-hot blade bit deeply into his shoulder, the Interrogator having been unable to stop in time. The smell of burning meat was strong in the air. The assistant fell to one side, still screaming, and pulled the sword out of the Interrogator's hand. Robin wrenched his arm free, viciously back-elbowed the assistant holding him from behind, and leapt up to drive his fist into the Interrogator's throat. The huge man staggered backward, coughing and choking, and Peter grabbed him from behind in a stranglehold.

Robin leapt forward, snatched up the scimitar, and spun round just in time to see the unharmed assistant charging toward him, arms outstretched. Robin stepped forward in a perfect thrust and lunge, and the assistant impaled himself on the glowing blade. Robin pulled the sword free and the assistant crumpled limply to the floor, as though only the blade had been holding him up. The other assistant stirred painfully behind the block, and groped for the long knife at his belt. Robin stepped over to him and kicked hard between wind and water, and the man stopped moving.

The Interrogator staggered backward, clawing desperately at Peter's arm round his throat, cutting off his air. Peter's weight was nothing next to the Interrogator's, but hatred and the unexpected chance for revenge had given him new strength. The Interrogator's eyes bulged as his lungs screamed for air, but he still had his wits about him. He realized how close to the furnace they were, and launched himself backward toward it, intending to crush Peter against the heated metal. Peter glanced behind him, and at the last moment spun on his heel and threw the Interrogator forward. The man's own weight slammed him against the furnace, and he screamed in pain and shock as the hot metal burned his flesh. Peter took a handful of the man's hair and drove the Interrogator's head against the furnace door again and again. The Interrogator buckled at the knees, and Peter thrust the man's head into the furnace opening, slamming the door against his neck to hold him there. Horrid screams rang from inside the furnace, but Peter hung on grimly. He grinned broadly, his eyes dancing.

"That's for five years of hell, you bastard," he said softly.

Robin started toward Peter, and then whirled around as a voice from behind him suddenly called a warning. An Arab guard stood before him, a massive ax swinging in a vicious arc toward Robin's head. Robin ducked at the last moment, and the wind of the ax's passing ruffled his hair. The guard quickly recovered his balance and pulled back his ax to strike again. Robin feinted at him with the glowing scimitar and then chopped sideways, putting all his strength behind the blow. The sword sheared clean through the ax's handle, the impact of the blow tearing the two pieces from the guard's grasp. The Arab stared stupidly at his empty hands, and Robin ran him through. He looked down at the dead man and scowled. If one guard had heard the commotion and come to investigate, then others must have heard as well and were undoubtedly already on their way.

Robin looked across at the prisoner who'd shouted the warning to him and saved his life. It was the Moor he'd traded glances with earlier. Tall and heavily muscled, he had dark skin covered with intricate tattoos. Even his shaved head was ornamented with them. He was an imposing figure, with an air of quiet strength that didn't only come from his broad frame. Robin approached the Moor and looked at him thoughtfully.

"You speak English," he said finally.

"The King's own." The Moor's voice was deep and calm, and barely accented. "Set me free." Robin raised an eyebrow, and the Moor stared steadily at him. "For pity's sake, Englishman. Mine is a sentence of death."

"Don't trust him!" said Peter sharply. He moved unsteadily over to stand by Robin, his starved frame trembling as much from hate and anger as from the exertions of his struggle with the Interrogator. "The man's a heathen, one of the ungodly vermin who've kept us here all these years."

"He saved my life," said Robin.

Peter sniffed. "For his own reasons, no doubt."

They all looked round sharply as the sound of raised voices and running feet came clearly to them from the corridor outside. Robin slammed the door shut and looked about him for something to use as a barricade. The Moor smiled slightly.

"Free me, and I'll show you a way out."

"Why should we trust you?" asked Robin flatly.

"Because if you don't, you are dead men."

Robin looked at Peter. "He's got a point."

The running feet drew nearer, and the door burst open as a guard charged in. Robin cut him down with a single well-judged stroke, and smiled at the Moor.

"A good point. One moment, if you please." He bent over the nearest assistant and grabbed the keys from his belt. It was only the work of a few moments to find the key that fit the Moor's chains and free him. Robin threw the manacles aside and glanced quickly at the open door. The running footsteps were very near. "They'll be here any minute. Show us the way out, friend."

"This way," said the Moor, heading quickly for the rear of the chamber. Robin looked at the blank stone wall behind the furnace, then shrugged, tossed the keys to the other prisoners, and hurried after the Moor with Peter at his side, leaning heavily on his arm for support. The Moor slipped a hand carefully behind the furnace and tugged at a hidden lever. There was a low grating sound, and a section of the wall swung back, revealing a dark, narrow tunnel. Robin wondered briefly how the Moor had known about the hidden exit, but quickly decided the matter could wait till another time. He grabbed a flaring torch from a wall bracket, and he and Peter followed the Moor into the tunnel. The door swung shut behind them, and darkness closed in around the narrow pool of light.

Robin shivered suddenly, and the torchlight danced. It was cold in the tunnel after the sweating heat of the torture chamber. He could hear guards clashing with the unchained prisoners on the other side of the wall, and grinned devilishly. A hand closed suddenly on his arm, and he jumped, startled. The Moor smiled, and took the torch from him.

"We must hurry," he said quietly. "It won't take them long to discover where we've gone."

"Where are we going?" asked Peter suspiciously.

The Moor's gleaming white teeth flashed briefly again in the gloom. "To the one place in Jerusalem that is even worse than the dungeons, my friend. The sewers."

He set off into the darkness, holding the torch high to spread the light as far as possible. Robin and Peter followed him through the narrow tunnel as it descended into the earth and finally opened out into a series of rough stone tunnels that crisscrossed beneath the city. An appalling stench filled the air, growing steadily worse until they stepped out of one tunnel and plunged suddenly into three feet of extremely filthy water. It was unpleasantly warm, and there were objects floating on the surface that Robin quickly decided not to study too closely. The Moor waded steadily forward, and Robin and Peter splashed after him. Robin screwed up his face and did his best to breathe only through his mouth, but the stench was still overwhelming. He'd thought his years in Jerusalem's dungeons had inured him to every form of filth and stink, but the sewers had a smell all their own. Robin grinned suddenly. It was still a vast improvement over being chained up in the torture chamber.

"You are fast with a sword, my friend," said the Moor unexpectedly.

"Five years I've waited for a chance at freedom," said Robin. "That makes a man fast."

"How much farther is it?" Peter asked. "These tunnels seem to go on forever."

"Not far now," said the Moor. "Can you make it, or should we carry you?"

"I can follow anywhere you lead, heathen," snapped Peter, but his voice sounded more tired than angry.

Robin looked at him worriedly. Rage and desperation had kept Peter going for a while, but it was clear he was fading fast. Robin tried to support more of his friend's weight without being too obvious about it. A sudden flash of light filled the tunnel ahead and stopped them where they were. The sound of raised voices came clearly to them on the quiet as armed men splashed through the sewers toward them. There was a brief rumbling from above, and then guards bearing swords and torches dropped suddenly out of the tunnel roof and into the water directly before them. The Moor glared quickly about him, and then plunged into a side tunnel. Robin and Peter hurried after him.

"Let us hope you can be as fast with your feet as you were with a sword, my friends," said the Moor breathlessly, "or I fear our new friendship is fated for a swift and premature end."

Robin slogged through the waist-deep water after the Moor, half dragging and half carrying Peter with him. He hoped the Moor had some idea of where he was going. Robin was so turned around he hadn't a clue where he was. But he'd trusted the Moor this far, so he might as well carry on trusting him. He smiled sourly. It wasn't as though he had much choice in the matter. The guards were catching up fast, even though the weight of their armor was slowing them down in the deep water. Robin glanced back over his shoulder, panting from his exertions, and cursed breathlessly as he saw half a dozen archers fitting arrows to their bows. He plunged on, trying to urge more speed out of Peter. Blazing arrows began splashing down around them, trailing clouds of thick, choking smoke.

"Poison air," snapped the Moor, without looking back. "Hold your breath."

Robin put a handful of rags to his mouth and breathed through that. He'd seen the Arabs use such tactics before in battle and knew how deadly the poisoned smoke could be. Already Peter was coughing harshly again, despite the rags at his mouth. Somehow they struggled on, splashing heavily through the filthy water, with the guards constantly closing the gap between them. The flaring torch illuminated walls crawling with slime, and the low-roofed tunnel seemed to stretch away forever.

Peter suddenly stumbled and fell, almost dragging Robin down with him. The Moor stopped and turned back as Robin struggled to lift Peter out of the water. A guard appeared out of nowhere and cut at Robin with his sword. He just managed to parry the blow, but had to let go of Peter to do it. Peter lashed out with his fist, catching the guard by surprise, but he hadn't enough strength for another blow. The guard thrust his blazing torch at Peter's face, and he couldn't get his hands up in time to protect himself. A dark hand shot out and closed on the guard's arm, bringing the torch to a halt inches from Peter's face. The Moor squeezed hard, and the torch fell from the guard's numbed hand. The guard lifted his sword, and the Moor's hand shot up and closed around his throat. Dark arm muscles swelled, and there was a dull crack as the guard's neck broke. The Moor threw the body aside, and hauled Peter to his feet.

"Thanks," said Peter hoarsely. "It seems I misjudged you."

"Save your breath," said the Moor, not unkindly.

The three of them plunged on into the darkness, cries from the pursuing guards echoing loudly in the cramped confines of the tunnel. The Moor darted suddenly to one side and into an opening so narrow he had to turn sideways to enter, and Robin and Peter followed in single file. The tunnel quickly opened out to form the bottom of a tall air shaft. The Moor held up his torch, but its light couldn't reach the top of the shaft. Robin stared up into the gloom and felt a breath of fresh air caress his face, smelling pure as the sweetest rose. The Moor started up the shaft, using jutting bricks in the shaft's walls like the rungs of a ladder. Peter watched him climb, and shook his head slowly.

"I don't think I can do that, Robin."

"Try," said Robin. "We haven't come this far to give up now."

He pushed Peter ahead of him and got him started up the shaft. He glanced back down the side tunnel. The pursuing guards sounded very close. He scrambled up the shaft after Peter, encouraging him with heartening words and the occasional push. The climb was long and arduous, and

Robin's muscles began to shake from the strain of it. The only thing that kept him going was the knowledge that it had to be even worse for Peter, and he hadn't complained once. The stonework was slimy and slippery, and the bricks weren't as secure as they might have been. Once a brick was torn out of the wall under Robin's weight, and he was left hanging by one hand over the long drop. He could hear the falling brick clattering away down the shaft, the sound growing fainter and fainter until it finally disappeared. He took a deep breath and let it go slowly. It didn't calm him as much as he'd hoped, but every little bit helped. He found another foothold and began to climb again. The air slowly grew fresher.

Robin finally reached the top of the shaft and found Peter and the Moor straining against a heavy iron grating that capped the shaft. Robin squeezed in beside them, put his shoulder against the grating, and heaved upward. It shifted slightly and then settled again. The smell of fresh air was tantalizingly close. Robin and the Moor heaved again, muscles straining. There was a slow rasp of metal on metal, and the grating finally tore free. Robin slid it carefully to one side, pulled himself up another step, and then cautiously raised his head through the opening.

It was night in the city, and Robin grinned broadly as he looked out on an empty street. He tensed as a roar of sound filled the night, and looked wildly about him before realizing it came from behind. He twisted round and just had time to duck back down into the shaft as a squad of mounted soldiers thundered right over him. Robin waited for the din to die down, and for his heart to start beating sensibly again, and then stuck his head back out into the night. He looked quickly in all directions and slowly relaxed as he saw nothing but the empty street. He pulled himself out into the cool night air and then reached back in to help Peter out. The Moor emerged so gracefully he made it look easy, and slid the grating back into place. Robin and Peter sat together in the street, breathing in great lungfuls of the fresh night air and leaning on each other for support.

Robin flexed his aching arm muscles and studied the scimitar he'd somehow held onto through the escape. It was no longer glowing with heat, but it seemed a good enough blade. He looked slowly about him and realized they'd emerged just outside the prison wall. If nothing else, it proved the Moor was a damn good navigator. Robin rose slowly to his feet, determinedly ignoring his protesting muscles, and Peter rose groaning to stand beside him. The Moor had been on his feet all the time, and was staring warily about him into the gloom by the light of his guttering torch. Robin grinned at Peter.

"God willing, we may finally be safe."

Peter smiled back at him, and then gasped suddenly in shock and horror. His smile stretched into a grimace, and he clutched desperately at Robin's arm. Robin stared disbelievingly at the bloodied arrowhead protruding from Peter's chest, and then the Moor was quickly at his side, and between them they hustled Peter into the sheltering shadows of the prison wall. Robin put a tentative hand on the arrow's shaft sticking out of Peter's back, but he hissed with pain the moment Robin touched it. Robin snatched his hand away and looked desperately at the Moor.

"There's no sign of the archer," said the Moor quietly. "He could be anywhere."

"We can't stay here," said Robin. "Peter needs help."

The Moor looked at Peter's wound, and then raised his eyes to meet Robin's. He didn't say anything. He didn't have to. Shouts of alarm came to them from inside the prison, and the sound of soldiers approaching from somewhere in the night. Robin slipped an arm around Peter's waist and steadied himself to take as much of his friend's weight as he could.

"Hold onto my shoulder, Peter. We must hurry."

Peter shook him off with an effort and leaned back against the prison wall. His face was ghastly pale, but his eyes were dark and knowing. "I'm not going anywhere, Robin. The wound is mortal. Leave me." He pushed himself away from the wall and stood stiffly on his own. "Our quest ends here. We can go no further together." He swallowed dryly and grimaced as even that small movement stirred the arrow within him. "You were always a good friend to me, Robin. Don't spoil it now. My mother . . . my little sister . . . tell them I love them. Tell them . . . I died a free Englishman."

Robin looked despairingly at the Moor, but found no support or comfort there. "His wound is by the heart. We cannot save him, and we dare not tarry here."

Robin tried to argue with him, but the words wouldn't come. Peter produced an insignia ring from a hidden pouch in his rags, and pressed it into Robin's hand. "Take this to my sister. Swear you will protect her for me . . . Swear it, Robin!"

Robin nodded reluctantly, as though by agreeing to the obligation he was somehow making Peter's death real and final. "I swear it."

Peter looked meaningfully at the scimitar Robin carried, and Robin handed it to him. Peter hefted the sword professionally and looked down the street to where he could hear soldiers drawing near. He moved slowly toward them, his legs trembling but his back straight and his head proudly erect. He began to stride more quickly, refusing to yield to the pain or the wound that was killing him. He broke into a run as he saw soldiers grouped before him, and brandished his sword at them.

"For England," he said, and smiled. It was the only battle cry he'd ever needed or believed in. "For England!"

He ran toward the soldiers sword in hand, and once again he was the great and powerful warrior who'd first come to the Holy Lands, seeking fame and glory and honor for his faith. All his old strength and skill blazed within him, and he cut down the first soldier to reach him with a single contemptuous blow. The other soldiers surged around him, like dogs set on a bear, and he stood his ground and would not yield. He swung his sword with savage skill and never felt the swords that cut and tore at him. He finally fell beneath their hacking blades, still trying to strike back at them.

The Moor dragged Robin away into the shadows. "Come! Make his sacrifice an act of honor."

Robin snatched one last look at the soldiers swarming around Peter, and then he and the Moor disappeared into the night.

Some time later, they stopped to get their breath in a deserted back alley. A dog nosing through the garbage snarled a warning at them, but slunk away when the Moor glared at it. Soldiers with torches raced by both ends of the alley, but the night and the shadows were dark enough to hide an army. Robin clutched the insignia ring tightly in his fist and shook his head slowly. England seemed a long way away. He turned uncertainly to the huge figure of the Moor beside him.

"It's time to say farewell, friend. God speed your way."

"Our way is together," said the Moor. "With the speed of Allah."

He grinned at Robin, who found himself grinning back.

The Moor might be a strange and enigmatic figure, but at least he had a sense of humor.

"Why?" Robin asked finally. "What holds us together?"

"You saved my life," said the Moor. "I must stay with you until I save yours."

"Thanks," said Robin. "But I go to England, a long way from anything you know. I relieve you of your obligation."

The Moor shook his head. "Only Allah can do that."

"And if I don't want you with me?"

"You have no choice . . . unless you think you can kill me." He grinned broadly, and offered Robin his hand. "I am called Azeem."

Robin sighed resignedly, and took the proffered hand. "And I am Robin. Robin of Locksley."

2

LOCKSLEY

Locksley Castle stood proud and tall, though its rough stone walls were scarred and pitted from long exposure to wind and rain. Ivy crawled along the walls and towers, and the water in the moat was green with scum. Locksley Castle had known better days. Night mists swirled around the towers and crumbling battlements like ghosts of yesterday, and only a thin plume of smoke rising from a single chimney gave any sign of life within.

In the hall, wrapped in a heavy cloak despite the crackling flames in the great open hearth, Lord Locksley sat alone at a long table, staring at nothing. Not an old man, but older than his years, head bent and shoulders bowed by the weight of too many sorrows. His hair was gray, his face lined, but still there was a strength, a power, in him that burned undimmed by years of worry. He sighed tiredly, lifted his goblet to his mouth, and then put it down again. He was drinking too much these days. The old dog lying before the fire yelped suddenly, hitching and snorting in its sleep as it chased something in its dream. Locksley smiled fondly at his dog. It had been a fine animal in its day, and had accompanied him on many a long hunt, but now its fur was brindled with white and gray, its legs creaked, and its wind was gone. Much like its master, in fact. Locksley smiled briefly at the thought, leaned back in his chair, and pulled his cloak more snugly about him. He felt the cold more these days. And there was no denying the world seemed a colder place with his wife gone to her final rest and his only son missing these past six years.

Locksley looked grimly at the correspondence lying scattered across the table before him, and had to fight down an urge to cast it all aside with one sweep of his arm. Papers and papers and more damned papers. Rents and tithes and taxes, judgments and politics, and all the other paperwork that filled too many of his days. None of it mattered. None of it really mattered, now that he was alone. Family and friends had either disappeared into the Crusades, or abandoned him when he refused to ally himself with the would-be kingmakers clustering around Prince John, their voices growing louder and more confident the longer King Richard remained abroad. Locksley scowled unhappily. The King had been gone too long, and when the cat's away, the rats will plot treason. There was apparently those who already hailed John as King, and pledged allegiance to him in open court. Locksley sniffed loudly. Damned if he'd do any such thing. His honor and his duty were not for sale. They were all he had left.

Locksley looked out over the long table, with all its empty chairs. He could remember when every chair had been filled with friends, allies, and advisors; brave men and true who fought to uphold the law and put down injustice. They had all left, one by one, on this Crusade or that, their eyes full of the Holy Grail, their heads stuffed with rousing sermons and dreams of gold and treasure beyond counting.

22

They went away, and never came back. Sometimes there was news, of deaths or injuries or brief sightings, but mostly there was just the silence, and those who sought knowledge of a loved one's fate had to chase down hopes and rumors in what ways they could. Locksley looked at the letter before him, like so many others he'd written down the years, to little or no response. The same old words, the same thin hope. He glanced across at the portrait hanging over the hearth. It showed a tall and proud young man, with a solemn face and laughing eyes. Robin of Locksley. Missing, captured, presumed dead.

Locksley picked up his quill, and put it down again. The words would do, or they would not. He didn't know what else to say. He looked over his letter one last time, the familiar words sounding in his head like an old, sad tune, its sharp edges worn smooth by time, but still able to pierce the heart of the listener.

Kindest sir, 'Tis rumored you fought in the Holy Lands with my beloved son, Robin, whom I have not seen for some six years now. Were you present at his capture near Acre? Do you know the name of the potentate who holds him? Does Robin still bear me ill will? A little news, please, kind sir. I would give all that I own for his release. . . .

All that, to a knight he barely knew by name, let alone reputation. But he had to try. He would not give up on his son. Locksley had no doubt that Robin would never have given up. If his son was still alive, he would fight till his last breath to return to England. If he was still alive . . .

Locksley looked round sharply as his dog scrambled to its feet and stood growling before the fire. It stared fixedly at the main door, tense and watchful, its lips drawn back from its teeth. Locksley pushed his chair back from the table, to give him room to maneuver, if he needed it. Vague shouts and scufflings came to him from the corridor outside, and Locksley drew a dagger from a concealed sheath beneath his robes and slipped it carefully out of sight under a pile of letters. Just in case.

The door burst open, and a desperate ragged figure stumbled in, fighting off an older man with frenzied, almost hysterical strength. Locksley relaxed a little. He knew them both. The ragged man pulled free, and bowed jerkily to Locksley. The older man glared at him, and turned to face Locksley with what dignity he could muster.

"I'm sorry you've been disturbed, my Lord," he said breathlessly, "but this person insisted on seeing you, and would not wait."

"My Lord, please!" said the ragged man. "I must speak with you!"

Locksley nodded to the older man. "It's all right, Duncan. I may as well see him, now he's here."

The elderly retainer bowed stiffly, and scowled at the ragged man, his lined, craggy face radiating disdain. He turned his back on the both of them, his bearing loudly proclaiming that he washed his hands of the whole affair. He stalked out of the hall and slammed the door shut behind him. Locksley had to smile. Duncan had been a Locksley family retainer all his life and had strong views on proper behavior at all times. So much so that he occasionally forgot just who was in charge. It did no harm to remind him, now and again. He was a good man, though, loyal and true, and Locksley would have cut off his own hand rather than risk losing him. He'd stayed on when his lord's brooding and occasional rages over the loss of his family had driven many of the other servants away.

Locksley realized that his mind was wandering again,

and he made himself concentrate on the man before him. He knew him . . . Kenneth Something-or-other, a peasant farmer in his early forties. He was a short, blocky man with the solid muscular frame you only got from hours of backbreaking toil, working the land from dawn to dusk, and sometimes beyond. Locksley realized suddenly that the man's clothes were torn and there was blood on his face, welling out from an ugly wound on his temple. Locksley leaned forward in his chair.

"You are Kenneth of Crowfall, are you not? What has happened?"

Kenneth's mouth worked soundlessly for a moment, struck dumb by grief, and then the words forced themselves out. "They've taken my Gwen. My daughter."

"Who?" said Locksley sharply. "Who has taken her?"

"Men on horses. In masks." Kenneth raised a trembling hand to his bloodied head and swayed unsteadily for a moment before regaining control. "We tried to stop them. My son is dead."

He swayed again, tears starting from his eyes, and Locksley rose quickly from his chair to provide a steadying hand. He knew how it felt to lose a son. "Take heart, Kenneth. We will avenge your son and save your daughter."

He strode across the hall to stare at a massive broadsword hanging in its scabbard on the wall. He smiled slowly, and it was not a pleasant smile. He reached up and took the sword down. The old familiar weight brought back memories and emotions he hadn't felt in a long time. This was what had been missing from his life—the call to arms, to fight for the good against evil. A simple problem that could be solved by simple, direct action. Just what he needed. He might be a little past his prime, but he was still lord of his domain, and no man could attack his people with impunity.

He smiled across at Kenneth, who straightened a little under his lord's gaze.

"Come, Kenneth, we have work to do this night."

It took a matter of a few minutes for Locksley to wake his staff and set them to what had to be done. He gave orders to his groom to prepare his mount, and sent messengers to the Sheriff to tell what had happened. He had no doubt the Sheriff would send men, but they wouldn't arrive till morning. And his own men were scattered across his lands, on his business, and could not easily be recalled. So he'd just have to do the job himself, as he had so many times before. When he was younger. Locksley pushed the thought aside, and growled at Duncan to help him with his chain-mail vest. The old retainer did so, shaking his head dolefully and coming up with reason after reason to try and dissuade Locksley from leaving. Locksley ignored him, settled his sword comfortably on his hip, and strode down to the courtyard with Kenneth and Duncan hurrying along behind him.

It was cold out in the courtyard, and a bitter wind was blowing out of the night. Locksley swung up into the saddle of his favorite charger and signaled for his people to open the gates. He felt strong and invincible, in charge of his life again. He felt young again. Kenneth stood at the horse's head, biting his lip impatiently as he waited for the gates to open. His head had been roughly bandaged, and there was a new determination in his face. Duncan hovered at Locksley's side, all but wringing his hands in his agitated state.

"Please, my Lord, you must not do this! Wait for men to ride with you, or at least wait till morning! There is an evil moon tonight."

Locksley grinned down at him. "Good will overcome,

Duncan. Trust in that. Look after things here, till I return. Kenneth, lead the way."

The ragged man nodded quickly, and headed for the open gates at a steady run. Locksley urged his horse after him. Duncan watched them go, and mouthed a silent prayer.

Locksley braced himself against the sudden chill. A low chanting, which could have been mistaken for the wind, emanated from the dárkness. Kenneth, who ran alongside Locksley, stopped short, hanging his head for a moment. Locksley pulled up his horse, a feeling of dread filling him.

From out of the gloom a group of figures appeared, drifting toward the castle. They carried torches and were dressed in masks—hideous gargoyle faces—and loose robes. Devil worshippers. As the figures drew closer, the chanting increased in volume and intensity, and an eerie malevolence hung in the air like a mist.

There was nothing Locksley could do but draw his sword. The chanting stopped abruptly when the Devil worshippers saw the crucifix sculpted into its hilt. Locksley stared at Kenneth, who returned his gaze with guilt in his eyes.

"I'm sorry, my Lord. I had no choice," he said softly.

The High Priest suddenly appeared before Locksley's horse, and thrust a burning brand in its face. The horse screamed and reared back, and Locksley was thrown from the saddle. He hit the ground loose and rolling, old battle instincts coming to his rescue, and was back on his feet in a moment. He glared wildly about him, brandishing the sword he'd somehow managed to hold onto, and forced himself to think past the laboring of his lungs. *Not as young as I used to be* . . . . He reached out for his horse, but the panicked animal was already off and running. Locksley cursed briefly, and threw himself at the High Priest. He slapped the burning brand from the Priest's hand with the

27

flat of his blade and slammed the man up against the nearest stone pillar. He set the edge of his sword against the High Priest's throat, and the Devil worshipper stood very still. Locksley spat blood from his mouth, and glared back at the hesitating guards and acolytes.

"Keep your distance, or watch your master die!"

Locksley took a little heart from the way his voice came out hard and unwavering, and grinned bloodily as the Devil worshippers looked at each other uncertainly. He turned back to the High Priest and ripped the mask from his head. Cruel, sardonic eyes met his, and Locksley gasped as he recognized the face.

"You . . ."

His sword wavered for a moment, and the High Priest brought his knee up sharply. Locksley gasped and fell backward, the sword spilling from his nerveless fingers. Arms took him from behind and threw him to the ground. The acolytes gathered around him, kicking him viciously and pushing at each other to get at him. Locksley curled into a ball to protect himself, but he could still feel his bones cracking and breaking, until a boot connected solidly with his head, and the world went mercifully vague for a while. The Devil worshippers finally tired of their sport and dragged him to his feet again. Blood soaked his face like a mask, and only his captors' hands kept him upright, but his head was already clearing.

The High Priest took Locksley's chin in his hand and forced his head round to face him. He smiled mockingly. "Don't look for help here, Locksley. You have no allies in this company. In fact, you are a most unwelcome guest."

Locksley met the man's gaze steadily. "The King shall hear of this!"

"I think not," said the High Priest. "No one here is going to tell him anything."

He gestured commandingly, and one by one the Devil worshippers removed their masks. Locksley stared in horror from one grinning face to another. He knew them all. Some he'd trusted, and a few he'd even thought of as friends. They looked at him now, and there was only death in their eyes.

"God help us," he whispered. "God help us all."

An albino crone laughed harshly and moved unhurriedly forward to stand before him. "Your God has abandoned you. One day, all England shall worship with us."

"Join us, Locksley," said the High Priest. "We are the future."

"Never," spat Locksley.

He tried to pull free, but there were too many hands holding him. They dragged him, struggling helplessly, to a massive stone pillar and tied a rope around his wrists. They laughed and spat on him as the High Priest threw the other end of the rope up over the high stone lintel. The guards grabbed the rope as it came down and pulled on it, hauling Locksley up off the ground. He hung there, twisting slowly, as the crone approached him. She smiled at the pain in his face, and her blood-red eyes were horribly eager. She pushed up his chain-mail vest and ripped open the shirt beneath. The air was cold against his bare skin. The crone stared at him, smiling.

"You will beg to join us . . . or you will beg to die."

The High Priest moved in beside her, holding Locksley's sword. He tested the edge of the blade and smiled approvingly. He moved slowly forward, and Locksley shut his eyes.

Up above the valley, Kenneth turned away as the first

agonized screams filled the night. He started toward the woods and then froze as masked figures appeared silently out of the dark to block his path. He tried to run anyway, but he didn't get far.

3

HOMECOMING

Rigging creaked and sails billowed as the French ship headed toward the English coast. Spray billowed up over the bow, flying on the air like mist, but drew no reaction from the man who stood there, still as a statue, watching his home draw slowly closer. The majestic white cliffs of Dover dominated the horizon, towering up into the cloudless sky. Gulls hovered keening on the breeze, and for the first time in a long while, Robin felt at peace. He was home again, his time in the East war nothing more than a bad dream, soon to be forgotten. England lay before him, just as he'd remembered and imagined it in the dungeons under Jerusalem.

England had come to mean many things to him during that time: a place of light and freedom, mostly, but also a place where honor and justice still prevailed. Such thoughts and dreams had kept him sane in the never-ending darkness; they kept hope alive when all else failed. The knowledge that beyond the heat and horrors of the East there still lay England, untouched by war and slaughter. A place where, if he could only reach it, he would find peace and contentment once again. Robin had done his duty, served his King, and suffered more than any man should ever have to. Now he was safely home, never to be tempted forth again by false promises of honor and glory in the heat of battle.

He stretched slowly, not taking his eyes off the white cliffs before him. He looked sturdier now, and much better cared for, but the long years of imprisonment had left their mark in his gaunt face and haunted eyes. He wore cheap and practical clothes under a pilgrim's cloak, and all in all he looked a far cry from the proud and fashionably garbed young man who'd left these same shores six years earlier. His own father would have trouble recognizing him. Robin smiled wryly at the thought. They'd parted with angry words after Robin had insisted on joining the Third Crusade despite his father's wishes, something Robin had had ample time to regret in the many desperate moments when it seemed certain he'd never see home or family again. A thought struck him, and he looked back over his shoulder, to where the Moor Azeem was standing silently to one side, watching impassively as the shore drew slowly nearer. What Lord Locksley was going to make of his son's new friend was anybody's guess. Like most Englishmen, Lord Locksley believed the only good Moor was a recently deceased one. Preferably with lots of gold and jewels on the body.

The ship finally dropped anchor, and Robin and Azeem sat together in a longboat while French sailors rowed them to shore. Robin stirred and twisted impatiently on the rough wooden seat as the beach drew nearer with tantalizing slowness. At the end he couldn't stand it any longer, and the Moor watched amusedly as Robin jumped over the side and waded through the surf to stand at last on England's shore.

He stood very still with his eyes closed, and drew in a deep breath, savoring the moment.

"Home at last," he said softly. "Thank you, Lord."

Behind him, the longboat finally nudged the land, and the French sailors jumped out into the shallows to haul the boat up the beach. Azeem climbed out of the boat with casual dignity and strode over to join Robin. The French sailors gave him plenty of room. For all the time they'd spent at sea with him, the French still weren't sure how they felt about Azeem. Robin didn't blame them. The Moor was an imposing figure, and not just because of his muscular frame and fearsome tattoos. Robin watched interestedly as Azeem sniffed his first English air.

"Well?" he asked finally. "What do you think?"

"A trifle thin and bland," said Azeem. "I'm used to air with a little more body to it. In Jerusalem there are streets where the scents are strong enough to knock you down and sit on your chest. That was real air. Air with character. Air you could chew. This English air is flat and weak by comparison."

Robin smiled. "I'm going to have to take you to London sometime. Still, given that your heathen religion doesn't allow you to drink wine, I suppose it's only natural you'd turn out to be a connoisseur of something else." He paused for a moment, looked at his feet, and then regarded the Moor narrowly. "My friend, you have escorted me safely home, and been a fine companion and friend. I beg you—free yourself from your vow. Return to the ship. Go home. I know how heavy your heart must be, so far from your family and native land."

Azeem shook his head firmly, arms folded across his massive chest. "It is because I love them so dearly that I cannot dishonor them by breaking my vow."

Robin spoke sadly. "I thought you'd say that."

He nodded at the French sailor who'd crept silently up behind the Moor, club in hand. The sailor grinned, and raised the club on high. He brought it swinging down, and Azeem sidestepped at the last moment without looking round. The sailor fell flat on his face. Azeem turned round unhurriedly, picked the sailor up as though he weighed nothing, and threw him into the surf. His friends quickly splashed out to recover him, showing as much concern as they could between fits of helpless laughter. Azeem turned a cold stare on Robin.

"No man controls my destiny. And especially not one who stinks of garlic and attacks upwind."

Robin laughed, clapped the Moor on the shoulder, and hoisted his modest bundle on his back. "Come then, Azeem, and travel with me. A few weeks will see us celebrating my return with my father. I'm sure you'll find lots to talk about. Stay with me as long as you wish, but if you wait for a chance to save my life, I fear you're in for a long stay. Our fighting days are done, my friend."

They set off up the beach together, Robin singing an old English drinking song, raucously but mostly on key. Azeem winced now and again but kept his own counsel.

Snarling and giving cry, the pack of hounds flowed across the open moorland in pursuit of their prey. Horsemen thundered after them, determined to be in at the kill. And in the lead, as always, was Sir Guy of Gisborne. A tall, imposing figure, even handsome if you overlooked the constant scowl and the missing left ear. The fastest rider, the keenest hunter, Gisborne always led the hunt. If only because no one dared challenge his position. Sir Guy had a short temper, and an impressive list of kills in duels.

He lifted his head and studied the moorland with narrowed eyes. The prey was obviously heading for the forest, hoping to lose the hunt in the woods. If it wasn't brought down soon, it might just get away. Gisborne was damned if he was going to let that happen. He'd been chasing the prey for the best part of an hour, and he'd promised himself the ears. And the death, of course. He grinned suddenly as his keen eyes detected a flurry of movement among the underbrush. He rose up in the saddle and pointed triumphantly.

"There he goes!"

The hounds' cry intensified as they caught the prey's scent on the wind and raced forward, heads down and bellies just clearing the ground. The prey risked a quick look back over his shoulder and then fixed his gaze on the forest ahead. Wulf was only a child, barely ten years old, but still he knew what would happen if the hounds and the hunt caught him. He plunged on, mouth gaping wide as he fought for breath. He'd done his best to throw the hunt off his trail, using every trick and scrap of local knowledge he had, but the hounds always found him out, flushing him from his every hiding place.

Pain stabbed in his sides and shuddered in his weary legs, and the air rasped in his straining lungs. The forest drew slowly nearer, but Wulf knew he wasn't going to make it in time. He was going to die. But he was damned if he was going to make it easy for them. He wondered if it would hurt much, and hoped he wouldn't cry.

At the edge of the forest, Robin and Azeem followed an old trial, heading north. Robin stepped out briskly, while the Moor followed in his own good time, studying the wild forest with an inquiring eye. The sheer abundance of both plant and animal life fascinated him. It was like an oasis without ending, an explosion of living things with none of the strict self-control of desert life. He stopped by the

remains of an old Roman wall to study a bird in flight, and
Robin stopped with him, his eyes caught by a flash of red
berries. He reached up and plucked a sprig of mistletoe
from the overhanging oak tree. He showed it to the Moor
with pride, and Azeem smiled back at him. Although he
tried to hide it, Robin was just as thrilled by the forest as the
Moor was, and had grown increasingly buoyant as they
drew nearer his home and old memories stirred at familiar
sights. Robin held out the delicate sprig for Azeem to
inspect.

"Mistletoe," he said dreamily. "Many a maid lost her
resolve to me, thanks to this little plant. . . ." He sighed
reflectively. "Seems a lifetime ago, now."

Azeem raised an eyebrow. "In my land we talk to our
women; we don't drug them with plants."

Robin laughed. "What do you know of women, my
honorable and dutiful friend? You haven't so much as
looked at a woman since we arrived here."

"In my land," said Azeem, unperturbed, "there are
women of such beauty that they possess a man's mind, so
much so that he would be willing to die for them."

He looked away, lost in his memories for a moment.
Robin smiled suddenly, as a piece of the puzzle that was the
Moor fell into place.

"Wait a minute. . . . Is that it? Is that why you were to
be executed? Because of a woman?" The Moor stiffened
slightly but did not answer. Robin crowed with delight.
"That's it! A woman!"

Azeem glared at him, but said nothing. Robin laughed
and danced around him, brandishing his sprig of mistletoe.
The Moor sighed heavily, and looked determinedly at the
skyline. "The hour grows late. It is close to sunset."

"Ha!" said Robin, throwing aside the mistletoe. "Who

36

was she? The Mullah's daughter? Another man's wife? You painted dog! What's her name?"

Azeem studied the darkening sky, removed his prayer rug from his backpack, and carefully unfolded it. He went to lay it down on the ground, and then hesitated. He glared up at the cloud-covered sky, and then turned the glare on Robin.

"Is there no sun in your cursed country? Which way is east?"

"Tell me her name," said Robin.

"Which way is east!"

Robin folded his arms and grinned at Azeem, obviously prepared to wait as long as it took.

"Damn you," growled the Moor. "She was called . . . Jasmina."

Robin pointed off into the forest. "That is east." Azeem threw his rug on the ground, and knelt down, facing east. Robin leaned over him. "Was she worth it?"

Azeem met his gaze unwaveringly. "Worth dying for."

He turned away and immersed himself in his prayers. Robin smiled, and moved a little away to let him get on with it. And then he looked round sharply as the bray of a hunting horn cut across the evening quiet, followed by the rising clamor of a pack of hounds in full cry. Robin moved to the edge of the wood to look out over the open moorland, and then stopped dead as a young boy burst through the trees, ran straight past him, and swarmed up the sturdiest of the trees like an oversized and somewhat desperate squirrel.

And then the hounds arrived in a roar of sound and motion, streaming past Robin to swarm around the base of the tree, barking at the top of their lungs and snapping and snarling in futile anger. The boy retreated even farther up the tree, well out of their reach. The dogs milled back and forth, giving Robin an odd appraising glance, but apparently too well trained to go after anything that hadn't been designated as prey. Robin felt decidedly relieved as he realized that, and stopped looking around for a tree of his own to climb. There was more noise and commotion as Gisborne and the rest of the hunt arrived, following the hounds. The horses came crashing through the trees and then stumbled to a halt as their riders caught sight of the small boy hiding in the branches. Gisborne glanced briefly at Robin, taking in his pilgrim's robe, and then ignored him. He signaled to his men to dismount and surround the tree. They did so quickly, while the dog handler cuffed the hounds into some sort of order. Gisborne leaned forward in his saddle and stared up into the branches.

"You're not playing by the rules, boy," he said mockingly. "Deer don't climb trees." He grinned at his men, but there was no warmth in the smile. "Perhaps he thinks he's a game bird. Shall we teach him to fly?" The smile vanished. "Cut the tree down."

The soldiers drew their swords and began to cut awkwardly at the base of the tree. Splinters flew on the air, and the tree shuddered under the heavy blows. The boy clung desperately to the branches, his eyes wide with fear. Robin's mouth was set in a grim line. He moved quietly over to the horses, surreptitiously lifted a crossbow out of a saddle pannier, and hid it under his cloak. No one noticed. Everyone's eyes were fixed on the boy above them. The tree creaked and groaned as steel bit deep into the wood, and the hounds stirred restlessly, eager for blood. Robin strode forward to stand between Gisborne and the tree.

"Hold!" he said loudly. "What creature is so fearsome that it takes six men to attack it?"

Gisborne stared at him blankly, taken aback that a commoner should address him so freely. An angry answer rose to his lips, but he bit down on it as he remembered the man was a pilgrim. It was always wise to allow pilgrims a little leeway. They could be anything from a saint to a leper. Gisborne summoned a polite smile from somewhere and nodded stiffly to Robin.

"Stand back, good pilgrim. This is no affair of yours."

"Have you treed the devil himself?" said Robin. "Let me see. . . . Ah ha! A small boy. A truly dangerous animal."

Gisborne controlled his temper with an effort. "This boy killed one of the King's deer."

"You starve us!" yelled the boy defiantly. "We needed the meat."

"Poaching is punishable by death," said Gisborne, ignoring the boy. "I only enforce the law. I advise you to move on, good pilgrim. This is the Sheriff of Nottingham's land, and his word is law here."

"Wrong," said Robin flatly. "This is my land, and my tree. Therefore, whatever is in it belongs to me. Call off your dogs."

"I grow dangerously tired of your wit," said Gisborne. "Leave now, while you still can." He glared at the watching soldiers, and they snapped to attention. "Don't just stand there, damn you! Cut down that tree!"

Robin looked at the soldiers. "The man who strikes that tree dies."

His voice was calm and even and very dangerous. The soldiers looked at each other, and then moved away from the tree to face Robin, their swords at the ready. Robin looked at the odds, and the thought crossed his mind that he might just have been a little hasty. And then he looked up at the wide-eyed boy in the tree, and the anger grew in him again. He was damned if he'd stand by and let such evil happen on his land. On the other hand, a dead hero is no use to anyone. He shot a quick glance at Azeem, but the Moor was still busy at his prayers, apparently oblivious to anything else. Robin looked back at Gisborne, who smiled coldly down at him.

"Well, stranger in a hood, may I know your name before I have you run through?"

Robin pushed back his hood to reveal his face, and smiled grimly at Gisborne. "I am Robin of Locksley, and this is Locksley land."

Gisborne stared at him for a long moment, his face utterly blank, and then the cold smile slowly returned. "Well then, Locksley, welcome home." He looked at his soldiers. "Kill him."

The largest soldier lifted his sword and stepped forward confidently. Robin parted his cloak to reveal the hidden crossbow, and shot the man neatly through the right bicep. The soldier staggered back a pace and dropped his sword, looking numbly down at the steel bolt protruding from his arm. The other soldiers looked at him, and then at Gisborne, who flushed angrily.

"Set the dogs on him!"

"Azeem!" said Robin loudly, "this might be a good time to redeem that vow of yours."

The Moor ignored him, still lost in his prayers. Robin had the strong feeling that sending up a few of his own might not be a bad idea. The soldier acting as dog handler moved purposefully toward the hounds. Robin threw aside the empty crossbow and produced his own, which had also been concealed beneath his cloak. If nothing else, his time in the Crusades had taught him there was no such thing as being too prepared. The dog handler opened his mouth to give the word that would set the hounds on their new prey, and Robin put a crossbow bolt right between his eyes. He fell back into the midst of the pack, and the hounds tore at him, maddened by the scent of blood.

One of the soldiers loaded a bolt into a crossbow. Robin

threw his empty crossbow into the man's face. The soldier staggered back, clutching at his broken nose. Gisborne spurred his horse forward, reaching for his sword. Robin ran to meet him, jumped up onto a tree stump, and used it to launch himself at Gisborne. His weight tore Gisborne from the saddle, and the two of them crashed heavily to the ground, Robin twisting in midair to make sure he landed on top of Gisborne. They landed hard, knocking the breath out of both of them, but Robin recovered first. He snatched the sword from Gisborne's hand and set the edge against his throat. Robin glared meaningfully at the advancing soldiers, and they stopped where they were and lowered their swords. Robin grinned at them, waited a moment to get his breath back, and then looked down at Gisborne.

"Now then," he said cheerfully, "if you would be so kind as to give me your name, sir, before I run you through. . . ."

Gisborne started to reply angrily with something that definitely wasn't his name, but broke off abruptly as Robin put a little more weight behind the sword at his throat. A thin trickle of blood ran freely as the keen edge gently parted the skin. Gisborne lay still, and tried very hard not to swallow. He took a long, shallow breath and answered very carefully.

"I am Sir Guy of Gisborne, the Sheriff's cousin. That little bastard was poaching the King's deer. I was just enforcing the law. . . ." He looked up at Robin's grim, unyielding face and his confidence began to slip. "Think what you're doing, Locksley! You can't seriously mean to kill me over a dirty little peasant brat. . . . Please, Locksley. Please!"

Robin remembered the boy's desperate face as he looked down from the tree at the pack of hounds, baying for his blood. He remembered the cold arrogance in Gisborne's face, and the naked hunger for blood and death in his eyes.

And in that moment Robin wanted to kill Gisborne so badly he could almost taste it. His face hardened, and then a sudden scuffling snapped his head round, just in time to see a soldier who'd been sneaking up behind him stop short, a scimitar sticking into the ground at his feet. The soldier froze. Robin looked across at Azeem, who was still kneeling calmly on his prayer mat. Robin grinned at him.

"Nice throw."

"Yes," said the Moor. "I thought so."

He rose unhurriedly to his feet, and the two remaining soldiers gaped at the dark figure as though it were the Devil himself. Azeem gave them a hard look, and they backed quickly away, dropping their swords to the ground. Robin looked down at Gisborne, still trembling beneath him, and sighed deeply. The moment had passed, and it wasn't in him to kill a man in cold blood, however deserving. He got to his feet, dragging Gisborne up with him, and shook him roughly. Gisborne made no move to defend himself, his eyes wide and staring. Robin pulled the man forward, so that they were face-to-face.

"I've seen enough blood spilled over vanity and stupidity to last two lifetimes. I give you your life, Gisborne. Now take your men and get off my land. And be sure to tell your cousin, the Sheriff, what happens to his scum when they pick on my people."

He swung Gisborne round and encouraged him on his way with a heavy swat across the arse from the flat of his blade. Gisborne leapt forward as though he'd been stung, and collided with Azeem, busy folding his rug. The Moor smiled slowly at Gisborne, his teeth flashing bright against his dark skin. Gisborne gasped soundlessly, and then ran for his life, as though all the devils in Hell were after him. Robin and Azeem stood grinning together as Gisborne headed for the horizon, followed by his two surviving soldiers and a rather confused pack of hounds. Robin chuckled briefly, and then turned and gave the Moor a hard look.

"You traveled ten thousand miles with me, all for a chance to save my life, and then you just sat there and left me to be butchered!"

Azeem walked over to his scimitar and nonchalantly plucked the sword from where it had stuck in the ground at the soldier's feet. Finally he looked back at Robin.

"I'll fulfill my vow when I choose. I don't know what you're complaining about. You're alive, aren't you?"

They both looked round sharply at a crackling of branches, as the boy descended cautiously from his perch high in the tree. He realized he was being watched, and froze where he was. Robin smiled at him reassuringly and put away his sword.

"Have no fear, boy. Come down. We'll not harm you."

The boy climbed slowly down, not taking his eyes off Robin or Azeem, and finally dropped to the ground to study them both warily. He stood in a half crouch, obviously ready to cut and run at a moment's notice, like a cornered animal, or a dog that's been beaten so often it's wary of everyone.

"What's your name, boy?" asked Robin kindly.

The boy sniffed quickly and wiped his nose on his sleeve, his eyes darting from Robin to the Moor and back again. "Wulf. Name's Wulf."

"Was Gisborne telling the truth?" said Robin. "Did you kill the King's deer?"

Wulf grinned. "Hundreds of them."

And with that he darted into the forest and was gone, so quickly it seemed as though the woods had swallowed him up. Robin blinked and looked at the Moor, who was shaking his head slowly.

"An interesting place, this England."

Robin clapped him on the shoulder. "Come, my strange friend. Just over that hill lies a warm hearth, hot food, and a mattress so deep you could drown in it. Home, Azeem . . . Home."

But something didn't sit quite right with Robin. England was not the same place he'd left.

Dusk had fallen. Robin stood looking at the ruins of what had once been Locksley Castle and found it hard to feel anything but numb. The proud, ancient castle had been torn stone from stone and burned by savage fires. The tall towers had been reduced to squat stacks of blackened rubble, and what could be seen of the castle's interior was gutted and deserted. Robin moved forward a few steps and then stopped, afraid to view the destruction too closely in case that would somehow make the horror real and irreversible. The castle had been home to the Locksleys for generations. It had stood for centuries before Robin's birth, and he had always assumed it would still stand long after he was gone. The castle had been home and sanctuary to him, a refuge from everything that ever threatened him. During his long years in the dark dungeons under Jerusalem, the image of Locksley Castle had burned within him, giving him strength and comfort. He never lost hope that one day he would return to Locksley Castle, and feel safe and cared for once again.

And now he was back, and the castle was a ruin, and all his hopes and dreams were shattered.

Robin forced himself to approach the gutted shell, and Azeem walked quietly at his side, knowing there was nothing he could say that would help. They clambered over the rubble and made their way into what remained of the courtyard. The great paving stones were cracked and smashed and littered with debris from the blackened walls. There were signs of fire on every side, and scattered dark stains on the ground could only be blood. There was dirt and filth everywhere Robin looked, and weeds flourished among the broken stones. Robin swallowed hard, and called out into the darkness.

"Father! It's Robin! Hello! Can you hear me?"

His voice echoed back from the scorched walls and empty battlements, dying quickly away on the quiet. Azeem put a gentle hand on Robin's shoulder and pointed wordlessly at the far wall. Hanging high up on the wall, partly hidden in the shadows, was a decaying human corpse. The features had rotted away, but moonlight glinted on a medallion round his neck. Robin recognized it the moment he saw it. The medallion bore the Locksley crest, only ever worn by the Lord of Locksley. Robin shook his head, knowing what it meant but refusing to accept it. His father couldn't be dead. He couldn't be. . . .

Rage and grief burned within him as he threw back his head and screamed out a wordless denial that carried far out into the dusk. He slammed his fist against the nearest wall, bloodying his knuckles. Azeem put a hand on his arm to stop him, but Robin didn't even know it was there. He stood with fists clenched and head bowed, like an animal at bay, panting for breath. And then, in the quiet, they heard an eerie tapping coming from somewhere close at hand.

Azeem drew his scimitar and looked quickly about him. There were shadows everywhere, dark enough to hide anything. Robin wiped at his eyes with the back of his hand and drew his sword. The prospect of an enemy cleared his mind like a shock of cold water. Someone had to pay for what had been done here. The tapping drew slowly nearer, rhythmic but erratic, like the sound of fingers battering against the underside of a coffin lid. Robin and Azeem stood together, swords at the ready, and out of the shadows before them came a hunched old man, wrapped in a threadbare cloak and hood, walking with the aid of a staff. Robin slowly lowered his sword, staring at the figure in disbelief.

"Duncan, is that you?"

The hooded figure stopped abruptly, and seemed to stand a little straighter. "Master Robin? It really is you! A miracle! I thought God had abandoned us."

Robin hurried forward and hugged Duncan to him, and was shocked at how thin and frail the old man had become. The Duncan he remembered had been a hard, sturdy man, for all his years. Anger flared up in Robin again, and he took Duncan by the arms and shook him roughly.

"Damn you, Duncan! How could you leave my father hanging there? Why didn't you cut him down?"

"Easy, my friend," said Azeem quietly, at his side.

"I'm sorry, my Lord," said Duncan. "I would have brought him down, if I could only see. . . ."

He pushed back his hood with trembling hands, and the moonlight fell harshly across his disfigured face. Deep scars crossed his cheeks and forehead, and his eyes were nothing but dark, empty sockets. Robin swallowed sickly, and let the old man go, but Duncan clutched at his arms with desperate strength, as though afraid Robin might disappear. Robin felt tears sting his eyes, but forced them back. There would be time for tears later.

"Duncan," he said finally, trying hard to keep the horror out of his voice, "What happened here?"

Duncan sniffed. "They say the Sheriff captured your father worshipping with Devil worshippers. They say he signed a confession before the Bishop."

"That's impossible!" snapped Robin. "My father was a

46

devout Christian. Everyone knows that. Did they have any witnesses?"

"One," said Duncan grimly. "Kenneth of Crowfall. He's dead too. The Sheriff gave orders for all that happened here, and the Bishop decreed all Locksley land forfeit."

Robin shook his head slowly, trying to take it all in. "Do you believe the charges, Duncan?"

"No. I never did. Not even when they took my eyes, for speaking out."

"Who? Who did this to you?" said Robin, and Azeem stirred uneasily at the rage and hatred in his friend's voice.

"Sir Guy of Gisborne," said Duncan flatly. "With the Sheriff looking on."

Robin hugged the old retainer to him again and stared over his shoulder into the dark with eyes that held too much anger to allow for any tears.

"There will be a reckoning for this, Duncan," he said softly. "I swear to you—there will be a reckoning."

4

ENEMIES

Nottingham Castle stood tall and grim and silent, dominating the surrounding city like a spider brooding over its web. The castle had been built as a fortress, to guard and oversee the northern trade routes, and its origin was clear in the dour and forbidding face it showed to the world. Gray stone walls towered up into the night, shimmering coldly in the moonlight, and strange lights shone at the narrow windows. Nottingham Castle was not a comfortable place to stay or visit, and never had been. While it was being built, the foundation stones had been splashed with the blood of Saxon slaves as they died beneath the headsman's ax, so that their ghosts would be tied to the site and their strength would support the walls for all eternity. Of course, that was only a legend, and one liable to earn the teller a beating or a cropped ear if overheard by anyone in authority. But everyone knew. Those who lived in the city of Nottingham turned their faces away from the castle and made the sign against evil if its name came up in conversation. The only thing more feared than the castle was the man who lived in it and held power over both castle and city. The Sheriff of Nottingham.

Some of this was in Sir Guy of Gisborne's mind as he strode down the silent, deserted corridor that led to the Sheriff's private quarters. The Sheriff did not look kindly on the bearers of ill tidings, but he had to know that Robin of Locksley had returned. The old lord had been a popular and much respected figure, and there were many who still refused to believe the charges brought against him. If Robin of Locksley were to rally them to his cause, and go searching for the truth, a great many things might be dragged out into the open that would not bear the light of day. Gisborne rounded the final corner and glared at the armed guard standing before the heavy wooden door. The guard bowed respectfully, but made no move to lower his halberd or stand aside.

"Move away, fool," Gisborne growled brusquely. "I have business with the Sheriff."

"Your pardon, Sir Guy," said the guard, still respectfully, "but Lord Nottingham has given orders that he is not to be disturbed."

Gisborne hit him with a mailed fist well below the belt and pushed the guard aside as he collapsed. He opened the door without knocking and stepped inside, his nostrils flaring at the heavy scent of perfume and incense that permeated the Sheriff's chambers. He closed the door carefully, stepped forward, and bowed formally to the figure seated before him.

The Sheriff of Nottingham was a tall, slender man in his early thirties, with sharp features and cold, dark eyes. The face was handsome in a brutal, unyielding way, and the faint smile that played around his mouth held little warmth and less humor. He dressed always in the finest silks and wore them with a casual elegance that was only a little studied. He sat in his chair as though it were a throne, and at his feet crouched a half-naked girl. The Sheriff casually stroked her bare shoulders as he studied Gisborne, and the girl trembled uncontrollably under his touch, like a pet dog expecting punishment. The Sheriff looked Gisborne up and down, taking in his battered and travel-stained appearance, and finally raised a single, elegant eyebrow.

"Well, cousin, I trust you can justify this intrusion. I'd hate to think you interrupted my pleasures for anything less than the most vital emergency. For your sake."

"I met a hooded man today," said Gisborne, meeting the Sheriff's gaze unflinchingly. "He bade me warn you not to harm *his* people."

The Sheriff looked down at the girl by his feet. She'd begun to pull her tattered clothes around her to cover her nakedness, but froze when she felt his gaze upon her. She slowly raised her eyes to meet his, and trembled again as he spoke.

"Who bade you cover up?" asked the Sheriff, in a calm, reasonable tone, and the girl pulled her clothes away again with quick, almost frantic movements. The Sheriff turned back to Gisborne. "This hooded man. Does he have a name?"

"Robin," said Gisborne. "Robin of Locksley."

The Sheriff smiled slowly. "So. The prodigal son returns. How unfortunate, for him. He's nothing but a whelp, Guy. This girl could best him."

"This whelp bested four of my men in the blink of an eye!"

"Your men were probably drunk. I notice that you survived unhurt, cousin."

Gisborne flushed angrily, but was careful to keep his tone neutral. "I barely escaped with my life. Locksley has a companion. A dark-skinned foreigner with the marked skin

50

of Islam. He proved himself quite deadly with a Saracen sword."

In the wall behind the Sheriff's chair, unnoticed by either man, a single burning eye studied the scene through a concealed spy hole, and then abruptly disappeared.

The Sheriff sighed heavily and cut off Gisborne's account with a casual wave of his hand. "Yes, yes, I'm sure you would have needed a whole army to fight off these two rogues. Desperate men, clearly." He stopped and smiled thoughtfully. "I trust young Locksley has visited his old family manor by now, and found the home fires still burning. . . ."

He chuckled happily, ignoring the growing storm clouds in Gisborne's face, and then he sat forward suddenly as a hidden bell tinkled ominously. It only rang for a moment, but the Sheriff was on his feet before the echoes had a chance to die away. He grinned broadly at Gisborne. "Time for portents, cousin."

Gisborne waited till the Sheriff had switched his attention to the girl at his feet, and then he rolled his eyes disgustedly. The Sheriff took the girl's hand in his and raised it to his mouth as though to kiss it. Her eyes were wide and her mouth trembled piteously, but she didn't dare pull back. The Sheriff pressed the shaking palm to his mouth and then bit down hard. The girl screamed, as much at the blood running down her arm as at the sudden pain. The Sheriff dropped her hand and licked her blood from his lips.

"Tonight, my dear, I will teach you that pleasure and pain can be one and the same."

He laughed softly, and then turned and left the room, knowing the girl would still be there when he returned. She could not escape, and after all, some pleasures were all the better for a little anticipation.

• • •

Gisborne followed the Sheriff down a long circular stairway as it wound into the dark bowels of the castle. He held his lantern high to spread the light as far as possible, but still the darkness pressed in close around them like a living, threatening presence. The Sheriff seemed quite unmoved by the gloom and was actually humming pleasantly to himself as they descended the stairs. Gisborne scowled unhappily and kept his free hand near his sword. His cousin had brought him this way before, in search of unearthly knowledge and advice, but it was not a journey he would have cared to make alone. Rats moved unseen in the dark, and other things, and the person who lived in these depths by preference was no friend of his. His foot slipped on the worn-down stone of the steps, and he cursed under his breath.

"Did you speak, cousin?" asked the Sheriff lightly.

"Since you ask, cousin, I'll say it's madness to consult the hag on these matters."

The Sheriff chuckled. "Fear not, dear cousin. In madness there is great power."

Gisborne said nothing, and the Sheriff chuckled again. All too soon the stairs came to an end, and the Sheriff led Gisborne down a long, narrow corridor to a bare wooden door. Gisborne looked briefly at the blasphemous designs carved into the wood of the door, and then looked away. The Sheriff produced a heavy brass key from a hidden pocket and turned it awkwardly in the massive lock. He pushed the heavy door inward, and light spilled out into the corridor. It was a pale, unhealthy light, and Gisborne hesitated a moment before following the Sheriff in and closing the door behind them.

It was a long room, the far end hidden in gloom and shadows. Alchemical instruments covered a sagging table,

52

and potions dripped and bubbled in long, slender glassware and pewter bowls. There was no other furniture, only dirty straw scattered across the floor. The place stank of filth and decay and burning chemicals. Gisborne put his lantern down carefully on the floor beside him, without first blowing it out. He took comfort from its clean and natural light. The room's only illumination came from a dozen black candles and a single glowing brazier. The Sheriff cleared his throat and addressed the dark shadows at the rear of the chamber.

"Mortianna? I've come for a reading."

Strange sounds answered him, drifting out of the darkness, harsh and unearthly. The shadows seemed to stir and grow, as though the name itself had power over them. A sudden cackle cut the air, and a wrinkled, monkeylike figure came dancing and spinning out of the shadows. Her milk-white skin and hair seemed almost to glow in the gloom, and she danced with a grace that belied her twisted form and many years. Sweat beaded on Gisborne's forehead, and he clenched his hands into fists. It was the same dance she'd performed before the standing stones on the night they'd been discovered by Locksley. Why should she repeat it now? She couldn't know about young Locksley returning. It wasn't possible. . . .

The albino crone spun to a halt before Gisborne and the Sheriff, and smiled knowingly at them. She could have been any age, from forty to a hundred. Her flesh was heavily lined and wrinkled, but her whole body blazed with unnatural energy. She dressed in the rags of what had once been a fashionable gown, and wore a grisly necklace of dried chicken feet. The Sheriff cleared his throat again, and the blood-red eyes darted to him.

"You called, Mortianna," said the Sheriff patiently. "Do you have something to tell me?"

53

The crone smiled, and scuttled over to one end of the table. She brushed glass and pewter aside, regardless of whether they were in use or not, and set a bare platter before her. She glanced back over her shoulder at the two men, her head cocked slightly on one side, like a watchful bird of prey. The Sheriff joined her at the table, with Gisborne hanging back as much as he dared. The crone gestured quickly with one hand and produced a large goose egg, apparently out of nowhere. She rolled it around in her hand for a moment and then tore the egg apart with her fingers. A foul mixture of blood and albumen splashed onto the platter before her. Gisborne recoiled in disgust.

"Good Christ, cousin. . . ."

"Quiet!" snapped the Sheriff, not taking his eyes off the crone. "Don't use that name here. Watch, and learn."

Mortianna grinned at them both and shook the contents of a small leather pouch out over the bloody platter. Carved wooden runes danced in the blood as the crone rattled the platter, watching the patterns they formed with burning eyes. Her gaze grew vague and fey, and froth bubbled at the corners of her mouth as words struggled to force their way past her lips. The Sheriff pressed in close, hanging on every word, trying to share the visions that passed before her unseeing eyes. He had visited Mortianna many times, and her rituals held no terror for him. He had done worse, in his time, and would again if he found it necessary. He studied Mortianna's contorted face with the avid concentration of a connoisseur, frowning over every word she hissed.

"I see the son of a dead man. . . ."

"Does he affect us?" asked the Sheriff carefully.

"He precedes the Lion-heart."

The Sheriff scowled, and exchanged a glance with Gisborne. "King Richard returns from the Crusades? That

54

would soften the spines of the barons, just when we need it least. Does he come soon, Mortianna?"

The crone swirled the platter, and the runes danced in the viscous blood. "You must make haste. . . ."

"But my plan is still intact?"

Gisborne looked skeptically at the bloody mess on the platter and wrinkled his nose. Mortianna saw it and snarled soundlessly. She leaned over the platter, and a rune splashed into the blood, apparently from nowhere. It floated on its own, a death's head symbol. Mortianna recoiled, howling in horror, and slapped the platter to one side, sending it crashing to the floor. She whirled on Gisborne, seized him by the throat with one bony hand, and bent him back over the table.

"Who?" she screamed, spittle flying into his face. "Who have you seen?"

Gisborne struggled for words, held helpless by the intensity of her emotions. "No one! I've seen no one!"

"You lie!" Mortianna released her hold on his throat and jumped back from the table, crouching on her haunches like an animal at bay.

"What is wrong?" asked the Sheriff. "Tell me."

"I have seen our deaths!" Mortianna whimpered, and spun round and round on her heels, as though fearing an attack that might come from anywhere. "There is a painted man! He haunts my dreams. . . . Dark as the night he is, adorned with strange and foreign markings!"

The Sheriff looked triumphantly at Gisborne, who nodded shakily. He'd told no one but the Sheriff about Locksley's strange companion. There was no way the crone could have known. . . .

"Do you still think this madness, cousin?" asked the Sheriff softly. "She has the power. She guided my father, and now she guides me."

Mortianna clutched the Sheriff's arms with trembling hands and thrust her face into his. "They threaten all! The man in the hood, the painted man! Kill them! Kill them both!"

She hugged the Sheriff tightly, hiding her face against his chest. He caressed her soothingly and smiled at Gisborne. "Cousin, I put this in your hands. Prove to young Locksley that allowing you to survive was a mistake. His last mistake."

5
MARIAN

Stray shafts of red-gold sunlight pierced the mist-shrouded trees as dawn rose over the ruins of Locksley Castle. A few birds sang tentatively in the woods, but most of the world was quiet, still half-asleep and unwilling to face the responsibilities of a new day. Robin sat beside his father's grave, staring at nothing. It wasn't much of a grave—just a low mound of earth with a cross fashioned from two sticks lashed together. The Lord of Locksley deserved better. But then, he'd deserved a better death too. Robin sat listlessly, the same thoughts running through his mind over and over, unable to settle. His father was dead, the Castle lay in ruins, his lands and heritage were forfeit. Every reason he'd had for coming home, every reason for surviving in the dungeons under Jerusalem, had been taken from him. In his hands he held the Locksley medallion, and he turned it over and over without looking at it, as though somehow it might suggest an answer, a reason to go on living.

Duncan and Azeem stood together, not far away, talking in lowered voices. They seemed to be worried about something, but Robin couldn't raise enough interest to care what. In the end, Azeem turned away to gather their few belongings together, and Duncan stumbled toward Robin, tapping at the ground with his staff. Robin heard him coming but didn't look round. At the last moment he raised an arm to stop Duncan treading unknowingly on his master's grave, and Duncan seized his hand gratefully.

"He loved you to the end, young master," said Duncan. "Never doubt it. He never gave up hope that one day you would return."

Robin stared at the crude cross on his father's grave and spoke to that rather than Duncan. "The last words we ever shared were spoken in anger. He called the Crusades a foolish quest. I accused him of killing my mother."

Duncan squeezed Robin's hand tightly, but didn't interrupt. They both knew there were things that needed to be said. Robin took a deep breath, and let it out again.

"I said . . . terrible things. I was angry. I wanted to hurt him. And now, too late, I wish to take it back. . . . Forgive me, Father. Please."

"He does, young master," said Duncan firmly. "But you have grieved enough for him. Now, it is time to think of yourself. You must flee, head north to safety. You have cousins there who will take you in. You cannot stay here. Gisborne will surely seek revenge against you and your companion."

Robin nodded slowly, and rose to his feet, gently disengaging his hand from Duncan's grip. Gisborne's name had given him the answer he needed. When all else failed, there was always revenge. He stared down at the rough mound of earth, and the tears that stung his eyes were as much from anger as despair. He drew his knife and held it out before him. The early morning sun gleamed on the blade, red as blood, red as hate. "Father, I swear I shall not

58

rest until you have been avenged. I swear it upon my honor and upon my blood."

He slashed deliberately at his palm, and blood splashed down onto the grave. Azeem hurried forward when Robin drew the knife, but stopped when he realized there was no immediate danger. Robin looked at him steadily.

"My world has been turned upside down, Azeem, but it's still my world. This isn't your fight. Go home."

Azeem sighed, and looked away at the horizon. "If I leave you alone now, my friend, you will only get yourself killed." He looked back at Robin, and each saw loss and suffering in the other's eyes.

Azeem put out his hand, and Robin shook it. Blood welled from their grip and fell to the ground, an unspoken pact of death and violence and justice, come what may. And then they shouldered their packs, took Duncan by the arms, and started off down the trail that would lead, eventually, to Nottingham.

It started to rain soon after, and the earth turned to mud that sucked at their feet. Dark clouds blocked out the sun, and the driving rain soaked them to the skin. Visibility shrank to a few yards, and the world became a place of looming trees and indistinct shadows. They pressed on through the storm, the gusting wind chilling them to the bone. They were far from the nearest village or hamlet, but from time to time they chanced across the burned-out shell of some house or barn. Robin had heard tales of harsh treatment handed out by the Sheriff's men to those who would not or could not pay their taxes, but he'd dismissed most of them as rumor or exaggeration. But the farther north he traveled, the more signs he saw of devastation and unrest, until it seemed to him that he was traveling through an occupied country, a people under siege.

The three of them stopped at a crossroads to check for directions, and stared silently at the rotting corpse hanging from a gibbet. Duncan stood patiently between Robin and Azeem as they stared at the dead man, and he shivered violently from the cold and the rain. Robin took off his hooded cloak and wrapped it round the old man.

"No, my Lord," said Duncan, shocked. "I cannot be warm while you are cold. It is not proper."

Robin smiled briefly. "New rules, old friend: There are no rules, for woodsmen such as us."

They walked on a while in silence, heads bowed to keep the rain out of their faces, until Azeem growled something under his breath in his own tongue. Robin looked at him inquiringly, and Azeem sniffed loudly. "Never have I witnessed a storm of such duration and determination. When does summer come to this land?"

Robin chuckled, in spite of himself. "This is summer."

Azeem gave him a hard look and shook his head slowly, and they trudged on through the wind and the rain. The storm gradually died away over the next hour, but the day stayed cold. Robin's spirits finally rose a little when he spotted smoke curling up into the sky beyond a narrow stretch of woodland, and he increased his pace. He led the way down a rough, winding path that brought them to an old dry-stone wall. Beyond the wall stood a large, blocky mansion with a thatched roof. Robin nodded slowly to himself and relaxed a little. It had been a long time since he'd visited Dubois Mansion, and he hadn't been sure he remembered the way. He often played at the mansion as a child, but that was all of fifteen, twenty years ago. The place looked a lot smaller than he remembered it, but then, it would.

"What is this place?" asked Azeem.

"Peter's house," said Robin. "I swore an oath to him,

remember? It's six years or more since he left here to come with me on a glorious adventure to the Holy Lands. Now I've returned without him. Still, we should find food and shelter here."

"And dry clothes?" asked Azeem.

"I don't see why not," said Robin. "The Dubois family and the Locksleys have been firm friends for generations."

He found the gate in the wall and led the way to the impressively large front door. He knocked politely, waited a while, and then pounded on the door with his fist. There was a long pause, and then a hatch slid open in the top half of the door, revealing the face of what had to be the oldest woman Robin had ever seen. He put on his best polite smile.

"No more beggars!" snapped the old woman, and she slammed the hatch shut.

Robin blinked, and then hammered determinedly on the door again. The hatch slammed open, and the scowling face reappeared.

"We are not beggars," said Robin quickly. "Tell the mistress of the house that Robin Locksley is at her door."

"Can't," said the old woman. "Her ladyship isn't here."

Robin smiled doggedly, ignoring the looks on his companion's faces. "Very well. In that case, is the child Marian at home?"

"Maybe she is," said the old woman. "And maybe she isn't."

She went to slam the hatch shut again. Robin thrust his hand into the gap to stop her. The old woman slammed the hatch anyway. Robin howled and jerked his crushed fingers free. The hatch slammed shut. Robin tucked his throbbing hand into his armpit and performed a little stamping dance of pain and anguish, while Azeem looked on interestedly.

"It seems hospitality in your country is as warm as the weather," he observed.

Robin gave him a hard look, and then glared at the closed door. He was wet and cold and tired, and had half a mind to burn the whole place down on general principles. Reluctantly he turned away. They couldn't afford to draw attention to themselves. He gestured for Azeem to help turn Duncan around so they could leave. And then he stopped and looked back as he heard the sound of bolts being withdrawn from their sockets. The door opened a crack. There was a brief pause, and then the old woman cleared her throat unhappily.

"Leave your weapons."

The three of them started forward. Robin began a graceful speech of thanks. The door opened just wide enough for the old woman to point a bony finger at Robin.

"Just you. Not them."

Robin started to protest angrily, and then stopped himself. Azeem, and particularly Duncan, needed warmth and shelter, but he obviously wasn't going to get any further with the old woman. She acted as though she were half–guard dog. Looked it, too, for that matter. His best bet was to wait and talk to whoever was in charge, and hope he could persuade them of his good intentions. He unbuckled his swordbelt and handed it to the Moor, squeezed Duncan's arm reassuringly, and stepped through the narrow gap into the gloomy hall beyond. The door slammed shut again, and inside bolts crashed back into their sockets. Azeem shook his head slowly, and hung Robin's swordbelt securely from his shoulder. Duncan shivered and pouted and kicked at the muddy ground.

"A pox on all Moors and Saracens!" he shouted suddenly. "Were it not for their ungodly ways, master Robin would never have gone off and left us, and none of this would be happening! Never been treated this way in my life." He muttered rebelliously to himself for a while, and then remembered there was someone else with him. He turned his head vaguely in Azeem's direction and tried to think of something to say. Polite conversation had never been one of his strong points. "Azeem . . . tell me, what manner of name is that? Irish, perhaps? Cornish?"

"Close," said Azeem. "It's Moorish."

The expression of sheer horror that crept over Duncan's face at that point did much to compensate Azeem for the day so far.

Inside Dubois Mansion, the old woman led Robin into the main hall, told him to wait there and not touch anything, gave him a last suspicious glare, and then stomped off and disappeared up the stairs at the end of the hall. Robin looked around him and tried to squeeze some of the excess water out of his clothes and hair. It was a fair-sized hall, dominated by the long dining table and the usual collection of deer and boar heads mounted on the walls. Robin remembered them from his childhood visits. He'd never liked them. He'd been convinced the eyes moved to follow him whenever he wasn't looking. On the wall facing the stuffed and mounted heads was the usual collection of ancestral portraits, most of the subjects looking as though they'd been in a really filthy mood when they'd had their portraits painted. Robin had never cared much for them, either. He heard quiet creaking sounds from the balcony above him and looked quickly up to see who was there. He felt obscurely guilty, as though whoever it was knew what he'd been thinking. A dim figure looked down at him, half-obscured by shadows.

"Who are you?" said a woman's voice.

Robin gave her his most charming smile. "My apologies for this intrusion. I am Robin of Locksley."

"You lie," said the woman flatly. "Robin is dead. Step more into the light, so that I can see your face. Now turn around."

Robin did so, still smiling determinedly. "What would you like me to do now? Dance a few steps? Who are you?"

"I am the maid Marian," said the figure haughtily.

"Then show yourself, child," said Robin. "You have nothing to fear from me. We knew each other well when we were younger."

The woman stepped forward into the light, and Robin had to fight down a strong impulse to take several steps backward. It was possible that somewhere in his many travels he might have met a fatter and uglier woman than the one looking down at him, but he was damned if he could remember it. The last time he'd seen a face like that, it had been sneering down at him from a cathedral roof.

"Marian," said Robin, hanging onto his smile, but only just, "the years have been kind. You haven't changed at all."

"Thank you." She smiled down at Robin. At least, he thought it was meant to be a smile. She remembered who he was, and the smile vanished. "With the King away, we must always be on guard against outlaws. And as relatives of the King, we must beware of kidnappers in these lawless times. So, you have spoken to me, as you wished. Now remove yourself from this household."

"I would, my Lady," said Robin graciously, "but I am sworn to protect you."

She laughed dismissively. "Protect me? Robin of Locksley was never anything but a spoiled bully."

Robin tensed suddenly as he heard soft footsteps behind him, but before he could turn round a sword point jabbed him firmly in the back. He raised his hands slowly to show they were both empty, and peered carefully back over his shoulder. Holding the sword at his back was a man dressed all in black, face hidden behind a metal fighting mask.

"As you can see," came the voice from above, "we are already well protected. Now leave."

"Wait, Marian, let me explain—" Robin broke off as the sword point jabbed him meaningfully in the back. At which time, Robin decided very firmly that he'd put up with enough for one day. He spun round to face his assailant, hand dropping automatically to where his sword should have been, and glared at the figure before him.

"You are truly courageous when set against an unarmed man. What do you do when you're feeling really brave— sneak up on them in the dark, when they're fast asleep?"

The figure gestured at the door with his sword. The moment the blade moved away from him, Robin kicked the masked man under the knee. He stumbled backward, caught off balance, and Robin slapped the sword out of his hand. It fell on the floor between them. Robin reached down for it, and the masked man quickly kicked it out of reach. He then drew a dagger from a concealed sheath, and Robin backed quickly away. There were only two exits from the hall, and the masked man was in the perfect position to block the way to both of them. He pressed forward, dagger at the ready. Robin turned and ran to the nearest wall. The masked man started after him, and then stopped as Robin turned back with an antlered deer head he'd torn from the wall. They faced each other over the horns for a moment, and then the masked man stepped forward and chopped viciously at the antlers with his dagger. The solid steel hacked through the antlers as though they were straw.

Outside the mansion, Azeem and Duncan looked round sharply as the sound of fighting came to them. Azeem hurled himself at the door. It shuddered under his weight, but didn't yield. Azeem hit it again, grunting with the effort.

Duncan glared sightlessly about him, brandishing his stick fiercely.

"Point me towards danger, Azeem! I'm ready for them!"

Azeem shook his head, and slammed his shoulder against the door again and again.

Back in the main hall, chunks of antler flew on the air as the masked man forced Robin to retreat with a whirlwind attack. He parried and thrust with the antlers as best he could, but they were quickly being whittled away by the dagger. Finally left with nothing but the nubs, Robin hurled the deer head at his assailant and threw himself after it. He managed to grab the hand holding the dagger, spun his assailant round, and smashed the hand against the wall until the dagger fell from numbed fingers. They struggled together, and Robin quickly realized he was by far the stronger. He waded into his assailant with both fists, and the masked man collapsed. Robin stood over him for a moment, panting for breath, and then reached down and tore off the metal mask. Long hair tumbled free, and Robin stared blankly at the beautiful woman glaring up at him.

The door flew open and Azeem burst in, scimitar at the ready. Robin looked round, startled, and the woman seized the opportunity to punch him viciously in the groin. Robin sank to his knees beside her and smiled with clenched teeth.

"Hello, Marian."

Some time later, when everyone had recovered somewhat, Robin and Marian walked together in the open yard before Dubois Mansion. Marian stared numbly at the ring Robin handed her, the insignia ring Peter had given him in a Jerusalem back street. Robin looked away, to allow her a little privacy as the news of her brother's death sank in. Rock-strewn hills surrounded the mansion on both sides, dotted here and there with grazing sheep. The rain had stopped, and sunlight was peeking through the clouds. Marian saw none of it, her gaze fixed on the ring in her hand, her mind in a Jerusalem street she'd never seen.

"You are sure?" she said finally. "You are sure he's dead?"

"Yes," said Robin gently. "He fought bravely, right to the end."

Marian looked at him almost challengingly, anger and anguish fighting in her voice. "Why would my brother wish me to be protected by the boy who set fire to my hair when I was a child?"

"Because he knew that years of war and prison can change a man."

Marian tried to answer him, but anguish choked her voice. Robin started to put an arm round her shoulders, but stopped when she tensed at his touch. He took his arm away, and Marian dabbed at her eyes with a handkerchief, refusing to give in to tears.

"I will forward your condolences to my mother in London," Marian said grimly.

"I would think you'd be safer with her."

"I have no interest in life at court, gossip mongering and currying favor," she scoffed.

"You're alone, then?"

"Hardly." Marian gestured at the ragged peasants crowding around the mansion's kitchen door for the simple food that was all the mansion had to offer. The peasants looked beaten down and badly malnourished, and carried their few possessions on their backs, like refugees from a war. Bones protruded from sunken faces, and silent children stared about them with frightened, hollow eyes. Anger brought the color back to Marian's face as she watched them. "These times have brought me many mouths to feed. While you and my brother were off playing boy heroes, the Sheriff of Nottingham has plundered the county."

She glared at Robin as though it were all his fault. He met her gaze steadily, just about holding on to his temper. "Yet you still have your land and your property, Marian. Why is that?"

"Because I give the Sheriff no excuse to take them!" snapped Marian. "I keep my mouth shut, and I don't make trouble. What else can I do? If I was gone, who would feed these people? I am the King's cousin. It's my duty to help these people until he returns and puts things to rights again."

They looked at each other for a long moment, pain and despair driving the anger from their eyes. Robin looked away first.

"Marian, why did the Sheriff kill my father, and destroy my home?"

"Because he can." Marian's voice softened, and she put a gentle hand on his arm. "Robin, don't believe for a moment the accusations they made against your father. Even if you did despise him."

Robin smiled sadly, still looking out at the gray-green hills. "When I was eleven, after my mother died, my father . . . loved . . . a peasant woman. I hated him for it, even after it ended, saying he'd betrayed my mother. So when I came of age I joined the Holy Quest and sailed for the East, seeking purification and perfection through adventure in a righteous cause. Instead, I found only blood and horror, and learned there are no perfect men in this world, only perfect intentions."

Marian studied Robin as he stood lost in old memories and present pain. This wasn't the Robin she remembered. There was sadness and hard use in his face, but there was strength too. "What are your intentions now, Robin?"

"To set things right," said Robin, and there were no

doubts or misgivings in his voice, only a harsh, implacable certainty.

Marian looked off at the horizon, and she seemed suddenly weary and frustrated. "More bloodshed? I'm tired of heroic, boyish gestures. . . . I'm tired of boys." She looked back at Robin, and smiled sadly. "Don't do anything foolish, Robin. These are dangerous times."

"Then times must change," said Robin.

They both looked round sharply as Azeem called urgently to Robin from atop the estate wall. The Moor was looking out across the countryside and scowling thoughtfully. Robin hurried over to the wall and climbed up beside Azeem. Down in the valley, a thick plume of dust was heading toward Dubois Mansion. Robin frowned. That much dust had to mean a fairly large group of horsemen. And it was too much to hope that their arrival during his visit was a coincidence. Someone must have recognized him earlier on and sent word to the Sheriff. He turned to Azeem for advice, and then stopped, mystified, as the Moor opened the pouch at his belt and produced two circles of ground glass and a square of leather hide. Azeem rolled the hide into a tube, stuck a glass into each end, and then raised the primitive telescope to his eye.

Robin watched curiously. He'd just about decided it must be something to do with the Moor's religion, when Azeem handed him the contraption and told him to look through it. Robin hefted the leather tube dubiously, gave Azeem a hard look just in case this was some obscure Arabic joke, and then gingerly put the telescope to his eye. Armed soldiers on horseback appeared before him, charging straight at him. Robin almost dropped the telescope, and grabbed at his sword to defend himself. At which point he realized there was no longer any sign of the soldiers, apart from the plume of dust down in the valley. A delighted smile spread slowly across Robin's face as he realized what the telescope had shown him. He looked at the leather tube with awe.

"A wonderous mechanism, Azeem."

The Moor shook his head slowly. "How did your uneducated kind ever take Jerusalem?"

Robin smiled. "God knows." He looked through the telescope again and scowled as it showed him Gisborne riding at the head of the soldiers.

"What is it?" called Marian impatiently. "What do you see?"

"The Sheriff's soldiers," said Robin.

"Coming here? Is this your idea of protection?"

Robin and Azeem leapt down from the wall. They shared a quick glance, and then Azeem ran for the stables while Robin went back to talk to Marian.

"I killed some of the Sheriff's men," he said steadily. "The cause was just, but I doubt I could convince the Sheriff of that. I fear I've placed you in danger by coming here."

"I can take care of myself," said Marian coolly. "Now get out of here and take your friends with you, while you still can."

Azeem reappeared with Duncan in tow, and two saddle-less horses. Robin winced. He hated riding bareback. The sound of approaching hoofbeats drifted up from the valley, drawing steadily closer. Robin hesitated, looking from Marian to his friends and back again.

"I told you I was sworn to protect you, Marian."

"And I told you, no more boyish gestures."

Robin shook his head firmly. "I'm not leaving. You need me."

Marian glared at him. Robin folded his arms across his chest and glared stubbornly back. At which point the yard's gate burst open, and mounted soldiers spilled into the yard with Gisborne at their head, scattering the peasants like frightened quail. Marian pointed dramatically at Robin.

"Stop these men!" she yelled loudly. "They're stealing my horses!"

"Damn the girl," said Robin, admiringly, and ran for the waiting horses. Azeem leapt onto one, hoisted Duncan up behind him, and dug in his heels. The horse thundered toward the gate, followed by its companion. Robin leapt aboard the second horse while it was still moving, made a rude gesture at Gisborne, and headed for the gate at full speed. A soldier slammed the gate shut, blocking their way. Robin and Azeem shared a quick glance, and then dug their heels in again. The two horses jumped the gate as though they did it every day, and raced on without slowing. Crossbow bolts filled the air around them. Gisborne swung his horse round to follow them and found Marian standing directly in his path. He glared down at her, all but frothing at the mouth.

"You have been sheltering woodsmen, Marian!"

"They're thieves, you imbecile!" said Marian, glaring right back at him. "Bring back my horses, or the Sheriff will hear of your cowardice!"

Gisborne smiled coldly. He knew she was lying. He also knew he couldn't prove it. "You're lucky he didn't steal your virtue too, Marian. Assuming you still have it to lose, of course." He turned his back on her and bellowed at his men. "A crown to the man who brings me Locksley's head! And someone get that bloody gate open!"

Robin urged his horse on and tried hard to think of somewhere intelligent to head for. There was nowhere to hide in the valley, and the hills were too steep and too rocky for the horses to manage. And up ahead lay mile after mile of open moorland. Robin racked his brain frantically for a way out of the trap he'd made for himself, but it didn't take him long to realize the only hope he had left was to try and outrun his pursuers. A narrow stream appeared before them, and Robin hung on grimly as his horse charged through the frothing waters without slowing. He glanced back to make sure Azeem was still keeping up, and was relieved to find the Moor right behind him, with Duncan clinging onto him for dear life. Robin almost smiled, but the sight just reminded him that Azeem's horse was carrying two riders, and there was a limit to how long the animal could maintain such a pace while carrying that kind of weight.

They thundered on, and the open land turned to scrub. The land rushed by in a verdant blur, and Robin glared about him, trying to get his bearings. Off in the distance a hill rose up into the sky, half its face taken up with a huge Neolithic horse carved into the chalk. A sudden chill ran down Robin's spine. If he was where he thought he was, there might be a chance after all. It wasn't a way out he would have chosen, and the sanctuary he had in mind might turn out to be worse than what lay behind them, but, any port in a storm. . . . He brought his horse to a halt, and Azeem followed suit.

"Any chance we've lost them?" asked Robin breathlessly.

The Moor reassembled his telescope and looked back the way they'd come. Less than half a mile behind, Gisborne was fanning his men out to encircle his prey. Azeem lowered the telescope and looked grimly at Robin.

"They're closing. My horse carries two, and yours is growing lame. We cannot outrun them."

"Leave me, Master Robin," said Duncan, struggling to get his breath after the punishing ride. "I'm just slowing your escape."

Robin ignored him and pointed at the mass of trees on the

72

skyline. "One chance, Azeem. We'll lose them in the forest."

"No, Master Robin!" Duncan turned his blind gaze in Robin's direction, his face a mask of horror. "Sherwood is haunted! We put our souls at risk just passing by it!"

Robin shrugged quickly. "Either we take our chances with the spirits, or we'll end up ghosts ourselves."

They raced for the trees, which spread out into an apparently endless expanse as they drew nearer to the forest. Robin glanced back over his shoulder. Gisborne had seen where they were heading and was signaling for his men to cut them off. Robin grinned as he saw some of the men hesitate. They didn't like Sherwood either. He looked back at the forest before him. Gnarled and grotesque trees loomed up ahead, and beyond them a seemingly solid wall of dark, forbidding growth. Robin could feel the hackles rising on the back of his neck. He gritted his teeth and plunged into the enveloping night of the forest, followed by Azeem and Duncan.

Gisborne's men thundered to a halt at the edge of Sherwood and disintegrated into a confused, milling mob of white-faced men and snorting horses. The soldiers peered in open trepidation at the deep shadows and the twisted trees, and muttered unhappily to each other. Gisborne glared at them furiously, and they wouldn't meet his eyes.

"What's the matter, damn you! There are only three of them!"

"It's not the men we fear," muttered a soldier at the back.

Gisborne cursed them all for fools and cowards and traitors, but not one man would cross the boundary into Sherwood Forest. Frustrated, Gisborne turned to face the trees and shouted at the mocking shadows.

"Robin of the hood! Son of the Devil worshipper!"

Some distance into the forest, Robin and Azeem and

Duncan sat quietly on their horses in the gloom, listening.

"Your father died a coward!" yelled Gisborne, grinning madly. "He cursed your name and squealed like a stuck pig!"

"That's a lie!" Robin made as though to urge his horse back out of the gloom, but Azeem stopped him with a hand on his arm.

"I was the one who strung his corpse from the castle wall!" called Gisborne tauntingly. "It will be my pleasure to do the same to you!"

Robin threw off Azeem's restraining hand, and the Moor grabbed at the horse's mane to hold the animal back. "You will gain no justice for your father by dying needlessly today!" he hissed. "Be patient."

Robin looked at him for a long moment, and then nodded reluctantly. Azeem released his hold, and Robin led the way deeper into Sherwood Forest.

6

SHERWOOD

No one knew how old Sherwood was. The ancient forest spanned acres beyond counting, and dominated every map of the North Country. Its boundaries were known and documented, but few had ever penetrated the secrets of its dark heart. Sherwood was perhaps the last remnant of old England, wild England, from the time before man and his works. Where life ran riot, hand in hand with its sister, death. Within Sherwood Forest laws were put aside, customs forgotten, and those who left the paths and entered its green embrace were rarely seen again. Sherwood was the haven of lost souls, the birthplace of dreams, the last refuge of the outlaw. The one place where no man pursued.

On their horses Robin and Azeem and Duncan moved slowly between the huge trees, leaving the waking world behind as they immersed themselves in the great green dream of Sherwood. The forest was majestic, breathtaking, almost primal in its power. Hundred-foot beeches and thousand-year-old oaks formed a cathedral's canopy high above them, and surrounded the narrow path like grim, brooding guardians. Moss and lichens undisturbed by the tread of man grew thickly on the forest floor, and everywhere there was the rich earthy smell of the living forest, thick on the air like bitter honey.

Robin fell into a kind of daze as he tried to take in everything he was seeing and hearing and feeling. The forest was too huge, too awesome to be fully comprehended, and he had to fight to stay alert. There might or might not be ghosts in the green, but there was bound to be danger of some kind. Sherwood's fell reputation was not unwarranted. A heavy breeze wafted through the trees, and the woods were suddenly full of an eerie howling. Bones rattled hollowly, and disembodied voices moaned and keened. Duncan wrapped his scarf over his mouth with trembling hands.

"Banshees," he explained in a shaking, muffled voice. "They fly in your mouth and suck you dry of blood before you can even scream."

The wind gusted through the trees, and the unearthly howling rose and fell. The horses stopped dead in their tracks and would go no farther, stamping their feet and rolling their eyes. Azeem drew his scimitar and glared about him, calling on Allah to protect him from evil spirits. Duncan clung desperately to the Moor as Azeem whirled this way and that, searching for an enemy he could face, and finding nothing but the endless green. Robin put a hand on his arm to calm him, and then reached out into the branches of the nearest tree and pulled out a string of hollowed wooden tubes. He pointed out more of the things to Azeem, and the Moor slowly relaxed as he realized there were dozens of them, scattered among the branches of the trees. Robin lifted one of the tubes to his mouth and blew across the hollow end. It responded with a low, chilling moan that died away the instant he stopped blowing.

"Here are your ghosts," said Robin, grinning. He threw the tubes aside and gestured around him. "Wind chimes. A child's toy put to good use. Easy enough to spot if you're looking for a natural source rather than a supernatural one." He cocked an eyebrow at Azeem. "You scare easily, my pagan friend."

Embarrassed and not a little chagrined, Azeem sniffed at the chimes and sheathed his scimitar again. "They but confirm what I already knew. This forest has eyes. I can feel them."

Robin nodded, and swung down from his horse. He waited while Azeem dismounted and helped Duncan down, and then the three of them moved slowly along the narrow trail, leading their horses.

Some time later they emerged from lush undergrowth that blocked the trail to find themselves facing a wide, fast-flowing river. Ahead of them, a huge waterfall cascaded down through a vale of trees and hanging branches, gushing and frothing around a series of wide stone steps. Robin stood in silence for a while, listening to the roar of the rushing water and marveling at the wonderous scene before him. Azeem stood at his side, awestruck at so much water running free, a sight never seen in his native land. Even Duncan seemed to understand some of the scene's majesty, listening to the waters fall and feeling the cool moist air on his face.

"In my dreams alone have I imagined such a place as this," said Azeem softly.

Robin smiled ruefully. "Then perhaps you can imagine a way for us to cross it." He looked up- and downstream, and spotted a possible crossing point where the rushing water was at its narrowest. He pointed it out to Azeem, who nodded agreement. The Moor watched thoughtfully as

Robin made his way down the bank and then stepped cautiously into the water, moving forward step by step and using a stick from the bank to test the depth. The river fell over a series of rocks, creating a tiered waterfall.

Robin splashed back into the shallows, surprised, and then froze where he was as the woods behind Azeem and Duncan suddenly came alive. Shaggy, wild-eyed men emerged from the trees in their dozens, armed with cudgels and scythes and hayforks. They looked more like savages than men, and a cold air of menace hung about them like a shroud. One of them pressed a spear point to Azeem's back before he could turn, and he stood very still.

A rough, raucous voice arose from the opposite bank, singing a nonsense song. Robin whirled around in the shallows and found that the far bank was thick with savage, watchful faces. The singing man stood among them, wearing a bright red jacket filthy with caked dirt and grease. He broke off the song as he saw he had Robin's attention, and smiled nastily.

"Beg for mercy, rich man!"

Robin met his gaze steadily. "I beg of no man."

"Ah, but this is our river," said the woodsman, "and no one crosses without paying a tax."

Robin looked unhurriedly about him, finding angry eyes everywhere and meeting them without flinching. He was outnumbered many times over, but the fact that they were still talking was a hopeful sign. As long as he was careful not to show fear or weakness, he might still be able to talk his way out. He looked back at the woodsmen in the red jacket, and held his head high.

"I will pay no tax. I have nothing but my cloak and my sword."

"Bullocks, mate," said a loud, jovial voice from back in the trees on the far bank, and the woodsmen parted and fell back as a huge, heavily muscled figure moved forward. He stood at the edge of the bank looking down at Robin, hands on his hips, and Robin had to fight hard to keep his face calm and unimpressed. The man was a giant, seven feet tall at least and easily half as wide. His sheer size was breathtaking, as though a part of the forest itself walked on two legs, primal and unstoppable. He grinned down at Robin, his eyes alight with silent laughter. When he spoke again, his voice was easy and unhurried.

"A man who travels with two servants and claims he's without money is either a fool or a liar."

"A liar," said the man in red.

Robin looked back at Azeem for some sign of support. The Moor arched an eyebrow, but otherwise made no move at all, the picture of indifference. Robin sighed quietly. It wasn't as though he'd expected anything else. He turned back to face the giant.

"Who are you?" he asked, politely.

"John Little," said the giant, as though Robin should have known. "Bestman of the woods."

"Bestman?" said Robin. "You lead this rabble?"

"I do. And don't call them rabble. They're good men, one and all." His gaze fell on the medallion hanging from Robin's neck, and his grin widened. "And if you wish to cross through Sherwood Forest it's going to cost you one gold medallion."

Robin gripped his family medallion protectively. "This is sacred to me."

"Sacred to us too, mush," said John easily. "That there medallion will feed us for a month."

The other woodsmen sniggered and giggled and nudged each other, clearly enjoying the spectacle of a rich man being outtalked by their leader. Robin decided there'd been enough talking. He drew his sword and the woodsmen fell

79

silent, their eyes hot and eager at the prospect of violence.

"If you want the medallion," said Robin steadily, "you'll have to fight me for it."

"Love to," said John, still grinning. He grabbed a long wooden staff from one of the woodsmen and stepped out onto the first tier of the waterfall. A young boy suddenly pushed his way through the woodsmen to stand at the edge of the riverbank, and Robin blinked as he recognized him. It was the boy called Wulf, whom he'd rescued from Gisborne's hunt.

"Be careful, Father!" the boy called to John Little. "I saw him wallop twelve of the Sheriff's men like they were made of paper!"

"Is that so?" said John, taking up a position on the middle of the rock. "I'm going to enjoy this."

Robin looked at Wulf, and then at the giant before him. "This is your father?"

Wulf nodded proudly. Robin shook his head and stepped onto the rock. He advanced cautiously on John, sword held out before him. He was just getting ready to launch an attack when a massive hand shot forward, grabbed the sword and wrenched it out of his grasp. Robin stood slack-jawed as John Little hefted the sword and then tossed it disdainfully over his shoulder. Robin realized he was gaping, and shut his mouth with a snap. John tossed him his quarterstaff, and Robin caught it automatically. John looked back, and one of the woodsmen threw him another staff. Robin tested the weight of his quarterstaff dubiously. He'd had some training with the staff when he was younger, but he wasn't sure any amount of training would be enough to offset the giant's strength and speed. He was going to have to think his way out of this one. Unfortunately, he didn't have a single useful thought in his head.

"All right, me old cock," said John amiably. "You ready for a good walloping?"

Robin glanced hopefully back at Azeem, but the Moor just smiled and nodded confidently at him. Robin turned reluctantly back to face the giant, and made up his mind that if by some miracle he came out of this alive and reasonably intact, he was going to have some very harsh words with the Moor. Preferably while sitting on his chest and throttling him. John suddenly surged forward, and Robin's mind snapped back to the matter at hand. He parried the first blow easily enough, though the impact jarred his wrists painfully, and then the staff was coming at him from all directions at once, and it was all he could do just to stay in the fight. Luckily John was so used to winning with his strength and speed that he didn't bother much with things like tactics or subtlety. Robin held his ground, waited for just the right moment, and then ducked an overconfident swing and brought his own staff hammering down onto John's foot.

The giant stumbled back, howling with shock as much as pain, and Robin pressed him furiously, putting all his strength into every blow. He landed two solid attacks to John's ribs, and then the giant brought his quarterstaff sweeping round in a short, vicious arc that Robin didn't have the strength to counter. He retreated a step, and John went after him with a blindingly fast flurry of blows. And so the fight went, back and forth, trading blow for blow and hit for hit, neither man able to claim the advantage for long, or land a telling blow. John studied him curiously, with something that might have been respect, and chuckled happily as he fought. And then Robin's foot slipped and he dropped his defense for a moment. John thrust the end of his staff into Robin's stomach, and he doubled up, gasping for breath.

"Oh dearie me," said the woodsman in red loudly, "seems the little rich boy is lost for words."

His fellow woodsmen found that hysterical, and clutched at each other as they howled with laughter. John tapped Robin smartly in the ribs, to make sure he wasn't faking, and then pushed him deftly off the rock and onto the next tier. The sudden shock of the cold water cleared Robin's head, and he quickly got his feet under him. He glared back at Azeem, who just smiled encouragingly. Robin growled under his breath and looked back at John Little. The giant leaned casually on his staff and grinned down at him.

"Feeling a little wet behind the ears, mate?"

The woodsmen fell about, and wiped tears of laughter from their eyes. Little John jumped down. Robin pulled himself up and advanced determinedly on John, trying to ignore the water that squelched from his boots with every step. They stood facing each other for a moment, both breathing hard and steady, and then they threw themselves at each other, and it began again. The two staffs blurred on the air, clashing together and flying apart so rapidly the watchers were hard pressed to follow what was happening. Robin slammed in a series of hard shots to John's ribs and was rewarded by seeing the giant's grin falter for the first time. John swung his staff in a wide arc, putting all his strength into it. Robin ducked at the last moment, and John lost his balance as the staff sailed on without connecting. He fell to his knees, wide open to any attack. Robin placed one end of his staff on the rock and pole-vaulted over him, landing elegantly on the other side of the river.

"Seems I've made it past you, John Little, and that makes me the winner. Or should I call you 'Little John'?"

John surged to his feet with a roar, and they came together for a third time, the staffs flying with vicious speed. Splinters flew from the crashing impact of wood on

82

wood, and then there was a loud, echoing crack as Robin's staff broke suddenly in two. John grinned broadly at him, and tried to hide the relief in his voice.

"Swimming time again, rich man."

He brought his staff round in a swift arc and clipped Robin neatly above the ear. Robin teetered backward, off balance, and John's hand snapped out to snatch the medallion from around Robin's neck just before he fell back into the river and disappeared beneath the foaming water. John stood at the edge of the water, waiting patiently, but Robin didn't reappear. The woodsmen moved forward on both banks and stared into the dark waters, but there was no sign of Robin anywhere. John sighed regretfully.

"A real shame, that. He were a brave lad."

He tested the medallion between his teeth to make sure it was really gold, and then looped it round his neck. At which point Robin burst up out of the water, grabbed John by the ankles, and tipped him headfirst into the river. John sent water flying in every direction as he disappeared beneath the surface and then reappeared clawing at the water in a panic.

"Help! I can't bloody swim!"

He broke off as his head went under again. Robin moved quickly over beside him and pulled his head above water.

"Do you yield?" he asked politely.

The giant spluttered incoherently and grabbed at Robin in terror. Robin evaded him easily, and John went under again, flailing desperately. Robin waited a moment and then hauled John's head above water again.

"Do you yield, Little John?"

"Yes!" howled John desperately.

"Good," said Robin. "Now put your feet down."

John stared at him blankly and then tried to stand up. His feet slammed against the river bottom, and he found that when standing the water only came up to his chest. Robin watched warily, and then relaxed a little as John smiled slowly.

"Well I'll be buggered. . . ."

Robin bowed formally to him and put out his hand. "The medallion, if you please."

The woodsmen fell deathly silent, and there was a long, tense moment as everyone waited to see what John would do. He looked thoughtfully at Robin, and when he spoke his voice was deceptively calm.

"Give me your name."

"Robin of Locksley."

Some of the woodsmen muttered uneasily as they recognized the name. The words "devil worshipper" came clearly across the water, and a few made the sign against the evil eye, but other voices rose, defending the late lord's memory and reputation. Of them all, only the man in red remained silent, staring strangely at Robin with surprise and anger and something else altogether.

"Well, Locksley," said John finally, "I'll say this for you—you've got balls of solid rock!"

He took the medallion from around his neck and handed it to Robin, and then swept him up in his massive arms and carried him to the far bank, chuckling loudly. The woodsmen laughed too, but this time there was no anger or mockery in the sound. John had accepted him, so they did too. John dumped Robin unceremoniously on the riverbank, clambered up beside him and gave him a comradely slap on the back that nearly sent him flying into the river again. He got his breath back after a moment, smiled at John, and then glared at Azeem as he came striding unhurriedly across the rocks with Duncan in tow.

"Thanks for your assistance," said Robin, his tone positively dripping sarcasm.

Azeem shrugged, unmoved. "You seemed more in danger of losing your pride than your life."

"Is it over yet?" asked Duncan. "Of course, if I'd had my sight I'd have boxed the scoundrel's ears for him. Why is everyone laughing?"

Night had fallen by the time they reached the woodsmen's camp. It consisted in the main of a number of uprooted trees, leaning together, covered here and there with rags and roughly tanned hides. A large bonfire crackled in the middle of the camp, over which chunks of unrecognizable meat were turning slowly on crude spits. The woodsmen sprawled about the fire, drinking, eating, arguing, and fighting, sometimes all at once. The newly rechristened Little John let things settle down a bit and then got everyone's attention by being louder and more persistent than anyone else. He set about introducing the woodsmen, but Robin quickly got lost in the mixture of names, nicknames, and histories. The one thing they all seemed to have in common was a background of ill treatment and worse luck.

None of them had come to Sherwood by choice. They'd been driven there by desperation and found in the band of woodsmen a rough sense of brotherhood and support that was new to them. They were a great, sprawling family that accepted no one's authority save their own. They accepted Robin and Duncan and Azeem's presence easily enough, though the Moor's dark skin brought him the kind of attention that would have made anyone else uncomfortable. Azeem, being Azeem, didn't give a damn. For most of the woodsmen, the East was a land of fantasy and tall tales, and Arabs were as unreal to them as spirits or demons. But once they discovered he was a fugitive from the law, just like them, they accepted him as just another woodsmen. More or less.

But one man at least was unwilling to accept any of the newcomers. The man in the red jacket, identified by Little John as Will Scarlet, stood off to one side, scowling darkly and taking no part in the celebrations. Instead he threw a dagger at a tree, over and over again. Robin quietly decided he'd do well to keep an eye on Scarlet. He realized Little John was still throwing names at him, and nodded quickly, as though he'd been listening all along.

"And finally," said Little John, "we come to this stumpy little fellow here. Name's David of Doncaster, only we calls him Bull."

Robin nodded to Bull, who winked back cheerfully. He was a squat little man of about five foot, with broad muscular shoulders and a barrel chest, who gave the impression of being nearly as wide as he was tall.

"Why do they call you Bull?" asked Robin politely. "Because you are short?"

"Nay," said Bull proudly. "Because I be so long." He started to pull down his trousers to prove it, but Robin quickly stopped him with an upraised hand.

"Thanks, Bull, but save it for the ladies."

Bull hauled his trousers back into place, amid general drunken laughter. Jugs of something decidedly alcoholic were being passed back and forth, and Little John was quick to note Robin's interest. He acquired a jug by grabbing it from the person sitting next to him, and presented it proudly to Robin.

"Mead. Made it myself. Guarantee you've never tasted anything like it in your life."

Robin sniffed cautiously at the dark liquid, took a decent mouthful, and then thought very hard about whether to swallow it or spit it out before his tongue shriveled. In the end the need for diplomacy won out by a very short head, and he got it down with an effort. Something hard remained in his mouth, and he spat it discreetly into his hand. It turned out to be a dead bee.

"That's from the wild honey," John explained helpfully. "And of course, I like my mead to have a little body."

A roar of appreciative laughter swept through the camp. Not for the first time, it occurred to Robin that it didn't take much to amuse the woodsmen. He pretended to take another swallow of the mead and then passed the jug quickly to the next man. The woodsman took a hearty swig, belched cheerfully, and then started to pass it to the man next to him. At which point he realized that that man was Azeem. He hesitated, and then pretended not to see the Moor, and went to pass the jug to the next woodsman. Robin froze both of them with a glare.

"Has English hospitality changed so much in six years? I've always known a friend of mine to be welcome at any table."

An uncomfortable silence fell across the gathering, and then the offending woodsman leaned confidentially toward Robin.

"He's a savage, sire."

Robin looked at the ragged figure, caked with mud and general filth, and then at the immaculately garbed Moor. "Of course he's a savage," said Robin calmly. "But no more than you or I. And don't call me sire. I'm no different from you, now."

The woodsman looked to Little John for counsel. The giant shrugged, and nodded. The woodsman turned to Azeem with a forced smile and offered him the jug. Azeem smiled politely, and shook his head.

"With regrets, I must decline."

Robin glared at Azeem. Little John bristled angrily. "An Englishman's mead not good enough for you, then?"

Azeem bowed to him formally. "My faith prevents me from partaking in such enjoyments."

Little John sniffed. "Your bleeding loss, mate." He snatched the jug back and presented it to young Wulf, sitting at his feet. The boy gleefully buried his face in the jug. Robin decided it might be a good idea to change the subject.

"John, how is it there are so many of you in hiding?"

Little John scowled. "Sheriff pronounced us outlaws. Put a price on all our heads. He said we owed him taxes, but we couldn't give what we didn't have. So we all ended up breaking one law or another, and here we are. Woodsmen."

"How do you fare, here in Sherwood?"

"Poaching, mostly. Plus a little thieving. We get by."

"While the Sheriff steals your land, and your families starve?" Robin looked at the woodsmen almost angrily. "You can't hide here forever. Your 'ghosts' will only keep the Sheriff's men at bay for so long."

"Well what in bloody blazes would you have us do?" snarled Little John. "We show as much as a toe outside the forest, they'll slaughter us like so many bleeding sheep!"

"So fight back," said Robin.

Silence fell across the camp as the woodsmen looked at each other to make sure they'd heard it right.

"Us, against the Sheriff's army?" said John incredulously. "You have got to be bloody joking!" He put his hand against Robin's forehead, as though checking to see if he was feverish, and the woodsmen laughed uneasily. John took his hand away and smiled indulgently. "Reckon I must have cracked that blasted noble head of yours!"

Will Scarlet suddenly pushed his way through the woodsmen to glare at Robin, his throwing knife in his hand. "Why does a rich boy care what happens to a band of woodsmen peasants?"

"Put a cork in it, Will," said Little John. "The man's our guest."

Scarlet turned his back on them all and stalked off into the gloom beyond the camp's light. Little John nodded reassuringly to Robin. "Pay him no heed. Our Will's just full of piss and wind."

"He's right, in a way," said Robin. "I was a rich man's son. But not anymore. When I killed the Sheriff's men I became nothing more than a common outlaw. Just like everyone else here."

John studied him with a wordly smile. "You're a daft bugger, Robin of Locksley, but you're a brave one, I'll give you that. Now drink up, laddie, and stop spouting rubbish. This is the best simple men like us can expect." He gestured grandly at the awesome solace of the forest. "Here, we're safe. Here, we are kings!"

Morning visited the campsite with the songs of birds and a steady pattering of rain. A steady drip on the forehead from an overhanging branch brought Azeem awake in a rush, and he sat up, cursing the world in general and the English climate in particular. His bones ached from the night's cold, and the damp had permeated all his clothes. He was beginning to wonder if he'd ever feel warm and dry again. He looked around him into the morning mists as the camp slowly came awake, the woodsmen coughing and hacking and sneezing as they emerged from their rough shelters like drowsy animals from their burrows.

"Kings," said Azeem softly.

He nodded to Robin, who was already up, sitting off to one side and brooding thoughtfully. Robin smiled briefly in reply, and the Moor walked away to find somewhere reasonably private to attend to his ablutions. Robin shook Duncan awake, and the old man sat up slowly, groaning with the effort. He was too old for such hardships as the night before, and they both knew it.

"What's the matter, old friend?" said Robin gently. "Too much mead?"

"Forgive me," said Duncan. "I fear I have overslept."

"Rest," said Robin. "Take it easy for a while. What day is it, do you know?"

"Sunday, I believe."

"Good. Do they still give alms to the poor at the mass?"

"They do," said Duncan grimly. "These days the need for mercy is greater than ever."

Robin eyed Duncan's cloak thoughtfully. "Then, old friend, I must ask you for a favor. I have a scheme in mind. . . ."

7

NOTTINGHAM

Driving rain swept the length of the empty road that led to the city of Nottingham. The sky was iron gray, promising more rain to come, and the cold wind had a cutting edge. A single figure plodded along, cloaked and hooded against the rain, tapping blindly at the road ahead with his staff. He slipped and struggled through the thick mud and kept his head bowed against the gusting wind. Nothing to draw the attention of any gentle passerby on horseback or in a carriage, just another ragged peasant making his slow, painful way to the city to beg for alms at Sunday mass.

The hooded figure pulled his cloak tightly about him and glanced at the city wall looming up ahead. A slight smile crossed his face as the cathedral bells rang out across the countryside, summoning the faithful to prayer, and judgment. The hooded man smiled. He was bringing his own justice with him, and heaven help the guilty. Whoever they were.

Marian Dubois hesitated before the cathedral confessional booth and then quickly opened the door and stepped inside before she could change her mind again. It was dark within the booth, a comforting gloom where sins could be confessed that could not be admitted or faced in the harsh light of day. Marian sat down stiffly, back straight and head erect, but her thoughts whirled confusedly and her eyes were dark and troubled. Something new had entered her life, something strange and threatening, and she knew she had to face and conquer it, or it would conquer her. The door opened in the booth next to hers, and her breath caught in her throat as she heard the Bishop settling himself comfortably. She'd thought she'd have more time before he arrived, time enough to find the right words to describe the thoughts and emotions that so unsettled her. The ornately carved wooden screen slid open, sticking a little just at the end, as it always did, and the familiar sound comforted her and eased some of her nerves.

"Forgive me, Father, for I have sinned."

"What is the nature of your sin, my child?"

The Bishop, as usual, sounded more bored than anything, but once again the familiar words gave her the strength to continue.

"I met a man, Father. . . ." Marian hesitated as she sensed the Bishop's sudden attention, but pressed on. "I don't know how to express it, but since meeting him, I . . . have doubts. Is it a sin to have doubts, Father?"

"What kind of doubts?" asked the bishop.

"I feel somehow . . . empty, Father. That perhaps my life is lacking. Is God testing me?"

The Bishop chuckled indulgently. "Every day, my child. Every day."

The hooded man stopped before the city gate and bent down to scoop up a handful of fresh horse dung from the road. He then proceeded to smear it very thoroughly over his cloak and clothes, spreading it well to obtain the maximum effect. When he finished he looked hard at his reeking hand, as though unsure what to do with it for the best, and then shrugged and just let it hang at his side. He lifted his head and surreptitiously studied the wall on either side of the gate, fixing its size and composition in his memory, in case he had to leave Nottingham in a hurry. His hood started to fall back, and he grabbed it quickly and pulled it low over his face. It wouldn't do to have anyone knowing that Robin of Locksley had come to Nottingham. Still, with Duncan's cloak and staff, and a rich miasma of horse dung to keep people at arm's length, he was fairly confident of not being recognized. He bowed his head, hunched over a little for effect, and walked toward the gate, tapping his staff ahead of him.

A long line of scrawny, ragged beggars was already filing through the gate, and Robin latched onto the end of the line. There seemed to be far more unfortunates than he remembered seeing on previous visits to the city. Apparently times had indeed changed for the worse while he was abroad. He tapped his way through the gate, and the armed guard on duty looked at him narrowly as he passed. Robin's heart beat a little faster as the guard's gaze followed him, and he let his free hand move a little closer to the sword hidden under his cloak. The guard called out for him to stop, but Robin only hesitated for a moment before continuing on his way. The blind man he was supposed to be couldn't have known whom the guard was addressing.

A hand fell on his shoulder from behind and hauled him roughly out of line. The guard spun Robin round and glared at him suspiciously. Robin cringed convincingly, and then his heart sank as he saw the guard up close for the first time.

The man had a dented nosepiece to his helmet, and a badly bruised and swollen mouth. It was the guard he'd smashed in the face with a crossbow, just the day before, one of Gisborne's men. Robin sighed inwardly. Some days, things wouldn't go right even if you paid them. Still, the guard hadn't got much of a look at him before encountering the blunt end of the crossbow, so Robin stared determinedly off into space, doing his best to seem blind, daft, and helpless. The guard let go of Robin's shoulder and scowled in disgust at what had transferred to his hand.

"Do I know you?" he said brusquely, wiping his hand hard on his trousers. "My God, you don't half stink."

"It's me blindness, your worship," whined Robin in a high-pitched voice. "I'm always falling down. . . ."

The guard started to lean forward for a better look at Robin's face, and then retreated quickly as the smell hit him. "To hell with this. . . . Get out of here. Go on, get the hell away from me!"

Robin reached out blindly and as if by accident clasped the guard's hand in his. He shook the hand firmly and then walked on, tapping briskly away with his staff. The guard looked in horror at his hand and hurried Robin on his way with a solid boot to his rear.

"Thank you for noticing me, your worship," said Robin brightly, and moved quickly off into the city. Behind him, the guard was desperately trying to clean his hand by scraping it vigorously against the rough stone wall.

Down in Mortianna's chambers, deep in the bowels under Nottingham Castle, the albino had cocked her head on one side to listen to the faint pealing of the cathedral bells. She sniggered briefly, and turned back to her own altar. A pentacle had been drawn meticulously in blue chalk on the bare floor, and before it stood a large upside-down crucifix.

Blood from a black rooster formed a circle round the unholy icon, and burned meats lay scattered before it in blasphemous mockery of the Christian host. A tall figure stood within the pentacle, wrapped in the white robes of a Devil worshipper. He bowed three times to the unholy symbols and then left the pentacle, bent down, and picked up one of the charred meats. He chewed on it hungrily and pushed back his robe's hood. The Sheriff had never cared much for dressing up, but it was a necessary part of the ritual, according to Mortianna, so he kept his peace and put up with it. He finished the last of the meat, tossed the bone over his shoulder, and wiped his fingers on his sleeve.

Mortianna glared at him. The Sheriff sighed and found a handkerchief to use instead. He then stripped off his robes, revealing a noble's traditional Sunday finery. He handed the robes to Mortianna, patted and tugged at his clothing here and there, to be sure everything was as it should be, and then smiled at Mortianna as the cathedral's bells rang out again.

"My other god calls."

Mortianna scowled at him from over her mixing bowl, where she was stirring something that boiled and seethed rebelliously. She looked at his finery, sniffed disapprovingly, and spat into the mixture.

"Appearances are important, Mortianna," said the Sheriff calmly. "You know where my true faith lies." He looked thoughtfully at the upside-down crucifix and then reached out and turned it the right way up. "Although sometimes, to be honest, I can't see much difference. Did my parents ever tell you why they wanted me instructed in the left-hand path?"

"It was their dying wish," said Mortianna shortly. "Trust me. You are everything your mother wished."

• • •

Sunlight streamed through magnificent stained-glass windows, giving the huge gloomy cathedral what little light and color it had. The architects had concentrated on being impressive, to the neglect of practically everything else, including comfort, and the result was a bleak and austere structure, sprinkled here and there on the upper walls with some really ugly gargoyles and a handful of somewhat conceited-looking saints. But still the pews were packed with worshippers, and the Bishop looked smugly down from his pulpit on his largely noble and fashionably dressed flock. A mass was, after all, an important social event, a chance to see and be seen and catch up on all the latest gossip. The Bishop leaned forward and let his hands rest casually on the lovingly polished wood of the pulpit. It really was an excellent piece of workmanship. He'd chosen it himself, and together with his magnificent, ermine-decked robes, he was sure it made him look every inch the Bishop. Or, to be more exact, a Bishop on his way up, and headed for better things. He raised his eyes to Heaven and continued with his prayers, ignoring the shifting feet and fidgeting of the less godly members of his flock.

"We beseech thy blessing, Lord," he said loudly, "on all your people, but most especially on our noble Sheriff, the Lord Nottingham. Grant him the wisdom to guide and protect our glorious city. . . ."

The Sheriff shifted with boredom in his seat, while Gisborne dozed beside him. As far as Gisborne was concerned, it might be his social duty to attend mass, but no one said he had to enjoy it. The Sheriff let his eyes drift idly over the congregation, and then paused as his gaze fell upon Marian Dubois. A beautiful woman indeed, if a trifle stubborn. So far she had managed to find one excuse after

96

another to keep him at a distance, but he had no doubt she would defer to him eventually. Everyone did, eventually. He had money, influence, position, and power, and no hesitation in using any or all of them to get what he wanted. And he'd wanted Marian from the first time he saw her. He would have her in the end, no matter how she twisted and turned. In the meantime, he was rather enjoying the chase. A little anticipation was good for the appetite. He tried to catch Marian's eye, but she stared deliberately straight ahead, ignoring him. The Sheriff sighed again, leaned back in his pew, and, for want of anything better to do, listened to the Bishop.

"Grant him also the strength to bring to justice the lawless men who threaten Nottingham's safety and prosperity. . . ."

At the rear of the cathedral, the poor and the afflicted stood crushed together in a heavily guarded crowd, suffering through the service and the sermon for the chance to beg alms from the rich as they left. There were the old and the young, ancients and babes in arms, all of them marked by suffering or starvation, all of them quite invisible to those who had learned not to see them. The Bishop finally ran out of compliments and platitudes, and rushed the service to its end. The congregation rose to its feet in a buzz of conversation, chatting pleasantly about this and that as they filed out of the cathedral. The poor pressed in on either side of them, hands outstretched, eyes pleading. They begged in broken voices for food, for money, for medicines, for themselves or their loved ones, the ill and the dying. The congregation passed them by, neither seeing nor hearing, though a few lowered themselves to toss a handful of small coins across the floor, for the fun of seeing the poor scrabble for it on their hands and knees. The more desperate fought each other for it, and then the cathedral guards quickly intervened to put a stop to anything that might disturb the peace of the cathedral.

Marian pressed coins into begging hands until her purse was empty, and then gently disengaged herself and moved away into a small side alcove lit by dozens of prayer candles. Every Sunday she brought what she could spare, and often a little more, but it was never enough. Every week there were more begging hands, more starving children with huge eyes and distended bellies. All too soon the time would come when her money ran out and she had nothing left to give. Who would feed them then? She smiled sourly as she remembered asking the same of Robin of Locksley the day before. She had no answer then, and she had no answer now. She lit a candle with a spill, and closed her eyes in silent prayer, a heart-deep, wordless cry for help . . . and then her eyes snapped open as a grubby hand closed on her wrist. She spun round, pulling free, and gazed in shock at the ragged, filthy figure before her. She started to say something, and then stopped at the sound of a familiar voice.

"Alms for a blind man," said Robin softly. "For one who cannot see your beauty."

Marian glanced quickly round to make sure no one was paying the two of them any undue attention, and then looked back at Robin. Her mouth was set in a flat line, but her eyes were sparkling. "Are you mad? What are you doing here?"

"Looking for answers."

"I have no wish to be seen with an outlaw. There's a price on your head."

"Really?" said Robin interestedly. "How much?"

"A hundred gold pieces!"

"Is that all? I'll have to work harder at annoying the Sheriff. I'm worth at least a thousand."

Marian almost smiled, but quickly turned it into a sniff. "For a thousand gold pieces I'd turn you in myself." She glanced back at the Sheriff, and then leaned closer to Robin, her voice little more than a murmur. "The Sheriff is putting together his own private army. He has every blacksmith in the county holed up in his castle making swords and armor."

Robin looked across at the Sheriff, surrounded by armed guards and groveling ring-kissers. Marian stirred uneasily as she saw hatred and loathing burn in his gaze. It was as though the kind, irritating Robin she'd met the day before no longer existed, pushed aside by a cold implacable warrior, unstoppable as death itself. Robin looked back at her, and it was all Marian could do not to flinch at his icy gaze.

"What is he planning, Marian?"

"I don't know," said Marian quickly. "But I've always known there's no limit to that man's ambition."

Robin's eyes warmed again as they met Marian's. "Nor to mine. . . . Thank you, Marian."

Something moved between them in that moment, and then Marian saw the Sheriff approaching over Robin's shoulder, and the moment was broken. "He's coming this way," she murmured quickly. "You'd better go. But Robin, before we meet again, do something for me."

"Anything," said Robin. "What?"

"Take a bath!"

They shared a quick grin, and then Robin pulled his hood well forward to hide his face, and disappeared through a nearby door. Marian composed herself and turned to face the Sheriff, hoping he wouldn't notice the pleasant flush in her face.

• • •

The Bishop entered his private chamber and immediately removed his miter and rubbed irritably at his forehead. Damned thing itched like crazy, no matter what he tried. He sighed and looked about him, his heart warming as always at the sight of his luxurious surroundings. Life had been good to him since the Sheriff had appointed him Bishop of Nottingham. He tossed the miter into a nearby chair and glared at it. Impressive to look at, but a pain to wear. He smiled slightly. Interesting symbolism in that, something to do with the pains of responsibility and how heavy it weighed. Possibly something he could use in his next sermon. He looked about him for a scrap of paper to jot it down on, and then froze as he heard a sudden movement behind him. He spun round, and a cold fist clutched at his heart as a hooded figure stepped out of the shadows. The Bishop swallowed hard and pulled his dignity around him like a shield.

"These are my private chambers, my son," he said stiffly. "There are priests without who will hear your confession . . . if that is what you wish. . . ."

The figure lifted its hands and pushed back its hood, and the Bishop gaped at a face he'd never thought to see again. Robin of Locksley bowed formally to him. The Bishop smiled warmly.

"I see a boy I knew in the man before me. Welcome home, Robin."

He reached out to Robin, and after a moment Robin leaned forward and kissed the Bishop's ring.

The Sheriff bowed formally to Marian and gestured for his people to stand back a ways, to allow the two of them a little privacy. He took Marian's hand in his and raised it to his lips. Marian smiled briefly and took back her hand as soon as politely possible. She wanted to move over a little,

100

to mask the door through which Robin had disappeared, but she was afraid any movement would just draw the Sheriff's attention to it. He smiled warmly at her, his eyes as cool as ever.

"You shine like the sun, my Lady."

"Thank you," said Marian. "To what do I owe the pleasure of your company, my Lord?"

"You have been meeting with young Robin of Locksley," said the Sheriff. He smiled at her slight involuntary reaction to Robin's name, and continued smoothly. "My cousin tells me the knave deprived you of some horses."

"Yes," said Marian quickly, turning her expression to one of bored distaste. "A most disagreeable experience."

"For subjecting you to such treatment," murmured the Sheriff, "I will hang him from my castle wall by his own entrails."

Marian looked at him calmly. "I would like to see that, my Lord."

The Sheriff moved a little closer and placed a hand possessively on her shoulder. "My dear, if you would only bring your household within the city walls, I could give your needs my most personal attention."

Marian met his gaze steadily, ignoring his touch as though it didn't exist. "Thank you, Lord Nottingham, but for now I prefer to stay in my family's ancestral home. I feel safer there."

The Sheriff's smile didn't waver, but his gaze was suddenly disturbingly cold and direct. He took his hand away from Marian's shoulder as though he'd always meant to, and produced a beautiful jeweled dagger from beneath his cloak. "Then please do me the honor of accepting this, as a token of my undying devotion to your safety."

The dagger was a work of art, and worth a small fortune, but Marian accepted it from him as though it were a butter knife. The door behind her seemed almost to be shouting out Robin's location, and the need to glance at it to be sure everything was all right was almost overpowering. Somehow she managed a polite smile for the Sheriff, and tucked the knife under her belt.

"My cousin King Richard will be deeply moved to hear of your concern for my welfare."

"Alas," murmured the Sheriff, "the King has many enemies, both abroad and at home. I fear for his safe return."

"Fear not, my dear Sheriff," said Marian sweetly. "He will return. And when he does, he will reward his faithful subjects, and punish all traitors."

The Sheriff smiled stiffly, bowed formally, and then strode past her straight to the door leading to the Bishop's private chamber.

Robin listened intently as the Bishop talked. His stare was cold and unwavering, despite the Bishop's repeated efforts to put him at his ease, and even in his rags and filth he was still somehow every inch the Lord of Locksley. The Bishop told of the previous lord's disgrace and death as kindly as he could, but more and more he found Robin's cold silence unnerving. He began to look around his chamber as though for inspiration. He was finding it increasingly difficult to face Robin's implacable gaze. He finally reached the point where Robin's father had confessed to devil worship, and he broke off abruptly, not knowing how to finish.

"How could you have believed such a thing of him? You of all people must have known how devoted he was to the Church."

The Bishop looked earnestly into Robin's eyes. "Three times I asked your father that very question, because his answer vexed me so grievously. I couldn't believe it of him either, but he swore he must meet his God with a clear conscience, and admitted everything. These times haunt me, my son. The power of the old religion is a terrible temptation when drought, famine, and war so plague the land."

Robin nodded slowly, sadly, as if that was all the confirmation he needed.

"You lie," he said flatly, and the Bishop could not answer him.

Robin turned away, as though just the thought of touching the Bishop sickened him, and the expression on his face was worse than any blow. Robin strode over to the door and pulled it open. And found himself face-to-face with the Sheriff of Nottingham, poised to enter. For a moment they just gaped at each other, and then the Sheriff looked past the figure before him to the guilt and panic written clearly in the Bishop's sweaty face. He looked back at the ragged, malodorous figure blocking his way, and didn't need to be told who it was.

He opened his mouth to yell for his guards, and Robin seized a dagger from under his rags and lashed out with it. The Sheriff stumbled backward, but the tip of the blade opened up a long gash across his cheek. He fell backward, clutching at his face. Blood spurted between his fingers. He screamed for his guards, and Robin whirled on the Bishop again. The Bishop recoiled as he saw the dagger in Robin's hand, all color draining from his face.

"Oh, for your soul's sake, spill no more blood in the House of God!"

Robin looked at him disdainfully and made for the door on the opposite side of the room. It burst open, and guards spilled into the room. Robin skidded to a halt and looked wildly about him. Guards were coming at him from both directions, and there was no other way out. His frantic gaze snagged on a thick rope that stretched up to the ceiling, and it only took a moment to follow it up to the enormous candled chandelier it was supporting. He grinned, grabbed the rope firmly, and then severed it with his dagger. The rope parted in an instant, and the down-rushing weight of the chandelier yanked him up out of harm's way, even as the chandelier crashed down on the guards below. Robin swung agilely onto a high window ledge, kicked out the glass in the window, and started to clamber through. Then the Sheriff called his name, and Robin stopped and looked back. The Sheriff was glaring up at him, pressing a blood-soaked handkerchief to his face, almost out of his mind with pain and rage.

"Locksley! I'll carve out your heart for this!"

Robin looked calmly down at him. "So. It begins."

He smiled at the Sheriff and then threw himself out the window. Arrows pierced the wall where he'd stood.

A groom holding the Sheriff's horse outside the cathedral was having a fairly boring morning when he had a sudden religious experience. A ragged holy man appeared out of nowhere, landed on the Sheriff's horse, and snatched the reins out of his hand. The groom stood and watched open-mouthed as horse and rider disappeared at a gallop.

Robin charged toward the city gate, scattering all before him. He plunged through the busy marketplace, being pelted with produce from various stalls, and pursued by all manner of curses, along with a few arrows from the quicker-reacting guards. The gate loomed up before him, and the guard on duty moved quickly to block his way. Robin grinned vindictively as he remembered a certain boot to his posterior. He grabbed a bulky sack from a nearby supply wagon and used it to slam the guard into the city wall. Robin rode out through the gate, laughing and urging his horse on to even greater speed. Arrows whistled down around him, none of them coming close, and Robin left the city of Notthingham behind him in a cloud of dust and the echo of his laughter.

8

THIEVES

Back in the heart of Sherwood, the woodsmen gathered around Robin as he reined his stolen horse to a halt. He grinned down at their astonished faces, exhausted but exuberant. Azeem called for water to be brought, and Robin nodded to him gratefully. Azeem took the bowl of water when it arrived and presented it to the panting, lathered horse. Robin gave the Moor a hard look.

"Why did you leave here without me?" asked Azeem, unmoved. "How am I to protect you if I don't even know where you are?"

"You've hardly raised a finger when you did know," Robin pointed out.

Azeem shrugged. "I like to have the choice."

As Robin swung down from the saddle, the woodsmen examined the horse admiringly, impressed by the rich heraldic finery the animal was wearing. Will Scarlet pushed his way to the front of the crowd, studied the trappings closely, and then turned an angry scowl on Robin.

"This is the Sheriff's horse," he said flatly, and the

woodsmen fell silent. They looked at Robin with frightened, accusing eyes, and Little John glared at him angrily.

"That's just great, that is. All the horses you could have stolen, and you had to pick the bloody Sheriff of Nottingham's! Why didn't you just leave him a note, saying, 'Please come into the forest after me and kick the hell out of whoever happens to be with me at the time?' There's no way he's going to overlook this; his pride won't let him. You've stirred up a real bloody hornet's nest now."

Robin smiled easily, entirely unperturbed. "Well, if the Sheriff's an insect, I gave him a damned good swat this morning. And I don't just mean losing his horse. I cut a remembrance into his face he'll carry to his grave. You worry about him too much. For all his office, he's just a man."

"A man with an army," growled Scarlet.

"Numbers aren't everything," said Robin. "I learned that in the Holy Land. If we organize and stand together, we can beat him."

Little John looked at him narrowly. "What's with this *we* business? You looking to join us?"

"No," said Robin. "I'm going to lead you."

He unstrapped from his saddle the heavy sack he'd picked up on his way out of Nottingham, and emptied out the contents. Great hams, whole cooked chickens, and massive cheeses tumbled out before the astonished eyes of the woodsmen. They fell on the unexpected feast with hungry hands, praising Robin with incoherent voices. Little John laughed, and clapped Robin on the back. Will Scarlet stood at the back of the crowd, arms folded stubbornly across his chest, refusing to even look at the food. His eyes were fixed on Robin, and there was nothing but hatred in his gaze.

• • •

In the Sheriff's private chambers in Nottingham Castle, the Sheriff sat stiffly in his chair, trembling more with rage than pain as his personal surgeon-barber prepared to sew up the wound in his cheek. Gisborne stood close at hand, ostensibly to receive orders and provide moral support, and watched interestedly as the surgeon heated the blunt-looking needle in a candle flame. At heart, Gisborne was a man of simple pleasures. The Sheriff glared at him.

"I want this brigand found, Gisborne! I don't care how many of the peasants support him. We'll starve the fight out of them. Slaughter their livestock . . . No . . . better still, *take* their livestock. That way, they'll think there's a chance they might get them back if they cooperate. I want Locksley's own people fighting each other for a chance to bring in his head."

Gisborne nodded thoughtfully. "Perhaps we should give him a nickname, cousin; something to make the peasants fear him. Locksley the Lethal, Reeking Robin, the Hooded Man. . . ."

"Call him what you will, but find him! I want this brigand dead by the next full moon, before the barons return and see what a fool he's making of us!" He glared malevolently at the waiting surgeon. "Sew, damn you. And make a clean job of it or I'll have your fingers stitched together!"

He braced himself as the needle neared his bloody cheek. Gisborne leaned in closer for a better look.

In the days that followed, the Sheriff's men were everywhere, enforcing the laws. Any who dared to object were beaten viciously, and sometimes worse. No town, village, or hamlet was spared. Houses were burned to the ground, to punish the stubborn or set an example to those who might

108

consider hiding goods or gold. Smoke blackened the sky all across the county, and blood from guilty and innocent alike soaked into the trampled earth. Sir Guy of Gisborne led the raids personally, and found it all great sport.

But even he was beginning to grow bored with it all by the end of the second week. He watched impatiently from his horse as his men sacked a small village on the border of Sherwood Forest, and drummed his fingers on the saddle horn. Barely mid-afternoon, and already he was two hours behind schedule. His soldiers smashed their way into the simple hovels, and emerged with whatever they could carry. Most would go to the Sheriff, some to Gisborne, and the rest would be divided among the soldiers. Gisborne believed in rewarding initiative, and besides, he liked to hear the peasants squeal.

Women and children ran screaming as the soldiers drove them from their homes, and the men of the village stood together and looked on silently, too frightened and too outnumbered to even think of interfering. There were screams and squeals from the villagers' livestock, as soldiers herded the animals together and urged them up onto a wagon for transport, and one farmer stepped forward suddenly, perhaps braver than the others or simply despairing at the sight of his livelihood disappearing. He looked doggedly up at Gisborne, his hands clenching and unclenching helplessly at his sides.

"You must not do this, sire! You'll starve us all! First the drought ruined the harvests, and now you take what little food we have left!"

"For starving people, you look fat enough," said Gisborne. "Perhaps someone has been bringing you food—a man in a hood, perchance?" He looked mockingly at the villagers crowded sullenly together behind the farmer, and then frowned suddenly as he recognized a familiar face. The woman might have been pretty under the dirt, but hard work and a harder life had scoured all the softness out of her. She glared at Gisborne, and held a small child protectively close to her as Gisborne leaned forward to address her. "Where's your husband, Fanny? The man they call Little?"

She met his gaze steadily, not bothering to hide her hate. "He died. Last winter."

"Is that so?" said Gisborne. "We hear that he is very much alive, hiding out in the forest with the Sherwood bandits."

"Must have been his ghost," said Fanny.

Gisborne urged his horse forward a few steps, till he was towering over Fanny and her child, but she held her ground defiantly. Gisborne kicked out suddenly, and the force of the blow threw Fanny to the ground. She landed hard and painfully, and the child wailed, but no one moved to help mother or child. No one dared. Gisborne and the soldiers laughed. Fanny rose slowly to her knees and spat on the ground between her and Gisborne. The farmer raised his voice again, his words stumbling as Gisborne turned his cold regard on him.

"God bless you, sire, but leave us the sow at least. She's with young. Her litter will feed us through the worst of the winter."

"Not now they won't," said Gisborne easily. "If I were you, I'd pray Robin Hood is brought to us before winter sets in."

He turned his horse away, laughing, and led the soldiers out of the village. The wagon brought up the rear, groaning under the weight of the livestock and other booty. Some of the peasants watched them go with hate in their eyes. Others looked angrily at Fanny.

110

• • •

A long line of refugees filed tiredly into the woodsmen's camp, deep in Sherwood. They carried their few remaining possessions on their backs, and all of them, men, women and children, showed signs of long hunger and brutal ill-treatment. They had come to the deep woods as so many had before—because there was nowhere else to go. Among them was Fanny Little, and the boy Wulf ran to greet her, howling his delight.

Robin and Azeem sat together on a giant tree trunk, silently watching the latest batch of refugees arrive. Robin had known there would be some, in fact his plans depended on it, but he'd never expected there to be so many. He looked down at the newly fashioned yew bow in his hands, but the sight of the refugees stayed with him. When all was said and done, their plight, their suffering, was at least partly his fault. He made himself concentrate on the job at hand, and carefully attached the gut string to the bow.

The refugees sank warily down beside the central fire, and told their tales to the woodsmen. It was a single, sad, familiar tale, already told many times over by previous refugees. Some of the newcomers asked timidly for food, or drink, but others just sat where they were, too tired to go any farther, too tired even for tears or complaints or the simple acts of living. A few spoke the name of Robin Hood, and Will Scarlet stepped forward to point him out. An old farmer advanced on Robin angrily and pulled open his tunic to show still-healing wounds from a recent beating. A woman held up a starving baby for Robin to see, its eyes huge in its shrunken face. More refugees drifted toward him, their faces hurt and angry. Azeem looked at Robin.

"If it's fame you sought, my friend, I think you have it."

Will Scarlet pushed through the refugees to stand glaring at Robin. "You brought this misery on us, Locksley."

"This is the Sheriff's work, Will," said Robin patiently. "He's trying to divide us."

"We are divided, rich boy," said Scarlet loudly. "I heard today the Sheriff has raised the value of your neck to a thousand gold pieces." He looked about him, judging the mood of the listening refugees and woodsmen. "I say we take him in; give him to the Sheriff."

There were general murmurs of agreement, mostly, but not all, from the refugees. Robin shook his head slowly, and looked at Scarlet as though he were a slow, and particularly dense, pupil. "Will, do you really believe the Sheriff will just give everything back, after I'm gone?"

"He'll give us the reward," said Scarlet. "And our pardons. We could live as free men again."

"He'll stretch your necks one by one," said Robin flatly. "No one defies the Sheriff and lives. You know that."

There was a long, deadly silence. Robin looked at Scarlet coolly. The refugees and the woodsmen looked uncertainly from Robin to Scarlet. He sneered openly at Robin.

"What would you have us do, rich boy? Fight armored and mounted troops with rocks and bare hands?"

"If needs be, with the one weapon that escapes you, Will—courage."

Scarlet's face turned as red as his tunic. He glared speechlessly at Robin, but in the end he was the first to look away. Robin tested the string on his bow once, rose unhurriedly to his feet, turned, and walked away. Scarlet drew a dagger and lifted it to throw at Robin's unprotected back. The boy Wulf yelled a warning, and Robin whirled round, aimed, and fired an arrow in one lightning-swift movement. The arrow slammed through Scarlet's hand while he was still aiming the dagger. He dropped it and stumbled away with the arrow piercing his hand, grimacing at the pain but savagely refusing the few offers of assistance he received. The woodsmen and the refugees murmured quietly among themselves, impressed by the feat of skill. Robin nodded his thanks to Wulf and then turned and addressed the watching crowd.

"You wish to end this? You wish to go home? Then we must stop fighting amongst ourselves and face that there is a price to be paid. You can't birth a child without pain; you can't raise corn without sweat. I, for one, would rather die, than spend my life in hiding. The Sheriff calls us outlaws . . . but I say we are free men. And one free man defending his home is more powerful than ten hired soldiers."

Robin glanced at Azeem. "The Crusades have taught me that. If you truly believe in your hearts that you are free . . . then I say we can win."

"You can't eat wood," said one peasant roughly. "We have nothing. The Sheriff took all our animals."

"And they have armor," said another.

"And all our money! Sheriff's men didn't leave us a farthing!"

"Then, by God, we'll take it back," said Robin. "All of it, and more."

Time passed, and summer faded into autumn. In Sherwood gold and bronze tatters wrapped the trees, and the thick mulch on the forest floor soaked up the sounds of those who walked the narrow paths between the trees. Cool eyes watched from the shadows, and silent figures appeared and disappeared before startled travelers, as though by magic.

But the Sheriff continued his onslaught. Even the Church was not exempt from his abuse. On one particular day, the Sheriff's men were surprised. . . .

"Please, sire, those belong to our Lord," an ancient, wizened priest begged the Sheriff's men.

"Now they belong to my Lord Sheriff," one soldier sneered.

Suddenly, out of the trees came a sound like screaming banshees. The men looked up. Whistling arrows thundered down, landing at the soldiers' boots, and Robin appeared, smiling grimly, a quiver full of white arrows on his back and a longbow in his hands.

"If you don't wish to meet your maker, you'll return to him that which belongs to him," he said, pointing his longbow at the men.

The soldiers glanced at each other nervously. But before the leader could speak, an arrow whizzed past his ear. The woodsmen stood, half-shrouded by the trees, in a group. The leader of the soldiers gulped and retreated slightly. The rest of his men threw down their weapons and booty.

"Good," said Robin. "Now tell the Sheriff, for every harm he does these people, I will visit it back on him tenfold."

There was no argument.

On a day in late September, when the sun was little more than a crimson orb hanging low on the sky, Baron Hardcastle rode nervously through the forest, his eyes darting from shadow to shadow, his heart jumping at every unexpected sound. Not for the first time, he wished he'd taken some other route, or at least assembled a company of armored guards to protect him, instead of relying on his two usual bodyguards. They were both good men, and loyal to the generous retainer he paid them, but if half the tales told of Robin Hood and his wild men of the forest were true . . . Baron Hardcastle swallowed hard and decided very firmly that he wasn't going to think about that anymore.

He mopped at his sweating face with a silk handkerchief, and glared about him into the gloom between the trees. He was worrying himself needlessly over nothing. These tales of woodsmen in Sherwood were just comforting stories made up by peasants as they huddled together in their filthy hovels at night. It was ludicrous even to think that the lower classes might dare to rebel against their rightful lords and masters. They knew their place. And by God, if they didn't, the army would soon ride in and teach it to them! The Baron smiled complacently, and started to put together a clever little speech he could casually drop at his destination, about how he'd braved the dangers of the infamous Sherwood Forest. . . .

And then the forest itself seemed suddenly to come alive, as figures boiled up out of the undergrowth on both sides of the trail. Their clothes were camouflaged with leaves and branches, and their faces painted artfully with greens and browns. The Baron looked back over his shoulder, and panic rose chattering in his heart as he discovered that more had appeared behind him to cut off his retreat. They all had bows with arrows nocked, held with the casual ease of those who knew how to use them, and in their cold smiles and colder eyes there was no trace of mercy. The Baron looked helplessly at his two bodyguards, but they had already raised their hands in surrender. The Baron would have liked to do the same, but he was too frightened to move. A voice floated casually down from an overhead branch, and the Baron looked up, startled.

" 'Tis a hot day, my friend. Far too warm to burden your horse with such a heavy pouch."

Robin Hood smiled down from the overhanging branch. The Baron started to splutter some kind of protest, looked at all the arrows pointing in his direction, and thought better of it. He reluctantly untied the heavy purse from his belt, hefted the solid weight of gold and silver for a moment, and then tossed it up to Robin, who caught it neatly with one hand. He bowed mockingly to the Baron.

"Many thanks for this generous contribution to our cause, my friend. This purse will fill many hungry bellies and warm many a cold hearth."

The Baron glared up at him. "The Sheriff will hear of this!"

"I hope so," said Robin. "And you can tell him from me, the current reward on my head is an insult. It's not nearly high enough."

And so it went, as the weeks passed. No rich man, be he noble or merchant, could pass through Sherwood without paying a heavy toll for the privilege. Armored guards were no match for an arrow shot from cover, and any attempt at pursuit simply resulted in men floundering aimlessly through the thick undergrowth as they were picked off one by one by unseen enemies. Money that had been extorted from the poor found its way back to them, and for the first time in a long time the villages and hamlets of Nottingham-shire faced the coming winter with something more than growling stomachs and empty hearts. The woodsmen captured livestock in daring raids, and returned it to those who needed it most. The name of Robin Hood was voiced everywhere in the North Country, and the harder the Sheriff tried to stamp it out, the louder those voices rang.

The woodsmen trained hard under Robin and Azeem's direction, firing arrows at dummy soldiers over and over again to refine their marksmanship. They trained with sword and ax and knife, and in between labored hard to build new homes in the forest. Rope bridges were built between the trees, far above the ground, linking dwellings constructed among the high branches. Hunters brought in fresh game every day, often the deer it had once been worth a man's life to hunt. Few now dared to enter Sherwood in pursuit of poachers.

Some of the barons took to traveling through the forest in heavily reinforced carriages, trusting in thick oak and steel panels to protect them. Robin in turn quickly came up with several new ways of bringing the carriages to a sudden halt, such as hidden iron hooks and chains that appeared just at the right moment to snag the carriages' axles as they passed and yank the axles right out from under the carriage. Once stopped, the occupants of the carriage could then be relieved of their valuables with the minimum of fuss and the maximum of efficiency.

Robin often headed these forays, not because he had any doubts in the method, but because he loved to see the expressions on the barons' faces. On one occasion, he broke into a carriage to find himself face-to-face with a fuming middle-aged baron and a lovely lady easily young enough to be his daughter. Robin helped her descend safely from the carriage, smiled charmingly, and deftly slid a large diamond ring off her finger. The lady made a small moue of disappointment, and Robin bowed gallantly.

"Milady, a woman of your rare beauty has no need for such decorations."

He kissed her hand, and she sighed deeply and batted her eyes at him. The Baron glowered at Robin.

"You should be ashamed of yourself, to address my wife in such a fashion!"

Robin cocked an eyebrow at him. "If this young lady is your wife, you're the one who should be ashamed of himself."

He and his men then disappeared into the woods with the Baron's purse and belongings, while the Baron was still trying to force an answer past his furious spluttering. His wife looked after the woodsmen.

"Who was that man?" she murmured dreamily.

"A thief!" snapped her husband.

"A prince of thieves," said the young lady, her eyes fixed on the woods.

As more and more goods and gold entered Sherwood and failed to leave it, the woodsmen moved more and more freely among the surrounding villages and hamlets, distributing their booty to those whose need was greatest. The grateful poor would no more have turned them in to the Sheriff's men than they would have turned against their own families. Bull drove his cart from one settlement to another, with Wulf and Fanny to help him unload the food, blankets, and clothes. All three wore weapons, openly displayed. The villagers cheered them on sight, and called down God's blessings on the name of Robin Hood, Prince of Thieves.

Posters appeared on trees at the edge of the forest, offering a reward of ten thousand gold pieces for the head of Robin Hood. The posters grew yellowed and tattered, but no one took up the Sheriff's offer.

Gisborne led his men into Sherwood again and again, employing the best trackers the Sheriff's money could buy, but never found a trace of Robin Hood or his woodsmen. Finding their tracks was easy enough, but the trails led nowhere, often just stopping dead, as though the woodsmen had simply vanished into thin air. The soldiers rolled their eyes and crossed themselves and muttered about the dark magics and secrets to be found in Sherwood's ancient heart. None of them ever thought to look up. If they had, they might have been able to pierce the camouflage of leaves and branches to make out a whole web of bridges, ropes, and sleeping platforms, and the woodsmen watching gleefully from their hiding places.

● ● ●

In his private chambers in Nottingham Castle, the Sheriff sat in his great chair and listened wearily as his chief scribe read from a long list of recent thefts. He did not see the burning eye that watched everything through the hidden spy hole, and his gaze barely lingered on the latest group of trembling young women brought before him by his guards, for his approval. They were all pretty enough, behind their fear, but the Sheriff concentrated instead on the scribe, who grew increasingly nervous under the Sheriff's unwavering stare. He cleared his throat, clutched his papers so tightly they wrinkled, and continued unhappily with his report.

"We have reason to believe, my Lord, that this Robin Hood person has taken as much as four million gold pieces, or goods to that value, in the last three months. Possibly even more."

The Sheriff gestured brusquely for one of the young women to turn around on the spot. She did so, timidly, and the Sheriff watched her coldly, absently picking at the scar on his cheek. He turned his gaze back to the scribe, and when he spoke, his voice was very calm and very dangerous.

"Very well, then. Increase the bounty on his hooded head. Make it twenty-five thousand crowns."

"Begging your pardon, my Lord," said the scribe diffidently, "but I really don't think it's going to make any difference, no matter how much you make it."

The Sheriff leaned forward in his chair and pinned the scribe with his gaze. "Really? And why is that, my good and trusted scribe?"

"Because, my Lord," said the scribe nervously, "because the poor, you see, they . . . Well, he gives them most of what he steals from the rich, so they . . . love him."

The Sheriff leaned back in his chair, an increasingly

heavy scowl furrowing his brow. The scribe checked unobtrusively how far he was from the nearest exit. The Sheriff hammered on the arm of his chair with his fist. "Robin Hood is stealing from my pocket, forcing me to hurt the poor, and they love him for it? They dare love him, and not me, their rightful lord? That's it! There'll be no more charity from this pocket! All public holidays are canceled, as from this moment. No more merciful executions! And cancel the kitchen leavings for the lepers and orphans. Remind me to come up with some new charity payments, so I can cancel them, too."

The Sheriff rose abruptly from his chair and strode restlessly back and forth, scowling furiously. The scribe hurried close behind him, scribbling down the Sheriff's words as fast as he could.

"All I hear these days are complaints," growled the Sheriff, a dangerous gleam in his eyes. "The treasury is shrinking, and all day and all night men of means plague my door, whining for tax relief and guards to ensure safe passage through Sherwood. And then they have the bare-faced cheek to complain they can't pay the taxes they owe me because woodsmen have stolen it all! If as much wealth had disappeared in Sherwood as the barons are claiming, the county would have been bankrupt by now. Why the hell can't the barons just stay out of Sherwood?"

"Because it's the shortest road from Nottingham to London," said the scribe automatically, and then he wished he hadn't as the Sheriff rounded on him.

"It's the *only* road to London, you obsequious little ferret! The only road that will take the barons to our would-be King John, and his court!" He broke off suddenly, as one of the waiting young women caught his eye. He glanced at her for a moment, and then nodded sharply. "You. To my bed. Tonight."

The scribe cleared his throat nervously, and the Sheriff rounded on him again. The scribe searched urgently for something to say that wouldn't get him into even worse trouble. "Sir Guy's patrols have found nothing then, my Lord?"

"Sir Guy couldn't find his own arse in the dark without using both hands!" snapped the Sheriff. "According to him there's no trace of the woodsmen's camp anywhere in Sherwood. The hooded viper simply slithers into the forest and disappears."

His wandering gaze settled on a bust of himself, standing on a side table. Someone had chiseled a scar into the stone cheek, to match the real thing. The Sheriff's face darkened dangerously as he glared at the bust, his hands clenching and unclenching at his sides as fury momentarily robbed him of his voice. The scribe took advantage of the Sheriff's preoccupation to stick out his tongue at the Sheriff's back.

Later that day, in Mortianna's chambers deep beneath the castle, the Sheriff pulled on his Devil worshipper's robes with even less enthusiasm than usual. The albino hag watched him narrowly from her blasphemous Devil's altar, already running with the blood of thirteen animal sacrifices.

"Something vexes thee?"

The Sheriff shrugged irritably, and Mortianna scurried over to place a cold palm on his forehead, testing for fever. He grimaced slightly at the unpleasant clammy touch, but had enough sense to say nothing. The hag might be withered and ancient, but there was no denying there was a power in her. He wanted that power, and would put up with much to get it. Afterward . . . there would be time for many things, afterward. He braced himself to meet the hag's burning gaze.

He picked up the cat-o'-nine-tails Mortianna had set out

for him, and flicked it a few times listlessly, his thoughts elsewhere. "In ten days time the barons will be here, and Robin Hood has stolen from me the money that would have bought their allegiance. I'm surrounded by fools and incompetents, who care nothing for my obligations! Tell me true, Mortianna, is there a traitor among my people?"

The hag raised a sharp fingernail and slashed it across the skin of her bony arm. Blood dripped onto the filthy stone floor as she watched unflinchingly. Finally she squatted down beside the pool of blood, spat into it, and studied the patterns that formed. The Sheriff crouched down beside her, trying to see what she saw in the blood. The hag rocked slightly from side to side on her haunches.

"Recruit the beast that shares your god!"

The Sheriff frowned. Mortianna was often obscure, but of late she'd been even harder to follow than usual. "Animals?" he said uncertainly.

"Nay, the dark ones from the north."

"Celts?"

"Yoke their strength, and make it yours."

The Sheriff nodded slowly. The northern savages were known for their wild cruelty, and a willingness to follow any cause for gold. It also helped that they worshipped the same dark forces as the Sheriff. Mortianna stared at him unblinkingly, her gaze smoldering with unguessed secrets.

"Put thine own issue on the throne."

"A child of mine on the throne of England?" said the Sheriff incredulously. "How?"

"Ally with royal blood."

"Well, obviously," said the Sheriff testily. "But who?"

Mortianna looked away from him. "That is not yet revealed." The Sheriff scowled unhappily, not entirely surprised. Mortianna dragged a stick leisurely through the blood and spittle before her. "A tongue offends thee."

"Whose?"

"One who writes all."

"My chief scribe . . ." said the Sheriff thoughtfully. "I might have known. Never trust a man who reads and writes. He dares wag his tongue at me?"

Mortianna nodded, smiling coldly. "Cut it out."

9

BEGINNINGS

A narrow road meandered through Sherwood, picking its way through the cathedral of giant trees. Only an occasional shaft of light pierced the forest gloom, and no bird sang. Sir Guy of Gisborne peered constantly about him as he led a troop of armored men along the rough trail. The continuing silence of the forest unnerved him. It wasn't natural. No birds, no insects—nothing. Gisborne licked nervously at his dry lips. The woodsmen were out there, somewhere. He couldn't see them, but he had no doubt they were there. He could feel the pressure of their eyes on his back. His men could feel it too. Their songs and chatter had slowly died away as they rode deeper into Sherwood, and now they all rode with one hand on their sword hilts. Gisborne looked back the way they'd come, and a little of his confidence returned. The woodsmen might have stopped other tax collections, but this time things would be different.

In the middle of the company rolled the tax wagon, a great armored box on wheels, large enough to hold all the tax money and half a dozen crossbowmen. The only door was locked and sealed, and the only openings were narrow bow slits in the sides. And yet, the sight of the wagon didn't raise Gisborne's spirits as much as he'd hoped. The tax wagon looked formidable, even impregnable, but it was clearly the work of desperation rather than inspiration, something designed in a hurry because everything else had failed. Because every other tax collection had been stopped and plundered by Robin Hood and his woodsmen.

The Sheriff was relying on this wagon to get through. He'd made that very clear to Gisborne. He'd also made it clear that the responsibility for the tax money's safety rested entirely with Gisborne, and if he failed, if so much as one gold coin went missing, then cousin or no, Sir Guy of Gisborne would wish his parents had never met.

He mopped at his sweating face with a handkerchief. It was a warm day, and the oppressive weight of his chain mail just made things worse. He pulled his horse over to the side of the trail, stopped, and took a long drink of water from his canteen. The company moved slowly by him, the tax wagon creaking and groaning loudly in the quiet, the weight of its contents forcing the wagon's wheels deep into the earth trail. The horses had to lean heavily into the traces to keep it moving.

Rumbling along behind came a cart loaded down with barrels of beer, pulled by a single, bored-looking horse steered by a fat, red-faced friar. One pudgy hand held the reins while the other held a jug that dipped at regular intervals into an opened barrel. Gisborne smiled sourly. At the rate the beer was disappearing into the friar, the abbey would be lucky to receive half the beer they'd paid for. The friar had been singing hymns on and off for some time now, in a loud, raucous voice, interspersed occasionally with drinking songs of somewhat disreputable origin. He sang with increasing feeling, and Gisborne increasingly wished that he wouldn't. Apart from anything else, the noise drowned out whatever warning sounds there might have been in the forest. Gisborne glared at the impenetrable shadows on either side of the trail. This time, whatever happened, he was going to get the gold through. It had gone beyond duty now, it was personal. Robin Hood had made him look a fool, and he would see the woodsman dead for that.

Without any warning, arrows came flying out of nowhere. An arrow hit a soldier in the throat, just above his armor, and he leaned slowly forward and toppled off his horse. Another arrow slammed into a barrel beside the friar, and he yelled and dropped his jug. A soldier behind the cart sat slumped in his saddle. Blood trickled down his face from the arrow protruding from his eye socket. Arrows filled the air as Gisborne drew his sword, urged his horse forward, and yelled to his people to keep moving. There was always the chance they could outrun the ambush and leave the woodsmen behind them. But the tax wagon was already moving as fast as it could, and Gisborne realized with a sinking heart that that wasn't going to be fast enough. Two more of his men fell in as many seconds, and the rest were close to panic.

Gisborne glared wildly about him, and finally spotted four woodsmen standing together at the edge of the trail. With their green clothes and painted faces, they were almost impossible to make out against the woods as long as they didn't move, but now they were firing arrows as fast as they could aim and let fly. Gisborne yelled to his men and pointed out the woodsmen. The armored soldiers rode their horses straight at the woodsmen, who immediately broke and ran back into the thick undergrowth. Briefly hidden from the advancing soldiers, they dropped into the trench they'd dug earlier, and pulled into place a matted screen of brush and grass that hid them from view. The mounted soldiers made their way slowly through the undergrowth, hacking blindly about them. As far as they were concerned, it was as though the forest had suddenly come alive and swallowed up the woodsmen.

The friar saw a chance to escape while the outlaws and the soldiers concentrated on each other, and whipped his horse on, but there wasn't enough room to maneuver his cart past the straining tax wagon. The friar cursed the wagon with some highly unholy language, and then stared openmouthed as Robin and Azeem swung down from the trees and dropped onto the roof of the tax wagon. They kicked the driver and his bodyguard off their seat, jumped down and grabbed the reins, and then steered the wagon off the road. Inside the wagon, crossbowmen clattered angrily at the narrow window slits but were unable to draw a bead on either of their new drivers. The friar quickly realized that he'd been given another chance, and grabbed at his reins again. At which point Little John dropped out of the overhead branches onto the cart, which shuddered violently under the impact, spilling the friar from his seat. He tumbled backward, hit his head on a beer barrel, and took no further interest in the proceedings. John grinned broadly, and steered the cart off the trail after the tax wagon. Both wagon and cart disappeared into the woods, and hidden woodsmen immediately raised another camouflage screen into place, covering their route.

Gisborne emerged from the undergrowth to find the trail completely empty, apart from a few riderless horses running for their lives, and the bodies of his own men. He looked frantically around him, and the forest stared impassively back, giving away nothing. Gisborne swallowed hard. The Sheriff was not going to be pleased.

Not all that far away, though comfortably out of range of Gisborne's hearing, Robin brought the tax wagon to a halt in a small clearing by a slow-moving river. He handed the reins to Azeem, climbed up onto the wagon's roof, and stamped hard twice to get the occupants' attention. Angry shouts and threats echoed from inside, and Robin waited patiently for them to die away.

"Surrender your weapons," he said loudly. "And I give you my word you shall all go free."

There was a pause, and then a sword blade jabbed viciously up through a slit in the roof, narrowly missing Robin's foot. He shook his head sadly.

"I feared as much. You just can't help some people."

He signaled to Azeem, who steered the wagon down the slight slope to the nearby river. Robin and Azeem waited until the last moment and then jumped clear as the wagon careered into the river, ploughed to a halt in the thick mud of the river bottom, and then toppled slowly over onto its side. Water flooded in through the narrow bow slits, and from inside the wagon came loud cries of panic, and an urgent request to renegotiate the possibility of surrendering. Some bright soul even tied a white handkerchief to an arrow shaft and waved it energetically through a slit. Robin grinned and gestured for the watching woodsmen to break the soldiers out of the wagon. The river wasn't deep enough to put the soldiers in any real peril, but he hadn't seen the point in telling them that.

A little later, after the soldiers had been disarmed, disrobed, laughed at rather loudly, and then roped together, Robin watched happily as his men carried the heavy iron strongboxes out of the waterlogged tax wagon. Little John smashed the lock on one of the strongboxes and pried open the lid. A sudden silence fell across the small clearing as the woodsmen crowded round the open chest. It was full to the brim with glittering gold coins, and it was a big chest. The woodsmen looked at the gold, and then at the other boxes still unopened, and burst into loud cheers, slapping each other on the back and jostling each other for a better look at the gold. Robin stood quietly, scowling thoughtfully at the opened chest. Little John slipped a huge hand into the mass of coins and stirred them slowly, feeling the solid weight of the gold against his fingers.

"Well bugger me sideways," he said softly. "I didn't think there was this much gold in the world."

"This treasure was gathered for a purpose," said Robin slowly. "I think it might be in our interests to find out what that purpose was."

His thoughts were interrupted by sounds of a brawl drifting over from the friar's cart. The friar was all but buried under a pile of woodsmen but was still struggling mightily. Two woodsmen were already stretched out on the grass, moaning quietly, and as Robin watched, a third fell away from the struggle with both hands clasped firmly between his legs. Robin nodded slowly, impressed.

"All right, get off of him!" he called loudly. "That's no way to treat a man of the cloth. Besides, I don't think I can afford to lose any more of you."

He had to drag a few men off by main force, but the rest broke away from the fight happily enough, now that they had an excuse to do so. They stood around the friar in a respectful semicircle, coughing and gasping for breath and leaning on each other for support. The friar stood with his back to his cart, looking decidedly battered but still definitely unbowed. He glared dismissively at the winded woodsmen, and then nodded brusquely to Robin.

"The good Lord's blessing on you, kind sir. These sinners were attempting to steal these libations, destined for the monks of St. Catherine's."

He indicated the barrels of beer with an unsteady wave of his hand. The friar was a man of average height, but decidedly more than average girth. His face seemed to be permanently flushed, his large nose blossomed redly with broken veins, and his grubby monk's habit was practically held together with new and ancient beer stains. His great round face was dominated by a pursed mouth in a scruffy beard, and disturbingly direct eyes. Little John grinned at him.

"Appears to me, reverend friar, that just possibly most of your liquor might have already found its way into your fat person."

The friar ignored him magnificently, and clambered up onto the driving seat of the cart. Robin moved quickly forward and grabbed the reins.

"A moment, my reverend friend. You travel with poor company when you travel with Nottingham's soldiers."

"Aye," said Bull. "Tax him, just like the others. His kind aren't short of a penny."

There were loud growls of agreement, not least from the woodsmen who'd been struggling to subdue the friar, and were only just beginning to get their breath back. Robin looked at the friar innocently.

"You see how it is, friend. My men are thirsty, and have much to celebrate. Surely the good Lord has the charity to spare us a few barrels?"

The friar gasped and crossed himself, with rather more drama than was strictly called for. "Lord bless me, sir, I had mistook you and your men for common thieves. So if you and they wish to share in the good Lord's brew . . ." He reached casually under his seat, pulled out a club, and hit Robin smartly round the ear with it. ". . . you must best me for it!"

Robin dropped the reins and staggered backward, his ears ringing. The friar quickly grabbed the reins and whipped up the horse. It ambled unhurriedly forward. The friar dipped his jug into an open barrel, took a good swallow of beer, and toasted Robin sardonically.

"Confess, Robin Hood," he called merrily over his shoulder, "that Friar Tuck is a better, holier, and braver man than thou art!"

A low-hanging branch caught him squarely across the forehead, and he toppled backward off his seat and onto the ground, smashing the jug of beer beneath him. The horse looked back, saw there was no longer any need to put himself out, and stopped the cart to resume cropping the thick forest grass. Friar Tuck rose groaning to his feet, and then shook his head slowly as he discovered what had happened to his jug.

"Alas, the Lord giveth, and the Lord taketh away. Mysterious are the ways of the Lord."

Robin staggered over to join him, and for a moment they just stood there, glaring at each other and rubbing their aching heads.

"Do you yield?" asked Robin finally.

Tuck sniffed haughtily. "I'd rather roast in Hell."

He kicked Robin's feet out from under him and then threw himself on top of Robin like a malevolent whale. Robin rolled aside at the last moment, and Tuck crashed onto the unyielding ground, knocking all the breath out of himself.

Later that day, the woodsmen at the camp were treated to the spectacle of Friar Tuck strapped firmly into the traces of his own cart and pulling it along through his own sweat and strength. He grunted and groaned loudly, and sweated profusely, but still kept the cart moving at a steady pace. There were real muscles under that fat, thought Robin, as he flicked the reins lightly from the cart's driving seat. He steered the cart into the middle of the camp, and women and children came running to greet their returning menfolk. There was almost as much interest in the strongboxes slung between the woodsmens' horses. The children jeered at the roped-together soldier prisoners, and flocked laughing round the panting Friar Tuck as Robin finally allowed him to rest. Tuck groaned feelingly, and clutched at his aching back as he straightened up.

"Thank you, Lord, for teaching me this humility. I really must do something for you someday."

"Here is your chance," said Robin, swinging lightly down from the cart to stand beside him. "Gathered here are the poor and the destitute. The meek of the earth, who have known nothing but misfortune and maltreatment all their hard lives. I brought them here to give them a chance to live in peace, to rebuild their lives anew after the Sheriff's men took everything from them. We have need of an honest man of God to minister to us. We are an unusual flock, but then you are an unusual friar. What say you?"

Tuck looked slowly around him in the sudden quiet, taking in the hopeful faces on every side. They didn't look much like the murderous savages he'd heard so much about. Instead he saw only poverty, hunger and unmistakable signs of ill-treatment—men with missing hands and ears, and women with whipmarks; a young girl with crippled legs and a young man who'd had an eye burned out of his face. The children gathered around him with wide eyes and hopeful smiles, and he had to look away from the signs of ill-treatment on their small bodies. He folded his hands in a moment of prayer. More than once he had prayed for a flock of his own, which only went to show you should be careful of what you prayed for. He looked up and smiled at Robin.

"The Lord moves in mysterious ways," he said quietly. "I accept."

Robin grinned, slapped him on the shoulder, and set

about freeing him from the cart's stays. "You will not regret this, good friar."

"Aye," said Tuck. "But you might."

Night had fallen by the time Gisborne reluctantly returned to Nottingham Castle. He went in search of the Sheriff, knowing that the longer he kept him waiting for a report, the worse it would be, and finally found him watching the blacksmiths work in the castle armory. The Sheriff had turned the armory into his own private weapons factory, and work never stopped there, day or night. The craftsmen worked in shifts, for more money than they had ever dreamed of, and the forges never cooled. Already there were swords and armor enough to equip a larger army than Gisborne could comfortably imagine.

He advanced slowly through the smoke and sparks, and eventually discovered the Sheriff drawing a sword from one of the furnace mouths. The blade glowed white hot as the Sheriff turned it back and forth admiringly. Gisborne approached him diffidently, but the Sheriff did not turn to face him.

"I bear bad tidings, cousin," said Gisborne quietly. "We were ambushed in Sherwood."

The Sheriff tested the sword against a nearby anvil, and sparks flew from the glowing blade. "Spanish steel, cousin—so much stronger than our native blades. Any losses?"

"Most of the men. Actually, all of them."

"And once again, you are the sole survivor, cousin. Interesting. And the gold?"

"It . . . disappeared. The forest just swallowed it up."

The Sheriff turned and looked at Gisborne for the first time. He was smiling pleasantly, but Gisborne couldn't read his eyes. "Robin Hood?"

"There were woodsmen, dressed in green. I saw them."

"Robin Hood," said the Sheriff, nodding slowly, thoughtfully. "Tell me, cousin, did you know that in the past, before we learned the art of steelmaking, a sword was tempered by thrusting a heated blade into the belly of a slave? Something to do with the sudden change in temperature. They still do it in the East, I understand. These days, of course, we follow more scientific ways."

He placed a reassuring hand on Gisborne's shoulder. "My dear cousin, we must be strong. We cannot allow this woodsman to make fools of us." His smile widened slightly, and he thrust the glowing sword into Gisborne's belly, and twisted it. Steam rose from the wound, and blood fell thickly to the floor as Gisborne slumped to his knees, his mouth gaping soundlessly. The Sheriff withdrew the blade, and Gisborne fell forward into a pool of his own blood, and lay still. The Sheriff smiled down at him.

"And I cannot allow a lieutenant of mine to fail me." He held the blade up before his eyes and studied it. "A good blade, fine steel. Perhaps the old ways are best, after all."

Early the next morning, two mounted figures hidden under heavy cloaks and hoods made their way slowly along a leaf-strewn trail at the edge of Sherwood Forest. The steady hoofbeats of the horses sounded clear and loud on the morning quiet. Two more figures, dressed in Sherwood green, moved silently through the undergrowth at the side of the trail, following the horses. Bull and Much, the Miller's son, were supposed to be out hunting game, but having stumbled on two such tempting targets, they were loath to give up on them. Much was tall, gangling, and not exactly the brightest of Robin's men, which was probably why he and Bull got on so well. They hurried a little to get ahead of the riders, and crouched in wait at the bend in the trail. Bull moved in close beside Much.

"You take the one on your left," he whispered hoarsely. "I'll take the one on the right."

"Right," said Much. "Which one's left?"

Shaking his head sadly at Much's ignorance, Bull raised his right fist and brandished it before Much's eyes. "This is left, clothead. The one you feed your face with. Right is the one you scratch your arse with. Don't you know anything?"

"I knew, really," said Much hotly. "I was just testing."

Bull hushed him urgently as the two riders drew near, and then the two of them leapt out onto the trail, blocking the horses' way. The riders pulled up, startled, as the two woodsmen nocked arrows to their bows.

"Hold!" said Bull, grandly. The horse before him reared up, and the rider's hood fell back, revealing the face of a beautiful young woman. The other rider threw back her hood, revealing a decidedly uglier woman. He grinned at Much. "Don't think much of yours."

Much ostentatiously ignored him, and gave the two women what he fondly imagined to be a ferocious scowl. "A donation, ladies, if you please."

The beautiful woman glared defiantly down at him, daring him to shoot. "A donation? For what, pray?"

"For safe passage through Sherwood," said Much. "Terrible dangerous place, this. Anything might happen."

"I am Marian Dubois," said the woman icily. "Does the name mean nothing to you?"

Much looked at Bull, who shrugged. "Everyone's equal in Sherwood, lady. Everyone pays the toll."

"Very well," said Marian, in a dangerously calm voice that would have had anyone who knew her diving for cover, "if you would have a donation, come and get it."

She reached into her cloak as though for a purse, and Much stepped forward eagerly, lowering his bow. At which point Marian leaned suddenly forward, grabbed a handful of his hair, and spun him around so she could set the dagger the Sheriff had given her against Much's throat. Her companion, Sarah, lashed out with her boot, catching Bull squarely on the nose. He dropped his bow and arrow, staggered backward, clutching gingerly at his bleeding nose, and stared up at Sarah with wide, reproachful eyes. Much felt the dagger's keen edge gently part the skin at his throat, and decided to stand very still indeed, and not swallow or breathe heavily or anything else that might upset Marian Dubois.

"You obnoxious little rodent!" snapped Marian. "How dare you attack us?"

"Just doing me job, milady," said Much, smiling tentatively.

"Really?" said Marian. "And who might your employer be?"

"Robin Hood," said Much, as impressively as he dared.

Marian scowled thoughtfully down at Much, and his blood ran cold. In his experience, people who looked at him thoughtfully were usually busy thinking of some new way to cause trouble for him. From a great height, Marian smiled at him coldly. "Take me to see this Robin Hood. I've a few things I'd like to say to him."

Some time later, Bull and Much, the Miller's son, led Marian and Sarah to the edge of a lushly ferned crevasse, not far from the woodsmen's camp. Both men had tried to persuade Marian to go straight to the camp, but she had insisted on being taken directly to Robin. Bull had felt his nose, and Much had felt his throat, then they both looked at each other and shrugged, and did what Marian wanted.

Bull stopped at the very edge of the crevasse and gestured for Marian to look down. She did so, and then froze where she was, stunned by the magnificent view below her. A high waterfall cascaded down from a stony cliff, thundering down into a hidden shadowed pool. Sheltered on both sides by the crevasse, the waterfall and its pool seemed like an innocent moment of Nature, kept separate from the world of man, untouched by his greeds and angers. But down in the pool, in the cool dark waters, a man was bathing. Robin Hood.

Naked and alone in the primal setting, unaware of any audience, he seemed more like a creature of the wild than a man. His muscles were broad and starkly defined, with little overlay of fat to smooth their harsh lines. Terrible scars covered his back, from whips and knives and hot irons, and other things Marian could not put a name to. There were more scars, on his chest and arms and legs. The fact that Robin had survived such wounds said as much about his strength of spirit as his body. Marian flinched away from the sight of so much pain, and for the first time began to understand some of the awful secrets of Robin's past, which had turned the boy she remembered into the man below her.

She fell back a step involuntarily as Robin strode unself-consciously from the waters and headed for his clothes, piled neatly on a rock well away from the waterfall's spray. Sarah looked away, pursing her mouth disapprovingly, but Marian did not, mesmerized by the casual strength and grace in Robin's movements. Bull and Much shared a smile, but kept their peace, having finally figured out which way the wind was blowing. Bull waited till Robin was more or less decent again, and then coughed loudly and called down to him.

"Robin! We got visitors!"

Robin looked up, shielding his eyes against the light, and then grinned broadly as he recognized Marian. He waved to her, and she managed some kind of gesture in reply. Robin scrambled quickly up the side of the crevasse, climbing surely and easily, and finally stood before Marian, panting a little from the exertion, but only a little. Marian felt a pleasant flush fill her face as their eyes met, and she was suddenly flustered, forgetting in a moment the clever, casual speech she'd been rehearsing all the way there.

"What are you doing here?" she blurted finally.

Robin's grin widened. "Taking a lady's advice."

In the woodsmen's camp, the beginnings of a village were slowly forming themselves out of chaos. Men were working on huts and defenses, women were working at cooking fires and laundry, and small children ran back and forth, getting under everyone's feet. Men and women emerged from the forest in small groups from time to time, with fresh game or wood for the fires. With their rangy, muscular forms, painted faces, and clothes the colors of the woods, they seemed a part of the living forest. Everywhere Marian looked, the camp was alive with movement and purpose. Friar Tuck sat grandly on a tree stump in the center of the camp, an open sack of grain before him, and an eager crowd of students sat at his feet.

"This is grain," said Tuck, taking a great handful of the golden stuff and letting it trickle slowly back into the sack. "Any fool can eat it, but the good Lord intended it for a more divine means of consumption. My friends, let us worship our Maker by practicing the noble art of brewing. . . ."

At the far edge of the clearing men were practicing archery, the arrows thudding into crude man-shaped targets. Little John put an arrow into the bull's-eye before him and laughed loudly, delighted with his shot. He smiled down at Wulf, as always at his father's side.

"Right, my lad, let's see how close you can get to that bugger."

Wulf took careful aim, not hurrying himself, and let fly.

His arrow sliced clean through Little John's, splitting it in two. Little John gaped for a moment, and then roared delightedly, and clapped his son on the shoulder. He yelled for the other archers to stop what they were doing and take a look at Wulf's shot, and grinned broadly as they gathered round Wulf, as proud of the shot as though he'd made it himself. The archers grinned at father and son, and took it in turns to slap Wulf on the back until he was half-dizzy.

"Good shot, Wulf," said Robin from where he'd been watching with Marian. "But can you do it amidst distractions? Can you make the same shot when you must?"

He gestured for the boy to fire again. Wulf confidently nocked an arrow to his bow and prepared to fire, squinting at the target with one eye. Robin leaned forward on Wulf's blind side and blew suddenly in his ear. Wulf jumped, and the arrow went well wide of its mark, only just hitting the target at all. Little John sniffed angrily, and glared at Robin.

"How about you, then? Can you do it?"

Robin smiled at Marian, stepped forward, and nocked an arrow to his bow. He drew back the string, and Little John yelled suddenly and clapped his hands together. Robin stood rock steady, holding the bow at full extension, concentrating on the target. Marian suddenly leaned forward and blew in his ear. Robin jumped and let the arrow go. It not only missed the target, it didn't even hit the tree the target was leaning against. Little John and the watching woodsmen howled with laughter and elbowed each other meaningfully. Robin looked at Marian reproachfully, and she got the giggles. Robin tried to put on a stern expression, as befitting a leader of men, but he couldn't keep an answering grin off his face.

He led Marian away from the chuckling archers and over to a massive ancient oak at the edge of the clearing. A simple hut had been built high above in the wide branches, almost hidden from sight. Rough steps had been cut into the side of the tree. Marian looked at them dubiously. Robin smiled encouragingly, and she lifted up her skirts and climbed more or less decorously up the tree. Robin followed after, shaking his head admiringly. The steps finished at a wide platform, and they both rested there for a moment till Marian got her breath back. She looked at the cramped little treehouse before her and wasn't particularly impressed.

"Take a look inside," said Robin. "I think you'll find it's worth the climb."

She sniffed, and entered the treehouse with an air of only doing it under protest, as a favor. The interior was dark and gloomy, though it smelled pleasantly of bare worked wood. Standing together in the middle of the floor were half a dozen large strongboxes. Robin strolled nonchalantly past her and flipped open the boxes' lids one by one. Marian's eyes widened, and despite herself she gaped speechlessly at the sheer amount of gold before her.

"Nottingham robs from the poor," said Robin. "We rob Nottingham, and give it back."

Marian shook her head slowly, still stunned. "So much gold . . . What does it mean?"

"The Sheriff has been squeezing this gold from the people, so that he can use it to bribe King Richard's enemies to rise against him. Not all the barons side with Prince John, and many that remained unattached are wavering. This amount of gold could buy Nottingham a lot of support."

Marian frowned. "Nottingham would never dare challenge the King himself, surely?"

"The King is not in England to be challenged," said Robin. "While he is away, he may lose his country." Marian looked at the gold, and then at Robin. He grinned impishly. "You thought I was keeping it all, didn't you?"

Marian felt the heat rise in her face again. Embarrassed and flustered at being caught off guard again, she reached inside her cloak impulsively and brought out the jeweled dagger the Sheriff had given her.

"Here. A contribution to your cause."

Robin stared at the finely jeweled hilt of the dagger, and then at Marian's slender, delicate fingers. They trembled faintly under his gaze. He took the dagger and their fingers touched for a moment, before Marian pulled away. Robin reached up and took the Locksley medallion from around his neck.

"A gift so fine deserves something in return."

"No," said Marian quickly. "The dagger is not dear to me. I mean . . ." She broke off, knowing she was saying everything wrong, but still having to fight down an urge to babble. "I must go."

She hurried out the door, leaving Robin holding both the dagger and the medallion. He flushed angrily, wishing he'd handled the situation better, and made as though to throw the dagger into the nearest chest. And then he stopped, and tucked it out of sight inside his tunic. He liked the feel of it there, like having a part of Marian close to him, always. He frowned, not sure where that thought was leading him, and then shrugged. He put his medallion back on again, closed the lids of the strongboxes, and followed her out of the treehouse.

He stepped out onto the platform, and found that Marian was already descending the steps cut into the tree trunk. Robin looked around him, taking pride in the aerial fortress of huts and bridges and platforms he had put together. It was good to know he could do some things right. He grinned suddenly, kicked the emergency rope ladder over the edge of the platform, and climbed quickly down after Marian. He soon caught up with her, and easily kept pace with her as she descended. She looked briefly at him, and then looked away as she spoke, her voice carefully casual.

"Do you really think the Sheriff's going to let you get away with all this?"

"He has to find me first," said Robin easily. "We have a rule here: once a body has seen the way to our camp, that body cannot leave. There are too many lives at stake to allow for any exceptions."

They reached the ground together, and Marian turned to face Robin, smiling slightly. "I know. Bull told me. That's why I insisted Sarah and I be blindfolded on our way here."

"Oh," said Robin. His face fell for a moment, and then brightened again. "Perhaps you might stay for dinner?"

Marian smiled. "Perhaps."

Night fell, and the scent of roast venison wafted across the camp as the woodsmen celebrated. Ask them what they were celebrating and they'd have given a dozen different answers, but really they were just celebrating their freedom, and the new purpose in life that Robin had given them. Wild music filled the clearing as musicians pounded out of their instruments something that could be danced or sung to, and if the tunes owed more to enthusiasm than skill, no one really gave a damn. Dancers whirled around the blazing campfires, among them Much and Sarah.

Azeem watched the dancers silently, sitting a little ways off from the rest of the woodsmen. The music sounded harsh and alien to his eastern ears, but the dances seemed familiar enough, as were the expressions on the faces of the dancing couples. Not for the first time, Azeem realized he was a long way from home, and those he had loved. A young child wandered up to him, eyes frankly curious, and Azeem smiled as he recognized Little John's smallest daughter.

"Did God paint you?" asked the girl.

"I suppose he did," said Azeem softly. "Allah loves wondrous variety."

He broke off as Tuck loomed suddenly out of the darkness, scowling fiercely. He dropped a heavy hand on the child's shoulder and hauled her away, ignoring her protests, his cold glare fixed on Azeem. "Keep thy heathen words from the ears of the innocent, or you will answer to me! You know nothing of our God."

Azeem looked at him steadily. "Is not my Abraham your Abraham?"

Tuck snorted loudly. "Think not to trick me with twists of the Devil's tongue. Come, girl."

He strode off into the camp, dragging Little John's daughter with him. Azeem stared after them, and if there was hurt or anger in his face, there was no one close enough to see it.

The music crashed to a halt, and the musicians paused to refresh themselves with more liquor before continuing. One musician was already so refreshed it was all he could do to sit upright. Duncan sat with them, nodding his blind head to the music when they played, and sharing a jug or two of something refreshing with them. For an old blind man he was doing quite well, until he tried to stand up, at which point his legs went off in different directions, and he collapsed back down again, swearing loudly that someone had tripped him. He sulked for a while, his dignity hurt, but he brightened up quickly enough once the musicians presented him with a fresh jug.

Will Scarlet swaggered suddenly into the firelight, holding a lute before him as though it were a weapon, and the camp erupted with cries and groans of protest. Scarlet ignored them all with magnificent disdain, struck a dashing

143

pose, and strummed at his lute as though it might fight back.

"This," he announced grandly, "is a song about . . . love."

> She was so young and round and fair,
> That I gave her my heart.
> And then that wench, despite my cries,
> Did tear it all apart.
>
> For she was not what she had seemed,
> And there, my friends, take heed.
> Beware of those who charm with lies,
> The way to ruin, they'll lead.

Will Scarlet finished the song and stood for a moment, glaring at Robin.

Robin and Marian sat side by side, arms almost touching, watching the proceedings. Marian in particular watched Scarlet as he disappeared into the shadows at the far edge of the clearing.

"A strange lad," she said, frowning. "He bears you ill will?"

Robin shrugged. "He's not the first to do so."

But it bothered him none the less, and Marian could tell. She studied him for a long moment and then, almost against her will, stretched out a hand to lightly touch his back.

"Tell me about these scars," she said softly.

"Why? Only the memory pains me now."

Marian met his gaze steadily. "I would like to know how a once arrogant young nobleman came to find contentment living rough with the salt of the earth."

Robin looked slowly about the woodsmen's camp, studying his people at their play, and knew his pride for them showed in his face. "I've seen knights in armor panic at the first hint of battle, and I've seen the lowliest squire pull a spear from his own body to defend a dying horse. . . . Sights like that change a man. Anyway, who says I am content here? I have my own hopes for the future."

"Ah," said Marian, raising an eyebrow. "A grander scheme?"

"No, a simpler one. A home, family . . . love."

Marian laughed softly. "Men speak conveniently of love when it suits their purpose. When it doesn't, it suddenly becomes a burden to them." She looked at Robin, and though her voice was casual, her eyes were serious. "Robin Hood, the Prince of Thieves . . . Is he capable of love?"

Robin's chest seemed suddenly tight, and his breath caught in his throat. The crimson and gold of the leaping fire played across her face like passing thoughts, and it seemed to Robin then that Marian had never looked more beautiful. He reached out and pushed back a loose curl from her forehead.

"He is ready to be tested, lady."

He leaned slightly toward her, and she did not move. Their faces drew closer, and their breathing quickened until they could feel each other's breath on their lips. And then a harsh, frightened yelling broke the moment, and Marian looked away. Robin cursed silently, and looked round to see the boy Wulf run to his father, tears streaming down his face.

"Come quick! Mother's dying!"

Inside Little John's hut, Fanny writhed in agony on her rough bed of rags and blankets, eight months pregnant. Friar Tuck sat at her side, giving her what comfort he could, and looked bleakly at Little John as he rushed in, followed by Robin and Marian.

"The child comes early," he said quietly, trying hard to keep the worry out of his face and his voice. "I fear all is not well."

Fanny screamed as a new wave of pain hit her, and Little John was quickly at her side, taking her hand in his.

"Hush, lass," he said gently. "You'll be fine."

Fanny shook her head, exhaustion as well as pain showing clearly in her sweat-streaked face. "This one's not like the others, John. Oh God, it hurts!"

Marian knelt beside her too and placed a gentle hand on her brow. The heat coming off Fanny's skin worried her, but she too kept her voice calm and soothing. "Courage, mother."

Azeem appeared in the doorway, and Robin gestured urgently for him to enter. Tuck bristled at the sight of the Moor, but reluctantly acceded to Robin's authority. Robin smiled reassuringly at Little John. "My friend has knowledge of medicines and healing."

Azeem gestured for them all to move away from the bed, and knelt beside Fanny. Tuck scowled, and watched his every movement closely. Azeem ignored him, smiled reassuringly to Fanny, and pulled back the blanket covering her. On her bare chest and shoulders lay a dozen black, squirming creatures. Azeem snarled angrily.

"By Allah, leeches! Barbarians, do you want to kill her?"

He started to pull the leeches off. Blood trickled from tiny wounds where they'd been feeding. Tuck grabbed him by the arm and tried to stop him.

"Leave them be, savage! Get away from her!"

Azeem shrugged him off with enough force to send the friar staggering backward, and removed the last of the leeches. He threw them onto the floor and crushed them under his heel. "Blood is like air. If she loses too much, both she and the child will die."

146

Little John looked to Robin for help, and he nodded firmly, hoping he was doing the right thing. Azeem examined Fanny's swollen belly with gentle hands, and then looked at her compassionately. "Your baby has not turned. It cannot be born without help."

Fanny clutched tightly at Little John's hand, but he was paralyzed with fear and confusion. Tuck stepped forward again and appealed to Robin, his voice trembling with outrage.

"You cannot trust this man! He is the Devil's seed, sent to lead us astray. Do not listen to him. He will kill her!"

"If you do not listen to me," said Azeem evenly, "she will certainly die. And the child too."

Fanny cried out again as the pain stabbed through her. Little John looked pleadingly to Robin, who put a steady hand on his shoulder.

"The good friar has done all he can, John. Let the Moor try. I trust him."

Little John looked at Fanny, and she nodded quickly, unable to speak. John swallowed hard. "So be it."

"Then their deaths will be on your head!" snapped Tuck. "I have warned you. My conscience is clear."

Little John reached out and grabbed the front of Tuck's robe, pulling him close, so that their faces were only inches apart. "Shut up, Tuck. Just . . . shut up."

John let him go, and Tuck stormed out of the hut. No one watched him go. Azeem turned to Marian, his manner calm and businesslike.

"Bring me a needle, thread, water, a skinning knife, and burning ashes. Quickly."

Marian nodded and hurried out of the hut. John looked at Azeem in horror. Robin took him by the arm and gently persuaded him to wait outside. He shut the door behind Little John, and then gestured for Azeem to move a little

away from Fanny. They talked quietly, heads close together.

"A skinning knife?" said Robin. "What the hell are you
planning to do?"

Azeem looked at him steadily. "The child must be taken
out, by the knife. It is the only way."

Robin shook his head slowly. "I've heard of such a thing,
but never seen it. Have you done this before?"

"I have seen it done many times. With horses."

"Horses?" Robin's voice started to rise, and he clamped
down on it before it could upset Fanny. "Azeem, if you fail
in this, and child and mother die, John will kill you! I
couldn't protect you."

"I know that," said Azeem. "But it must be done, or they
will both surely die." He looked round sharply as Marian
burst into the hut with the things he'd requested. Azeem
took them from her, one at a time, and finally nodded his
approval. "Robin, hold the woman steady."

He heated the knife in the red-hot ashes, while Marian
slipped a piece of wood between Fanny's teeth, for her to
bite on. Azeem waited as long as he dared, and then took
the knife from the ashes. The blade glowed a sullen red.
Robin took hold of Fanny's shoulders firmly, while Marian
held her head.

"This will hurt, lady," said Azeem gently. "But the pain
will pass, and you will forget. Are you ready?"

Fanny nodded quickly, and squeezed her eyes shut as
Azeem advanced on her.

Outside the hut, Little John paced up and down, his great
hands clenched into helpless fists. Wulf walked at his side,
close as a shadow. Families sat quietly together close by,
trying to reassure John with their presence. Friar Tuck sat a
little to one side, clutching his wooden crucifix tightly, and
murmuring prayers in quick succession. Groans and cries

came from inside the hut, suddenly building into screams. Little John stopped pacing.

"Will you listen to me now?" snapped Tuck. "The barbarian is killing her!"

Little John moved uncertainly toward the hut. Wulf tried to restrain him. And then the screams broke off, and a new sound filled the night—the lusty wailing of a newborn babe.

Inside the hut, Azeem muttered with awe in Arabic as he tended to Fanny, who had finally fainted. Robin handed the bloody, struggling infant to Marian, who enveloped it in a blanket. Their eyes met over the squalling bundle, and something passed between them in that moment, something more than just the shared experience of the birth. Marian looked away, and hushed the crying baby. Robin looked back at Azeem, still bent over the unmoving mother.

"Is she gone?" said Robin quietly.

"No, merely passed out from the pain and the shock. She will live. She is strong. By Allah, she is strong." Azeem looked up at Robin, and smiled. "Strong as a Moorish woman. See, she is stirring already."

Marian gently placed the baby on Fanny's breast as she stirred, and it was the first thing she saw as she opened her eyes. Marian smiled at them both.

"Your son, my Lady."

Little John strode proudly through the camp, holding the swaddled baby up for all to see. He all but danced through the cheering throng, roaring with pride and joy, as though he'd done all the hard work himself. Tuck sat quietly to one side, not having moved from his seat by John's hut. Azeem appeared at the hut door, exhausted and still covered with Fanny's blood. Tuck jumped to his feet and approached Azeem, his face set and grim. Azeem stood his ground. Heads turned, and silence spread quickly across the clearing. Robin watched tensely from the shadows, ready to interfere if necessary. Tuck stopped before Azeem, and for a long moment they just stood there and looked at each other.

"This day," Tuck said finally, "God has taught me a fine lesson." He offered Azeem his hand. Azeem looked at it. Tuck didn't withdraw it. "Please. I would be honored."

Azeem nodded, and shook the friar's hand. Tuck laughed richly, and pulled the startled Moor into a crushing bearhug.

"Come, my barbarian friend," boomed the friar, releasing him. "We shall open a barrel together, you and I, and I shall do my damndest to save your heathen soul."

"Alas," said Azeem quickly, "I am not permitted—"

"Our God made this brew, brother," said Tuck sternly. "Do you dare insult his works?"

Azeem smiled. "Since you put it that way . . ."

The woodsmen cheered and applauded as Tuck and Azeem went off in search of holy beer. The musicians threw themselves into a wild jig, and the dancing began again. Marian stood watching from the edge of the firelight, still smeared here and there with blood from the birthing. Someone coughed politely behind her, and she turned with a smile on her lips for Robin, only to find Will Scarlet standing diffidently before her. He had cleaned himself up since his unsuccessful attempt as a troubadour, and actually looked quite presentable. He was tall and dark and handsome, not unlike Robin in some ways, and he offered her a single flower with something that was very nearly charm.

"If it pleases you, my Lady, might I have this dance?"

Marian smiled at him, and searched desperately for a polite way to turn him down. And then she looked past Scarlet and sighed inwardly with relief as Robin appeared out of the shadows. Scarlet turned quickly to see what she was looking at, and froze as he saw Robin. Something dangerous moved in Scarlet's face, and Marian tensed, expecting trouble, but Robin just smiled easily.

"The lady is spoken for, Will."

Marian smiled apologetically to Scarlet, who nodded slowly, as though he'd been expecting something like that to happen anyway. He turned and strode off into the darkness, ignoring Robin, still holding his single flower. Robin and Marian looked after him for a moment, and then turned and looked at each other. Marian reached out and wiped a smear of blood from Robin's cheek, and he did the same for her. Their eyes met, and their breathing deepened. Robin grinned suddenly, swept Marian off her feet and into the midst of the dancing mob, and there was no need for words at all.

Dawn rose unhurriedly through the early morning mists that cloaked the riverbank. The day was quiet with the expectant promise of things to come. Swans glided majestically by, appearing and disappearing in the mists like silent ghosts. A simple raft stood waiting by the riverbank, tended by an old ferryman wrapped in a thick cloak against the morning chill. Sarah led her horse and Marian's onto the wide raft as Robin escorted Marian down the sloping bank. Marian studied the raft dubiously and cocked an eyebrow at Robin.

"Why does it have to be this way?"

"So you can't find the way back," said Robin. "Or be forced to tell some other the way." He reached out and brushed away the long curl of hair that constantly fell across her brow. "It was good to see you again, Marian."

She smiled. "It was good to be seen."

They might have said more, but from behind them came

the sound of Bull leading Duncan and Robin's white horse down to the riverbank, and the moment was gone. Duncan looked confused, and even more unhappy than usual. Robin took Marian's hands in his.

"I have two favors to ask of you."

Marian smiled impishly. "Only two? Very well, good sir, the first."

"Take Duncan with you," said Robin quietly. "I fear for his health and his safety, with what may lie ahead here. Feed him and keep him warm. My family owes him much."

Duncan gripped blindly at Robin's arm as Bull led him past. "Master Robin, you wish me to leave you?"

"Old friend," said Robin gently, "I need you to escort Lady Marian home. I fear for her safety in these troubled times."

Duncan relaxed a little, and nodded understandingly. "Of course, Master Robin."

Bull led him down to the raft. Marian looked at Robin. "And the second favor?"

Robin looked at her steadily. "You are Richard's cousin. You can get word to him of Nottingham's plans. He would believe you."

Marian looked back at him just as steadily. "If I did such a thing, and the Sheriff found out, I could lose all that I have. There are people depending on me too."

"Will you do it for the King?"

"No. But I will do it for you."

She kissed Robin quickly, and then turned and strode over to the raft, where Sarah was already pulling her blindfold into place. Duncan smiled as he heard Marian come to stand beside him.

"He loves you, my Lady," he said quietly. He sensed her surprise, and smiled. "I may be blind, but some things I can still see."

Marian looked back at the riverbank, holding her blindfold in her hand as the ferryman slowly poled the raft down the river. Robin stood on the bank, staring after her. Their eyes met, and neither looked away until both of them had been swallowed up by the early morning mists.

10
BETRAYAL

Marian waited impatiently for the Bishop to join her, and stalked back and forth across his study, shooting anxious glances at the door anytime she thought she heard someone coming. She breathed deeply to calm herself, and clutched to her breast the letter she'd written, as though afraid someone might burst in and take it. She finally made herself stop pacing, and sat down in one of the sinfully comfortable chairs. It wouldn't do to have the Bishop see how disturbed she was. He might start to wonder about the letter's contents. It was bad enough that she was risking her life to get word to the King. She would never forgive herself if she imperiled the life of an innocent as well.

She looked round the great study, for something with which to distract herself, and found she was seeing the room with fresh eyes. There was nothing really unusual in the study, just the usual comforts and fittings, and the thick rugs that covered the floor from wall to wall. The kind of things you expected to see in the house of a man of noble birth. A man of means and riches. But Marian remembered the way the woodsmen lived in Sherwood, and their quiet tales of how they used to live under the Sheriff's oppression. She looked at the expensive furniture and the thick, deep rugs, and all she could think was how much food and other essentials that much money could have bought, if spent on the needy. The table could have fed a family for a year. That crystal decanter and the wine it held could have clothed a family against the winter's cold. Marian scowled unhappily, unsure where her thoughts were leading her. Did the rich man have a right to feast, while the poor were starving?

The door swung open suddenly, interrupting her thoughts, and Marian rose almost gratefully to her feet as the Bishop entered. She curtsied gracefully to him, kissed his ring, and then handed him her letter. The Bishop took it, and then raised an eyebrow fractionally as he saw the letter was already sealed with red wax bearing the imprint of the Dubois signet ring. He looked at Marian, and she met his gaze steadily.

"This is a personal matter, my Lord, but one of vital importance. It must go today, and I could think of no one else I can trust."

"I understand, my child," said the Bishop. He turned the letter over and over in his bejewled hands, as though looking for some sign of its purpose, and then smiled reassuringly at Marian. "This letter shall go at once with my most trusted emissary. He is waiting just outside."

He called out the open door, and a courier entered the study and bowed formally to the Bishop and Marian. He looked professional but anonymous, like all his kind. As someone who inevitably brought bad news sooner or later, it paid to be easily overlooked. The Bishop passed him the letter, and he slipped it into the leather pouch at his side without looking at it. Marian stepped forward and looked at him earnestly.

"You must travel immediately to France. Put this letter directly into the hands of the King, and no one else. If it cannot be delivered, destroy it." The courier bowed again in acknowledgment, his expression calm and completely unmoved. Marian's mouth settled into a firm, stubborn line. "One thing more. My lady-in-waiting, Sarah, will accompany you."

The courier looked to the Bishop, who frowned unhappily. "My dear, is this wise? I cannot vouch for her safety. The voyage is fraught with danger."

"I appreciate your concern," said Marian, "but Sarah is an accomplished rider, and well able to take care of herself. I must insist that she accompanies your courier."

The Bishop's eyebrow stirred again at the word "insist," but he smiled and nodded. "As you wish, my child. As you wish."

Sarah and the courier left the Bishop's residence within the hour. Marian stood and watched them both until they disappeared into the distance. So she never saw the courier rein in his horse some time later, and come to a sudden halt. Sarah drew in alongside him, and asked what was wrong. The courier explained that something seemed to be wrong with his horse's foreleg. Sarah leaned over to take a look and the courier struck her viciously across the back of her neck with his cudgel. Sarah fell limply from her horse into the thick mud of the trail, and lay still. The courier smiled once, and rode back the way he'd come.

In Nottingham Castle, in the Sheriff's private quarters, the Sheriff and six carefully chosen barons stood in a circle around a wide table covered with a cloth. There was something on the table under the cloth, but its shape was uncertain. Both the Sheriff and the barons were wearing the

156

robes of Devil worshippers, some of them more easily than others. They were singing a harsh, dissonant song, older by far than the language in which they were singing it. If they had known to whom and what the song was originally sung, they might have chosen something else for their ritual, but the barons saw the Devil worship trappings as little more than a means to power, and the Sheriff didn't give a damn. The song finally came to its end, with promises of blood and blasphemy, and the Sheriff moved among the barons, handing them each a small golden casket. One by one the barons opened their gifts, and then looked at the Sheriff. Baron Forrester upturned his casket, and a few hundred gold pieces spilled out, clattering on the bare floor. Forrester kept his gaze on the Sheriff the whole time, and did not speak until the last coin had fallen silent. He had fought in many battles, and had a soldier's capacity for quiet, controlled rage.

"What," he said finally, "is this supposed to be?"

"A down payment," said the Sheriff.

Baron Whitehead sniffed dismissively. "You promised us wagons of gold. Are your other promises equally untrustworthy?"

The Sheriff looked at him for a moment, as though fixing the Baron's broad, ruddy face in his memory, and then turned away and swept the cloth from the table, revealing a three-dimensional model of England, Wales, and Scotland, overlayed with a single great pentagram.

"There are greater things than gold," said the Sheriff. "I offer more land and power than you've ever dreamed of. When I rule England, this island shall be divided between the seven of us in this room. I offer every wench in Wales for your loins. Cornwall, with all its tin and silver. Scotland, to rule as a King. What is gold, compared to that?"

The barons looked at each other. Baron Leicester snorted loudly, unconvinced, open scorn twisting his dark, saturnine features. "You would recruit us to treason, and yet you cannot even get gold safely through your own forest." He looked from one baron to another, smiling unpleasantly. "My Lords, why should we risk life and limb for a man who cannot even snare the common bandit who marked his pretty face?"

All the barons smiled at that, and a few even chuckled. The Sheriff's hand rose briefly to stroke the scar on his cheek, but his calm expression and polite stare didn't waver.

"You make a good point, my Lord. How can I control all England if I cannot control my own county? The answer is simple: for a special problem, hire special help. Ordred, you may come in now."

The door swung open, and the barons looked round, startled. A huge figure filled the doorway, and some of the barons gasped despite themselves as the figure had to lower his head to get under the lintel. The floor seemed almost to shake under his weight as he advanced slowly on the barons, and they all but huddled together as he finally came to a halt before them—a great colossus of a man in black armor, his helm roughly shaped into the head of a dragon. He raised his visor, revealing flat, broad features, dominated by the deep tribal scars on his cheeks, and the cold implacable ferocity in his eyes.

"Dear God," said Whitehead finally, forgetting where he was. "It's a Celt. You would ally us with those savages?"

"Why not?" said the Sheriff. "Who better to deal with outlaws? Ordred and his men will bring me back my gold, and the heads of the men who took it."

Baron Forrester studied the huge Celt, trying hard to look unimpressed, as a soldier should. "What can these . . . mercenaries do, that our men cannot?"

The Sheriff looked at the Celt chieftan, who strode unhurriedly over to the open fire, blazing in the hearth against the autumn chill that was slowly seeping through all of the castle. He reached down, and grabbing a burning log with his bare hand, he removed it from the fire and held it out to show it to the watching barons. The two nearest fell back a step involuntarily, and then tried hard to look as though they hadn't. Ordred thrust the burning wood into the palm of his other hand and held the fire there unblinking for a full five seconds before throwing the log back into the fire. Steam rose from his palm, but the Celt's face showed nothing of pain or injury. For a moment there was an awed silence, and then Baron Leicester deliberately broke the mood with a derisive snort.

"Since you have no gold, Nottingham, how do you plan to pay these savages?"

The Sheriff smiled at him easily, quite relaxed and unconcerned. "Another good point, my friend. You seem very skilled at finding flaws in my plans. What am I to do . . . ? Ah. I know."

He reached out and casually lifted a two-handed ornamental sword from the wall. He swung it round in a swift, vicious arc and slammed the heavy blade into Leicester's neck. The impact threw the baron back against the wall, blood flying from the great wound in his neck. He stared at the Sheriff in horror and clutched at his neck with both hands, as though he could somehow force the wound closed. Blood spurted between his fingers. The Sheriff smiled at him, holding the sword ready for another blow. The Baron sank to his knees, and the Sheriff struck again, putting his back into it. The heavy blade tore Leicester's head from his shoulders, and it flew across the room to land on the model of England, staining its hills and rivers with blood. The barons fell back from the table, crying out in

159

shock and horror as Leicester's head stared at them with empty eyes. Some turned as though to run, but the Celt was between them and the door. They crowded together like frightened children, and turned reluctantly back to face the waiting Sheriff. He stood leaning on his sword, smiling calmly. He wasn't even breathing hard. There was a splash of blood on his face, but he made no move to wipe it off.

"I've always favored the direct method in dealing with problems," he said cheerfully. "Including Robin Hood. Does anyone here have any problems with that?"

The barons shook their heads mutely.

"Good," said the Sheriff. "I'm so glad we had the chance for this little chat. Is there anything more you'd like to say to me before you leave?"

The barons looked at each other, and finally Baron Forrester cleared his throat nervously. "Assuming Ordred and his men can recover your gold and deal with the woodsmen, you must still wed royal kin before we can act openly."

Baron Whitehead nodded quickly. "Then your claim to the throne will appear legitimate, and many men of influence will join with us who might not be swayed by just gold and promises."

The Sheriff of Nottingham smiled. "Rest easy, my friends. I already have someone in mind."

Marian Dubois woke suddenly from a restless sleep, convinced she had heard something. She sat up in bed and looked uncertainly about her. Moonlight pouring through the window showed her the room was empty, but as she concentrated she heard dim shouting and hammering sounds from some distant part of the house. She swung out of bed, pulled on a heavy robe, and picked up the single candle she kept lit for night emergencies or early morning trips to the privy. If that damned hostler had got drunk again. . . .

She bustled out the door and then hesitated uneasily in the passage, listening. Moonlight splashed the length of the empty passage, but the sounds seemed louder, as though they were slowly drawing nearer. A sudden chill ran down Marian's spine and along her arms as she realized for the first time just how vulnerable she was, living in a great, isolated mansion with only a handful of servants, most of them women. She shook her head quickly. She had to think clearly. She went back into her bedchamber, pulled open a drawer in a desk, and took out a plain, vicious-looking knife. She hefted it once in her hand, and then left the room and strode quietly along the passage and down the stairs, candle in one hand, knife in the other.

The hall was empty, but the sounds were definitely louder. Marian stood uncertainly at the foot of the stairs, trying to determine how close the sounds were. It sounded as though half an army had invaded her house. She could make out individual voices, some angry, some frightened, and the sounds of doors slamming. If the house had been invaded, they were almost certainly after her. In which case, the sooner she got the hell out of the mansion and away, the better. She'd worry about where she was running to later, when she had time. She nodded grimly to herself and padded silently down the hall to the kitchen at the rear of the house. From there it was only a short run to the stables. But she couldn't just run away and leave her people to the mercy of the invaders. . . . And she couldn't abandon Duncan, blind and helpless, after he had been entrusted to her care. Her pace slowed as she wrestled with her conscience, but finally she scowled unhappily as she realized she had to go. She couldn't do anything to help her people on her own. She had to get away and get help.

Marian entered the gloomy kitchen stealthily, knife at the ready. The light from the candle didn't travel far, and the shadows were very dark. Something moved just at the edge of her vision, and she whirled round, raising her knife, her heart jumping in her chest. A cat ran away from her, streaking across the floor to the back door, and Marian relaxed a little.

"Get out of here, Nicodemus," she said quickly. "Go find some mice and earn your keep."

The cat glared back at her, hissed defiantly, and disappeared into the shadows. Marian shook her head and smiled, and an arm grabbed her from behind, choking her with a vicious neck hold. Marian struggled furiously for a moment, and then stopped as she felt the point of a sword pressing against her ribs.

"Drop your blade," said the man behind her. His voice was low and breathy, almost amused. Marian swallowed dryly.

"It's only a knife. What's the matter? Do you feel overmatched?"

The hold across her throat tightened, cutting off her air, and the sword point jabbed painfully between her ribs. Marian dropped the knife, and her attacker released his hold and pushed her forward violently. She crashed painfully into the kitchen table and spun round, glaring at the soldier before her as she massaged her bruised throat. The soldier was large and muscular, wearing battered chain mail but no identifying badge or colors. Sword for hire, probably. Whoever was after her didn't want word of her situation to get out too quickly. The soldier smiled unpleasantly and lifted his sword a little so it pointed between Marian's breasts.

"I'm supposed to take you alive, girl, but no one said I couldn't have a bit of fun first. I've never seen the body of

162

a noblewoman. Take off the robe, bitch. Or I'll do it for you."

Marian tried not to flinch away from the sound of his voice, the look in his eyes. There was no point in reasoning with him. The fire in his blood had taken him beyond sense or judgment. With a little luck, it might also have taken him beyond common sense. Just because she had dropped her knife, it didn't mean she was helpless. She lifted one hand to the throat of her robe and undid the first button, taking her time before moving on to the second. His eyes followed her movements hungrily. Marian reached surreptitiously behind her with her free hand. The pepper pot was just where she remembered it being, and she quietly levered off its lid as she undid the third and fourth buttons on her robe. The soldier's breathing deepened, and he leaned forward slightly. Marian brought the pepper pot round quickly and let him have the entire contents right in the eyes.

The soldier screamed hoarsely as his eyes caught fire, and flailed blindly about him with his sword. Marian ducked under a wild swing and kicked him square in the groin. The soldier fell to his knees, tears streaming down his face. Marian darted over to the fireplace and grabbed a heavy iron cooking spit. She lifted it with both hands and poised herself to drive the point through the soldier's chest. The door behind her crashed open, and more soldiers burst into the kitchen. They fell upon her before she could turn, wrestled the spit away from her, and dragged her out of the kitchen and into the night.

Out in the courtyard there were soldiers everywhere, running in and out of the mansion and dragging away protesting servants. Shouted orders and answers rang on the night air. Some of the soldiers had burning torches in their hands, and Marian's blood ran cold. An older soldier came over to stand before her, cold and unsmiling and very professional.

"Do as you're told, my Lady, and no one need be hurt. Give me any trouble, and I'll have my men kill all the servants and burn this place to the ground. Do I make myself clear?"

"Yes," said Marian. "Very clear. I won't give you any trouble. Who are you? Why are you doing this?"

The soldier smiled. "Someone wants a word with you, my Lady."

Duncan stood listening at the stable door. The time he'd spent living in darkness had sharpened his hearing, and he'd been the first to hear the soldiers arriving. By the time he'd got his old bones out of bed and moving the soldiers were everywhere, but even so he hadn't had much trouble avoiding them. He was a lot more used to moving around in the dark than they were. But what to do, what to do . . . He couldn't fight these people, but perhaps he could carry word to the man who could. Master Robin would know what to do. He always knew what to do. Duncan groped silently through the stables to where the horses were tethered. He had to be quick. It wouldn't take the soldiers long to get around to checking the stables. He quickly located Robin's horse by its smell, as familiar and distinctive to him as a voice. There was no time for a saddle, but he managed to fit a bridle and reins with a little cooperation from the horse. He patted the animal's neck fondly and whispered in its ear.

"This night, old friend, I must depend on your eyes."

He found a mounting block and clambered onto the horse's back. He took up the reins, braced himself, and dug in his heels. The horse shot forward, burst out of the stables, and charged across the courtyard, scattering sol-

164

diers left and right. Duncan hung on grimly as the horse sped off into the night, and he headed the animal in what he remembered as the right direction for Sherwood. He urged the horse to as fast a speed as he dared, and listened for the sound of pursuit. He couldn't hear any hoofbeats apart from his own, and the night seemed quiet. Presumably the soldiers thought he wasn't important enough to worry about. Duncan smiled grimly. He'd show them. He clung tightly to the reins and urged the horse on.

He didn't see the dark figures that followed silently behind him on foot.

He followed the trail to Sherwood easily enough. It was a well-used road, and the horse knew the way from before, so all Duncan had to do was keep the animal pointing in roughly the right direction. But eventually the horse slowed to a stop, and whinnied uncertainly when Duncan tried to persuade it on. Duncan scowled. He vaguely remembered a crossroads at some point in the road, and he came close to panic as he realized he couldn't remember which route led to the forest. Choose the wrong road, and he could end up miles from Sherwood. And he would have failed his master's love. He took a deep breath, let it out in a long shuddering sigh, and loosened his hold on the reins.

"It's up to you now, boy," he said hoarsely. "Take us home. Take us to Master Robin."

The horse whinnied softly at the name, hesitated, and then trotted down the left-hand path, toward the forest.

Duncan never knew how long the journey took. For him it was an endless dark nightmare of unfamiliar sounds and turnings. The cold night air sank into his bones and the wind cut viciously at his bare face and hands. He'd had no time to find a cloak, and his thin nightshirt and trousers were little protection against the bitter night. The steady pounding of the long night leeched the strength out of him, mile by mile, until it was all he could do to cling on, but he still knew when the horse finally brought him to Sherwood. The familiar night sounds and smells of the living forest comforted him, and put new hope in his heart. He listened intently as the horse carried him along. The waterfall. Where was the waterfall? He strained his ears against the rustling of branches and the soft hooting of a nearby owl, and then he straightened up slightly, as from far away he heard a faint rumbling and splashing. He smiled, relieved, and headed the horse in that direction.

He was very tired now, sitting slumped on the horse's back, only holding on by grim determination. Sometimes it seemed to him that he heard noises in the dark behind him, as though someone might be following, but when he stopped the horse to listen all he ever heard were the quiet sounds of the forest. So he pressed on, one tired old man trying to do his best for those he loved.

And death and damnation followed behind him.

High in the trees, a lookout saw the lone rider approaching and fired an arrow into the midst of the camp, to alert the woodsmen. Robin looked round, startled, as the arrow thudded into the ground. He rounded up half a dozen woodsmen with quick jerks of his head, and together they moved silently to the edge of the clearing. The night seemed quiet enough. Robin frowned up at the lookout, who pointed out the approaching horse and rider. Azeem quickly assembled his telescope and stared through it, straining his eyes against the night, and then he lowered the telescope and looked blankly at Robin.

"It's Duncan."

"Duncan?" said Robin incredulously. "What's he doing back here? And how the hell did he find his way back on his own?"

He was off and running toward the rider before anyone could come up with an answer. Azeem followed quickly after him. The horse whinnied as it recognized Robin, and Duncan stirred at the sound, and almost fell. Robin caught him and eased him gently to the ground. The old man seemed frailer and more fragile than ever, but he gripped Robin's arm with desperate strength. Robin tried to calm him, but the fear and need that had driven Duncan for so long wouldn't let him rest. He tried to speak, but his dry throat only produced a croak. He beat at the ground with his fist in frustration, close to tears.

"Easy, Duncan," said Robin soothingly. "What's happened?"

Duncan swallowed hard, and forced words out. "Master Robin, thank God . . . Nottingham's men attacked us."

"Marian . . ." said Robin. A cold hand clutched at his heart. "What's happened to Marian?"

"They took her," said Duncan. He broke off as harsh coughs shook him like a rag doll. "But I found you. I did well, Master Robin, didn't I?"

An arrow thudded into the clearing behind them, followed by another and another. Arrows came whistling in from all sides of the camp as more lookouts raised the alarm. Woodsmen milled about confusedly, grabbing for weapons and looking for the enemy. Azeem raised his telescope again and stared out into the night. After a moment he lowered it and looked at Robin with what might have been horror in his eyes.

"Allah save us. . . ."

Robin snatched the telescope from him and looked through it. Off in the distance, at the top of a rise, still and silent in the bright moonlight, a small army of mounted Celts lay spread out behind a huge figure in black armor. There were hundreds of them, wearing hides and skins and leather armor, and headpieces in the forms of wild animals. Their faces were scarred and painted in the ancient way, and waiting motionless in the moonlight, they seemed more like ghosts than men—memories from England's dark past, from the time before civilization, when savagery ruled the land.

Robin lowered the telescope, and Will Scarlet snatched it from him. Robin looked down at Duncan's tired, proud face.

"Duncan . . ."

Scarlet threw the telescope at Azeem and whirled on Robin, his face flushed with fury. "Damn you, nobleman! This stupid servant of yours has led them straight to us!" He turned and ran back to the clearing; shouting the alarm.

Duncan tried to sit up, horror in his face. "What?"

"Celts!" called Bull, running after Scarlet. "Hundreds of them! They're coming!"

Up on the rise, the Celt Chief Ordred looked impassively down at his enemy, running back and forth in their pathetic little village, like frightened mice. There would be sport this night. Blood and fury and the despoiling of the enemy's women. He heard a horse moving up beside him, but didn't look round. He knew it was the Sheriff. No one else would dare approach him at such a time. He turned unhurriedly in his saddle, and bowed formally. The Sheriff nodded briefly in acknowledgment, and stared down at the clearing. He wore a full suit of chain mail, gleaming cold and silver in the moonlight. Behind him, waiting patiently at the base of the rise, stood row upon row of crossbowmen. The Sheriff finally looked away from the clearing, and turned a cold gaze on Ordred.

"Remember, I want prisoners."

The Celt chief stared down at his prey, and when he

spoke his voice was as much an animal's growl as anything human. "We came to fight."

"Nevertheless," said the Sheriff sharply, "I need prisoners. Kill and burn to your heart's content, but make sure that some survive for me to try and hang later. The forms must be observed. That is the civilized way."

Ordred drew his sword and raised it above his head. He tilted back his great dragon helm and roared in Gaelic at the full moon. The massed ranks of Celts put back their heads and answered him with a long, ululating howl that chilled the Sheriff's blood. The chieftan urged his mount forward, and his men followed him. In seconds they were streaming down the rise to the woodsmen's camp like a vast unstoppable tide. The moonlight gleamed brightly on their swords and axes, and their fixed, staring eyes.

Little John screamed orders to his men as they ran frantically to prearranged stations, readying themselves to cover the retreating women and children as they scrambled up rope ladders into the safety of the trees. Newer arrivals readied their weapons and their courage and looked for a good place to make a stand. The thunder of the Celts' horses filled the night, and the ground shook beneath the woodsmen's feet. They clutched their swords and axes, nocked arrows to their bows, and stood silently, waiting. Robin had drilled them many times on what to do in the event of an attack, but none of them had ever really thought it would happen. No one was ever going to find the camp. It was too well hidden, the ways in and out too well guarded. But now the Sheriff and his men had found them, along with an army of savages from the north, and all the woodsmen's plans and training didn't seem nearly enough.

Robin and his small group raced back to the camp, the Celts all but snapping at their heels. The savages' war cries were deafeningly close, but none of the woodsmen had time to breathe enough to spare a backward glance. The closely crowded trees slowed the horses down, but that was all. Robin dragged Duncan along with him by brute force, but quickly realized that the old man was just too weak and exhausted to make it to the clearing. And trying to carry him that far would get both of them killed. He stopped suddenly, let go of Duncan, and turned to face the Celts, nocking an arrow to his bow. He aimed and fired four arrows in swift succession, and four of the leading Celts were thrown from their saddles as though they'd been swept away by invisible hands. The charge didn't falter, and the Celts swept on.

Azeem ran back to stand beside Robin as he coolly fitted another arrow to his bow. The Celts were very close now. The Moor's eyes narrowed as he expertly judged speeds and distance, and then, at just the right moment, he slashed out with his scimitar to the left and to the right, and two Celts who would have ridden past him were cut screaming from their saddles. Their blood flew on the cold night air as Azeem moved quickly in to finish them off. Another Celt bore down on Robin while the Moor was preoccupied. Bull started to yell a warning, realized there wasn't time, and threw his dagger with desperate strength. It sank to its hilt in the Celt's throat, and the savage groped blindly at the weapon that had killed him, before slumping forward over his horse's neck.

Duncan stumbled on toward the camp. He could hear what was happening around him, and could smell fresh blood in the night, though he didn't know whose. Men were dying, and it was all his fault. He'd led the enemy here. He stumbled over a dead body, and his breath almost stopped as he knelt down to search the dead face with his fingers. He breathed easily again as his fingertips stumbled over tribal scars, and he scrabbled around on the blood-soaked earth till he found the savage's sword. He straightened up with the blade in his hand, and a look of bitter desperation on his face. He cocked his head to one side, concentrating on the sound of the horses as they drew near, and then he lashed out with his sword at the last moment. He felt the blade bite deeply into something as it passed, and someone screamed in rage and pain. The two Celts following close behind hit Duncan at the same time, their blades all but cutting him in two. The horses that came after trampled him underfoot.

Robin was fighting back to back with Azeem when he saw the old man go down, but the press of horses around him made it impossible to do anything. Finally the press weakened, and Robin fought his way through the riders to reach the old retainer's side. He knew Duncan was dying the moment he saw him, but the old man had enough strength left in him to grip Robin's hand as he knelt beside him. His mouth moved, but Robin had to lean right over to hear the few whispered words.

"Forgive an old fool, Master Robin."

And then he was gone. Robin just knelt there for a moment, unable to believe it. Duncan had been there most of his life. Servant, companion, friend. And the Sheriff had used and discarded him as though he were nothing. Robin rose to his feet, sword in hand, a cold rage giving him new strength and purpose. More Celts were thundering out of the night toward him. Robin sheathed his sword, nocked an arrow to his bow, and killed a Celt with it. He fired again and again, punching ragged holes in the massed ranks before him, but he ran out of arrows long before he ran out of targets. He put his back against a tree, drew his sword again, and looked around him. He wasn't far from the edge of the clearing. He could see Little John and Will Scarlet still trying to organize the camp's defenses as Celts charged into the clearing, scattering the woodsmen before them.

Robin yelled Little John's name, and he looked briefly in Robin's direction.

"Get them into the trees, John! We can't beat them on the ground, but they can't follow us into the trees!"

"Damn right," growled Scarlet and made for the nearest ladder. Little John grabbed him by the shoulder and pulled him back.

"The others can go, but we stand our ground till Robin and the others are safely back! Now lift that bow and show us some of that skill you're always boasting about!"

Men and women ran desperately for the trees and the rope ladders as the Celts swarmed into the camp. Arrows rained down from above, throwing riders from their horses, but all too often shafts bounced harmlessly back from upraised shields. Celts had experience with arrows. Bull fired and fired until he ran out of arrows, and then he scrambled up the nearest ladder. Someone else was right behind him, but the woodsman only managed two or three rungs before he was snatched from the ladder by a rider leaning out from his saddle. Bull watched helplessly as the Celt rode on, dragging the screaming woodsman behind him and finally impaling the man on the jagged edge of a broken branch.

Savage cries and laughter rang on the night as the Celts cut down men and women alike. Blood flew on the moonlit air and soaked the trampled earth, and from every direction came the screams of the wounded and the dying. Will Scarlet darted back and forth among the riders, cutting about him with his dagger as he tried to reach the nearest ladder. A Celt loomed up before him, blocking his way, and Scarlet threw his dagger into the painted, grinning face. It lodged squarely in the Celt's left eye, and he fell backward out of his saddle without even a scream. Scarlet grinned nastily, pulled himself up onto the horse's back, and used it as a springboard to reach the rope ladder.

Robin and the others finally burst into the clearing, shocked and breathless at so much death and destruction in so short a time. Bodies lay everywhere in pools of blood, and wooden huts burned brightly against the night. Robin snatched up a quiver of arrows from a fallen woodsman, but the Celts were everywhere now, and for every Celt that fell it seemed there were two more ready to take his place. More arrows filled the air as the Sheriff's crossbowmen finally reached the scene. Robin swore dispassionately and yelled for every woodsman still in the clearing to take to the trees. He drew his sword and made for the nearest rope ladder, pushing Azeem and Little John ahead of him.

Swords and axes cut at them from every side as they fought their way forward, foot by foot. Azeem got to the ladder first and swarmed up it as though he'd been doing it all his life. Little John clambered after him, the ropes creaking and groaning under his great weight. Celts rushed across the clearing from one side to the other, mounted and on foot, blood dripping thickly from their blades. Robin cut desperately about him, trying to open up enough space for him to reach the ladder, but there were just too many Celts crowding around him, and he knew it was only a matter of time before one of them got in a lucky blow. He'd always been a better archer than a swordsman. Little John yelled down at him to grab a rung of the ladder and hang on. Robin found a little extra strength from somewhere and opened up just enough room for him to snake his free arm round the ladder's bottom rung. The woodsmen on the platform above hauled the ladder up into the air, taking Robin with it. The Celts screamed in fury as their prey escaped them, and Robin pulled his legs up as high as he could to keep them out of reach of the Celts' swords.

He clung onto the ladder for dear life as it rose into the air, and looked down with grim fascination at what had been done to his camp, to his people. For as far as he could see, Celts moved unopposed through the clearing, cutting hands and ears from the fallen woodsmen for trophies, and torching any structure that looked as though it might burn. All that remained now was the aerial fortress, and the people it held.

Robin finally reached the platform, and many hands helped him up off the ladder. He nodded his thanks and looked quickly about him, taking in the situation. Men and women and children crowded everywhere on the platforms and rope bridges, but even so there were nowhere near as many as there should have been. Robin shook his head sickly, and his mouth tightened. There would be a time for vengeance later, but for now his first priority had to be the safety of those who'd survived. It was clear there were no more of his people left alive below, and he called for all the rope ladders to be pulled up out of reach of the Celts. The woodsmen hauled up the ladders, bringing with them a few Celts who'd clung to the bottom rungs. Robin gestured, and the woodsmen cut free those ladders. The Celts fell screaming forty feet and more back to the ground.

The woodsmen and the Sheriff's crossbowmen exchanged arrows for a while, to no great effect, and then the soldiers suddenly broke off the attack. A sudden silence fell across the night, broken only by the crackling flames of the burning buildings. The Celts stood at their ease, watching expectantly. The woodsmen stirred uneasily and looked at each other. They were safe in the trees, safe from the crossbowmen's arrows and the Celt's torches. Any Celt foolish enough to try and set fire to one of the great trees would be cut down by a dozen arrows before he got anywhere near it, and the Celts knew that.

And then, from out of the darkness, a ball of fire the size of a man's head flew through the air and smashed into the treetops. A hut burst into flames, the sudden heat leaping out to ignite the rope bridge beside it. A woodsman screamed shrilly as his clothes and hair caught fire. Men and women fell back from the blazing heat, and screams filled the treetops as the burning man fell from the platform and plummeted to the ground below like a howling comet. His screams stopped when he hit the ground, but the flames kept on burning. More fireballs came blazing out of the night to smash into the aerial fortress, and smoke and flames spread quickly among the panicking woodsmen. Flaming arrows arched up from the Sheriff's crossbowmen, starting new fires, but Robin just stared dumbly out into the dark. *Catapults. They're using catapults.* He'd anticipated and planned for everything but that.

A blazing arrow thudded into the platform by his feet, and he reached down absently, pulled it out, and dropped it back into the clearing. He snapped awake, and yelled for his people to stand their ground and use the water buckets he'd had installed in the huts in case of emergency. Woodsmen staggered back and forth in the thick, choking black smoke, dousing flames wherever they could, but the fire spread faster than they could react, and the dry wood of the fortress burned fiercely.

And the fireballs and the fire arrows just kept on coming.

Little John moved purposefully among the woodsmen, soothing and steadying them with calm words. Water buckets moved along rope pullies, and where they couldn't reach, people formed human chains to keep the water moving to where it was needed. Robin ran back and forth across the rope bridges, firing arrow after arrow down at the crossbowmen below, to protect the woodsmen as they worked. Will Scarlet ran across a bridge that was already afire, carrying a bucket of water. The ropes were all but coming apart under his feet, but he wouldn't let himself look down. The treetops were hotter than hell, and the water pullies weren't worth spit, but he was damned if he'd give up. Will Scarlet never gave up.

The rope bridge finally collapsed under him, and he threw himself forward onto the platform. He landed on the edge, started to slip back, and scrambled forward until he was safe. He looked down, and snarled happily as the mass of burning ropes fell onto the Celts below. He handed over his half-empty bucket of water to a pair of desperate hands and wiped sweat from his face as he seized a moment to get his breath back. Black smoke swirled about him, and his breath hitched painfully in his chest. He crouched down on his haunches to get below the smoke, and for a moment it cleared, showing him the Sheriff sitting calmly on his horse at the edge of the clearing, enjoying the sight of so much death and destruction at his command. Scarlet snarled and reached for his bow, but the wind changed and the smoke rolled back, and the moment was gone.

Robin fired his final arrow into the shifting smoke, leaned tiredly against a hut wall, and looked helplessly about him. The fire had taken an unbreakable hold on the aerial fortress and was spreading into the trees. There was no point in fighting it any more. The fire had beaten them. All that was left to him now was to save as many of his people as he could. He organized a small gang of archers into giving covering fire as men, women, and children scrambled down emergency ladders and ropes. They hit the ground some distance from the clearing and scattered into the sheltering woods. And found Celts waiting for them there too.

Bull found himself surrounded by four smiling savages, their eyes gleaming coldly in their painted faces. Bull drew his sword, put his back to the nearest tree, and spat out a defiant challenge. The Celts moved in together, and he lifted his sword to meet them.

Tuck fought off a Celt with his staff, and pummeled him to the ground. He could feel the man's bones breaking under his blows, and muttered prayers of penance under his breath. He didn't see the second Celt moving in behind him. The savage drew back his sword for a killing thrust, and Azeem appeared out of the darkness and ran him through. Tuck looked round quickly at the Celt's death rattle, and nodded acknowledgment to the Moor. They disappeared into the trees together.

Up in the treetops, Will Scarlet grabbed Little John by the arm and pointed furiously through the shifting smoke to where Robin was running along a rope bridge, away from the fire and the fighting. Scarlet's face was flushed with anger and something that might have been disappointment.

"Where's your precious hero going now, then?" he yelled above the clamor of the night. "Saving his own damned neck!"

Little John looked away, and his blood ran cold as he saw his son Wulf standing at the edge of the clearing below and picking off Celts with his bow as coolly as if he were still at target practice. John yelled for him to get the hell away while he still could, but the boy couldn't hear him. John leaned out from the platform to try again, his eyes fixed on his son. Wulf finally looked up at his father, and immediately fitted an arrow to his bow and drew a bead on him. John froze where he was, and Wulf fired. The arrow slammed into the Celt who'd been climbing silently up an overlooked ladder, just below John. The woodsman just had time to stare into the Celt's glazing eyes before the dying man released his hold and fell away into the thick smoke. John looked back at his son to congratulate him on his shot, and the proud grin disappeared as he saw three of the

Sheriff's men overpower Wulf and drag him away. Little John howled with helpless rage and scrambled down the ladder to the clearing below. He didn't know he was crying, and wouldn't have cared if he had.

Robin raced along the rope bridge and into a blazing hut, shielding his face against the roaring flames with an upraised arm. The heat was almost unbearable, searing his lungs as he breathed as shallowly as possible. He glared about the smoke-filled hut, his nose wrinkling at the smell of his own singed hair. Fanny was lying on a bed at the rear of the hut, shielding her baby with her own body. Robin got her on her feet, wrapped his cloak about them both, and protected the baby between his body and Fanny's. And then he led her through the fire and the blazing doorway and out onto the platform. The heat was agony for an endless moment, and then they were past the flames and out into the night.

The rope bridge was only wide enough to take them one at a time, so Robin pushed Fanny ahead of him, encouraging her all the while with calm, reassuring words. She pressed on with gritted teeth, one step at a time, refusing to give in to the heat. The baby was mercifully calm, watching the inferno of fire and smoke with wide, awed eyes.

Robin looked back over his shoulder. The hut and the platform they'd left were now a mass of flames, pumping black smoke into the treetops. Sparks from the blaze had set fire to that end of the bridge, and the fire was moving along the ropes after Robin and Fanny. He yelled for her to hurry, and the raw urgency in his voice spurred her on. Flames surged along the ropes in fits and starts, and the bridge creaked and sagged threateningly. Fanny scrambled safely onto the next platform, hugging the baby to her, and looked back to see Robin struggling toward her through the thick smoke. Fire burned on either side of him. The ropes parted suddenly beneath his feet, and Fanny screamed as Robin fell helplessly into the smoke and disappeared, one hand reaching briefly out to her as though for help. And then he was gone. Fanny called his name again and again, but there was no reply, and in the end she turned away, sniffing back tears so as not to upset the baby.

Down below, on a burning branch, hung a simple medallion, bearing the Locksley family crest. A Celt snatched it from the branch, tested the gold between his teeth, and tucked it into his belt before disappearing back into the smoke of the burning camp.

It was early morning, and the rising sun bloodied the sky as the Sheriff's men herded a ragged crowd of woodsmen, women, and children toward Nottingham, and their fate. Many were injured, or suffering from burns or smoke, but the soldiers drove them viciously on, using whatever cruelty was necessary to keep them moving. The Sheriff strode among the listless woodsmen, searching for Robin's face and demanding he reveal himself. No one said anything. The Sheriff shouldered people out of his way, the scar on his cheek showing blood red against his pinched white face. Robin Hood had to be here somewhere. He had to be, or it had all been for nothing. He finally came across the boy Wulf, and grabbed him by the shoulder. His fingers dug in painfully, but the boy hardly reacted.

"Where's Locksley, boy?" asked the Sheriff hoarsely. "Where's Robin Hood?"

"Dead," said Wulf dully. "Mother saw him fall."

The Sheriff looked at him for a long moment, and then let him go. He stood very still, eyes far away, as the woodsmen trudged on, taking the boy with them. More soldiers brought up the rear, staggering under the weight of recaptured loot.

. . .

In Nottingham Castle, in the Sheriff's private chapel, the Bishop and Marian Dubois held a private mass. She knelt before him, head meekly bowed. It was a quiet, peaceful scene, and only the soldiers standing between Marian and the two doors made it clear she was a prisoner. The Bishop's droning Latin was a comfort as Marian's mind raced helplessly. The Sheriff had to know something, but how much? If she wasn't careful, she might end up condemning herself out of her own mouth. Marian smiled grimly. She hadn't survived this long on her own without learning how to guard her tongue.

The Bishop broke off suddenly as the door opened and the Sheriff strode in. He was dressed in his finest clothes, and there was no mistaking the look of triumph on his face. He smiled at Marian, and she shrank inwardly from the gleam in his eyes. Without having to be told, she knew something had happened. Something awful.

"My Lady Marian," said the Sheriff. "So sorry to have kept you waiting."

Marian rose quickly to her feet. She would not kneel before him. "By what right do you drag me from my home and keep me prisoner?"

"You misunderstand my intentions," said the Sheriff easily. "I have brought you here for your own safety and protection."

"Protection from whom?" said Marian, icily.

"From yourself, my Lady. It seems you have been consorting with the woodsmen."

Marian held her head erect and met his gaze unflinchingly. "Where do you hear such lies?"

The Sheriff reached inside his tunic and brought forth the letter Marian had written for King Richard. Marian's heart lurched as she saw the red wax seal had been broken.

"Where did I hear? From your own hand, my Lady."

Marian looked speechlessly at the Bishop. He shrugged. "I'm sorry, my child. But it was clear to me that you were being led astray."

"And now, Marian," said the Sheriff. "What am I going to do with you?"

11
SECRETS

The Sheriff took Marian out onto a balcony overlooking the main courtyard, and showed her what was left of her world. In the cold of the morning, covered in mud and blood and untreated burns, the remains of Robin Hood's woodsmen stood huddled together in chains and shackles. There were men and women and children, all of them silent and uncomplaining, numbed by pain and loss and the quiet horror that comes to every animal caught in a trap. Soldiers moved unhurriedly among them, sorting them into small groups and herding them off to the dungeons below. More soldiers stood around the courtyard with weapons at the ready, watching the woodsmen with cold, flat eyes, hoping someone would be stupid enough to start something, so they could step in and finish it. No one did.

Marian looked down at them all, seeing face after face she knew, and thought her heart would break. For her and for them, the woodsman camp had been part of a sweet, simple dream of freedom, but now the dream was over, and harsh reality had taken its place. And just when she thought she couldn't hurt any more, she found herself looking down at her missing lady-in-waiting, Sarah. The woman she had unwittingly sent into danger and betrayal. Someone had beaten Sarah viciously not so long ago, and the marks of it were still clear on her face, and in her frightened, pleading eyes. Marian looked away. She'd never felt more dejected or more helpless in her life. The Sheriff moved in beside her.

"It's over," he said calmly. "The day of the woodsman is now a thing of the past. Today, I have returned justice to this county." He paused and looked at Marian as though expecting a response, but she had nothing to say. He smiled slightly and looked out over the prisoners gathered below. "I've decided to hang ten of the ringleaders, as an example. As a wedding gift, I have it in mind to be generous, and grant you the lives of the rest of the woodsmen and their families. And your treacherous lady-in-waiting, of course."

He gestured for the soldiers below to separate the children from their parents and herd them into a small group below the balcony. The children went quietly where they were pushed, eyes empty and downcast. One small girl reached up to hold a soldier's hand trustingly. Marian swallowed quickly, and fought to keep her face calm and her voice steady as she turned to face the Sheriff.

"And who exactly am I supposed to marry?"

"Search your heart, Marian," said the Bishop, stepping out onto the balcony to join them. He glanced briefly at the woodsmen below, grimaced fleetingly at their filthy condition, and smiled charmingly at Marian. "Would not a union between you and the house of Nottingham offer renewal, a chance to heel the wounds of this land?"

Marian looked at him with such contempt that the Bishop fell silent and looked away, unable to meet her fierce, accusing gaze. Marian smiled humorlessly. "Only one man

183

truly cares about the wounds of this land, the same man who was doing his best to heal them. Robin Hood."

The Sheriff reached inside his tunic and brought out a gold medallion on a chain. He placed it gently in Marian's hand. She looked down at the medallion, at the proud Locksley crest, and the tears she'd held back for so long burned in her eyes. "No," she whispered finally. "This isn't true. I won't believe it."

"There is a corpse, if you require further proof," said the Sheriff. "I'm afraid it's burned quite horribly, but you can view it if you must."

Marian's eyes squeezed shut, and her hand clenched around the medallion till her knuckles showed white, but she never made a sound.

"I'm truly sorry, Marian," said the Sheriff. "I had no quarrel with Locksley, till he went against me. He was strong and brave. A worthy opponent. I like to think that in another time and place, we might have been friends. But instead he wasted his life on foolish dreams and hopeless fancies. How many more lives would you waste?"

He waited, but Marian had no answer for him. He took her firmly by the hand and led her back inside, down passages and stairways, and finally out into the courtyard, where the children were still waiting with their guards. The Sheriff gestured easily at them.

"So beautiful, so full of life . . . so beautifully unaware of how short and precarious life can be." He squeezed her hand gently. "Marian, our bonding could allow these children to grow up as our allies. You must understand—I cannot allow them to grow up as my enemies." He waited patiently for a response, but Marian only stared at the children, as though he weren't there. The Sheriff took her chin in his hand and turned her head around to face him. "I will share everything I have with you. I will only hear a 'yes.' "

Marian's jaw tightened, and though she was looking at the Sheriff, her eyes were still full of the children. "Very well, my Lord. I have no choice. Yes."

The Sheriff smiled and released her chin, and turned to the Bishop, who had just joined them, puffing slightly from the exertions of the stairs. "Ah, my old friend. Take the lady Marian to her chambers, and see to her comfort. I'm sure in time she will come to see the benefits of our betrothal."

The Bishop extended a hand to Marian, but she swept past him and strode back into the hall in a fast walk that was almost running, as though if she could only move fast enough, she could leave it all behind her. She still held Robin's medallion tightly in her hand, and she whispered his name once as she left the light of the courtyard behind her and plunged into the gloom of the castle.

In what was left of the woodsmen's camp, a cold breeze moved slowly across the clearing, disturbing the dark ashes and stirring the occasional curl of acrid smoke. Blackened corpses lay everywhere, some still reaching out charred, stiffened hands, begging blindly for help that never came. The huts of the village were nothing more than scorched frames and blackened timbers. Dead houses for dead men. And everywhere, the smell of burned meat.

Little John, Azeem, and Friar Tuck wandered through what was left of the camp, searching for some trace of life, some sign, something to give them hope that not all was lost. Something to give them a reason to carry on living. But everywhere they looked there was only death and destruction and the end of dreams. Little John stopped suddenly, and knelt down to pick up a half-burned, but still distinctly carved bow.

"Robin . . ." he said softly. The others nodded. It was almost a prayer. He shook his head sadly, looked up, and his heart missed a beat as a dark figure stepped out of the trees to face him. Little John rose quickly to his full height, holding his staff out before him, ready to fight. And then he realized who was standing before him, and his blood ran cold.

"Dear Lord, what have I called up? Robin, I pray you, return to your rest. . . ."

Robin smiled tiredly. "I'm no spirit, John. Though I might have been, had a branch not broken my fall. If the Sheriff thinks me dead, he might show mercy to my people."

Little John laughed suddenly, and crushed Robin to him in a fierce bearhug. "It wasn't just the Sheriff who'd given you up for dead! I should have known you'd survive, no matter what the Sheriff brought against you!"

As John released him Robin looked about him, taking in the carnage and destruction that was all that remained of what had so recently been a thriving community. "Better perhaps if I had died. I'm the cause of all this."

Little John put an arm across his shoulders and gently pulled him away. "Come. A few of us are still safe. Seeing you alive will raise their spirits."

They led Robin off into the trees, but though they turned their backs on the dead camp it still traveled with them, in their hearts.

In a dungeon deep under Nottingham Castle, the ten woodsmen marked for death stood chained to walls encrusted with dried blood and grime. They stood quietly, far beyond protesting their pain or condition. Putrid water lapped about their ankles, and sometimes things moved in it, though mostly it was too dark to see what. A rat swam past Will Scarlet, and he kicked at it listlessly.

"Leave it alone," said a voice from the dark. "That's our dinner."

A few of the woodsmen managed some kind of chuckle, but it was a quiet, lost sound in the gloom. They all knew that none of them would ever leave this dungeon again, save to visit the torturers or the gallows. Their deaths had already been decided; all that remained was when and how. The only hope they had left was that it would be quick.

A heavy key turned in a lock, and the woodsmen looked in the direction of the sound as they heard heavy bolts being drawn back. A few of the woodsmen tried to stand straight despite their chains, but most were too beaten down even for that small show of defiance. The door swung open, and the woodsmen had to turn their heads away as light from blazing torches filled the dungeon, pushing back the darkness. The Sheriff stepped down into the filthy water with only the faintest of grimaces and looked unhurriedly about him as half a dozen guards spilled into the dungeon on either side of him. The Sheriff never had believed in taking unnecessary chances. Even a chained animal can be dangerous, especially when it knows it has nothing left to lose. He strode over to the nearest woodsman and smiled down at him.

"Would you prefer pain, or death?"

The woodsman looked at him steadily, eyes still half-closed against the harsh new light, but neither his chains nor his squalid condition could detract from his dignity as he faced his tormentor. "Give me death," he said flatly, and there was a growl of agreement from the other woodsmen.

The Sheriff pretended to consider the matter for a moment, and then nodded to his guards. "Torture him."

The guards unlocked the woodsman's chains and dragged him away, ignoring his struggles and curses. The Sheriff turned to the next woodsman. "And you—pain or death?"

The woodsman thought fast. "Pain?" he said tentatively.

The Sheriff nodded to his guards. "Torture him." He stepped back and smiled round at the watching woodsmen as the second man was dragged away, kicking and screaming. "You see, it makes no difference what you say. You will all be tortured." He turned to a frightened woodsman. "I've heard Robin Hood still lives. You will tell me all you know about Robin Hood. Where he might be hiding . . . everything. And when I have wrung every last drop of information out of you, you will all be hanged. Then we will catch Robin Hood and do the same to him."

"There's a quicker way," said Will Scarlet. "Let me out of here and I'll kill him for you."

There was a shocked gasp from the other woodsmen, and then they burst into angry shouts and threats. The Sheriff gestured to his guards, and they moved quickly among the prisoners, shutting them up with threats and blows. The boy Wulf rattled his chains furiously as he glared at Scarlet. The Sheriff moved over to stand before Scarlet, studying him interestedly, as one might a new form of insect found under a stone. Scarlet met the scornful gaze steadily.

"If he is alive, I know where to find him," Will Scarlet said. "I can get close to him. I'm one of his men; he'd never suspect me."

Wulf lunged forward against his chains, snarling like an animal. "He knows you always hated him, traitor!" One of the guards shut him up.

The Sheriff ignored him, his gaze fixed on Scarlet. The woodsman smiled coldly. "Robin Hood is a trusting fool. He'll believe me because he couldn't bear to think one of his own people might not love him. But even if he doesn't, he'll just kill me, and you'll have lost nothing."

The Sheriff drew his sword and moved in close. Scarlet tried to shrink back against the unyielding wall as the Sheriff pried his mouth open and delicately slid the tip of his sword between Scarlet's teeth. "If you fail," said the Sheriff calmly, "and Locksley doesn't kill you, I will personally cut out your lying tongue."

He withdrew the blade, but did not sheath it. Scarlet swallowed dryly, and tried to smile. "If I succeed, I want my freedom and the bounty on his head."

"Of course," said the Sheriff. He turned to his guards. "Torture him." He smiled at the stunned Scarlet with mock apology. "It will look better."

He laughed softly as the guards unlocked Scarlet's chains and dragged him away, and the cold ugly sound seemed to echo on in the dungeon even after he was gone.

The day passed, and the night, and dawn broke again over Sherwood as Robin filled in the last but one grave. Exhausted beyond pain or tiredness, kept moving only by grim determination and the guilt that gnawed constantly at his thoughts, Robin Hood patted down the dirt on the low, raised mound, and straightened up slowly to look about him. The clearing had been turned into a cemetery. Graves without number filled the open space where once a village had stood, full of life and laughter and hope. Friar Tuck moved slowly among the mounds of earth, planting crude crosses made from the blackened wood of burned-out huts. He muttered a blessing over each cross, adding the proper name in the few cases where the body had been undamaged enough by fire to be identified. There weren't many names. The fire had been widespread and unforgiving.

None of the dead Celts were buried in the clearing. They

had been dragged out into the woods and left to rot. Robin leaned on his shovel and allowed himself a few moments' rest. The early morning mists hung across the clearing like a shroud, giving the graveyard an almost peaceful look, but Robin knew better. There would be no peace for anyone lying in this ground as long as their deaths went unavenged. He heard footsteps, and looked up to see Azeem approaching, carrying Duncan's body in his arms. Robin nodded to Azeem, and the Moor lowered the dead man gently into his waiting grave.

"My pride brought us to this," said Robin quietly.

"No," said Azeem. "You gave these men pride. You gave them a life worth fighting for."

Robin looked down at Duncan in his grave. The old man looked small and vulnerable, like a broken toy. "I was a fool to let him leave. And a bigger fool for thinking I'd planned it all so perfectly."

Azeem looked at Robin steadily. "I once heard a wise man say, 'There are no perfect men in this world, only perfect intentions.'"

Robin took in the Moor's calm, forgiving face and swallowed hard, fighting for control of the emotions that were tearing him apart. "You were an honor to your countrymen yesterday, Azeem. You fought better than twenty English knights."

He lifted his shovel, but couldn't bring himself to drop earth on his old companion. Azeem reached out and took the shovel away from him. "I will do it. Get some rest, my friend."

Robin nodded slowly, and walked unsteadily away. After a while, he came to a slow-running brook a little way beyond the clearing. He knelt down beside it and splashed the icy water across his face and the back of his neck. The shock snapped him fully awake for the first time that morning, and he knelt there gasping for breath. It was well past time he started using his wits again. He'd been running on raw emotion ever since the attack, but now it was time once again to take up his responsibilities as the woodsmen's leader, and start working out what the hell he was going to do to put things right again. If there was anything he could do. He stared unseeingly at the water before him as he brooded, and then suddenly realized there was another reflection in the water apart from his own. He looked up quickly, and gaped at the figure standing beside him.

"Getting careless, Robin," said Will Scarlet. "There was a time I wouldn't have been able to sneak up on you like that."

Robin scrambled to his feet, grinning broadly. "Will! I thought you'd been taken!"

"I was," said Scarlet.

"Then how did you escape?"

"I promised to kill you."

The words seemed to hang on the quiet morning air, heavy with intent and unspoken emotion. Scarlet looked past Robin, and Robin turned to see Little John standing behind him. The giant woodsman glared at Scarlet.

"I'll wring your scrawny neck, Will Scarlet! Bull, fetch us a rope!"

"No!" said Robin sharply. "There's been enough killing here."

"It'll never be enough," said John. "Not as long as traitors like this are still alive."

He grabbed Scarlet by the shoulder and hauled the unresisting woodsman back into the clearing to show him the many graves. Azeem was just finishing tamping down Duncan's grave. He looked curiously at Scarlet, who stared impassively back. Bull and Fanny appeared in answer to John's shouts, and glared angrily at Scarlet. Tuck stared at him with icy contempt. Little John shook Scarlet roughly by the shoulder.

"No one escapes the Sheriff's dungeons. Not unless they're lining their pockets with the Sheriff's gold!"

"Search him," Fanny snarled. "He'll have a blade hidden on him somewhere."

Bull nodded agreement, his sword in his hand, ready for Scarlet to try anything. Scarlet looked unflinchingly at his accusers, and said nothing. John patted Scarlet down roughly, and then pulled open his shirt. Everyone gave some kind of gasp. Scarlet's chest was covered with a vicious tracery of barely healed cuts and fresh burns. John let go of Scarlet's shirt, and he adjusted it to hide his wounds with a kind of dignity.

"Damn me," whispered John.

"Let him speak," said Robin.

Scarlet looked briefly at each face in turn, and when he spoke his voice was eerily calm. "I bring a message from the Sheriff of Nottingham. Ten of our men are to be hung in the city square on Saturday, at high noon."

"What about my boy?" said Fanny.

Scarlet looked at her almost apologetically. "Wulf is to be hanged, as one of the ten."

Fanny turned away, and buried her face in Little John's chest. He patted her shoulder gently, rage burning coldly in his eyes.

"There's more," said Scarlet. "The hangings are to be part of general celebrations for the Sheriff's marriage."

Bull snorted derisively. "And what lucky wench gets to play with the Sheriff's codpiece?"

Scarlet looked directly at Robin. "The lady Marian has agreed to be his bride."

"Marian?" Tuck frowned. "The Sheriff takes a bride of royal blood?"

Little John nodded angrily. "Aye, and with King Richard gone, our Sheriff'll be set to take the bloody throne as well!"

And then they all realized what the news had to mean to Robin, and there was an awkward silence as they looked at him apologetically. But of them all, Robin had been the only one who showed no surprise. He looked unwaveringly at Scarlet, his face set and grim.

"You were supposed to use this news to get close to me, and then kill me. Right, Will?"

Scarlet smiled slightly. "Not straight away, of course."

"What are your intentions, Will?"

"That depends on you, Locksley. I never trusted you; that's no secret. Well, now's where we get to the truth. You said a lot of fine things to us, at one time or another—about pride and honor and having the courage to fight injustice. You still feel that way, after all that's happened? Are you ready to finish what you started, now it's just you, and there's no army of woodsmen to hide behind?"

Robin looked at him silently for a moment, and then looked out over the clearing full of graves. Little John hurried to his defense.

"Leave the man be, Will. It's over. We'd be mad to go against the Sheriff's men on our own."

Scarlet ignored him, his gaze fixed on Robin. "Will you stay, and keep us fighting till every man jack of us is dead? Or will you turn your back on us, and run like the spoiled little rich boy I always took you for?"

Robin glared at him, stirred to anger at last. "Where does this intolerable hatred for me come from, Will Scarlet?"

"Where did it come from, Robin? From knowing our father loved you more than me!" There was a stunned silence. Scarlet nodded, visibly hugging his sense of injustice to him like an old familiar friend. "You and I are brothers, Robin of Locksley. I am the son of the woman who replaced your dead mother . . . for a time. Your anger drove them apart."

Everyone looked from Will to Robin and back again. There was a resemblance, now they were looking for it. Robin walked slowly forward to stand before Will Scarlet, face-to-face.

"I didn't know, Will."

"Nor did our father," said Scarlet hoarsely. "My mother never told him. She was too ashamed to go back to him, after she'd left." He looked at the others, watching in astonished silence. "So know this: I have more reason to hate Robin than anyone, but . . . I have found myself daring to believe in him."

Robin hugged Scarlet to him, and the two men stood locked in a fierce embrace, trying to crush away the years that had separated them. The others exchanged confused, delighted grins. A lot of things had suddenly become clearer. The two brothers finally released each other, both trying to pretend there weren't tears in their eyes. Robin grinned at his friends.

"I have a brother! I always wanted a brother."

"Today we are all brothers," said Azeem. "If not by blood, then by fire." He gestured meaningfully at the graveyard. "Do we forget what these people have given to the cause we believed in, and go our separate ways . . . or do we band together as brothers should, and save those who would save us, if things were different?"

Tuck moved forward to stand at the Moor's side. "If my heathen brother stays, I stay!"

"Aye!" said Bull. "Brothers together, to the end!"

Little John laughed, and shook his head. "Bloody hell. We're all bloody in."

Robin looked around at all the grinning faces, and smiled

proudly in return. "The game is not yet lost, my friends. Not till we write finish to it."

In the dungeon under Nottingham Castle, the ten condemned woodsmen hung limply in their chains, resting from their torture, waiting for it to begin again. None of them had been spared the whips or the knives or the hot irons, not even the boy Wulf. In the dark some moaned, some prayed, and some sobbed openly. No one spoke against them. And whether they had talked of Robin or not was a matter for their own consciences, and no one else's. From outside, faint but clear, came the sound of gallows being built.

Wulf bit his lip to keep from whimpering, and stared up at the thin chink of light set high up on the wall. It wasn't large enough to be called a window, but it was the only light there was. The light was growing dim as the evening drew on, and as the light disappeared Wulf's hopes went with it. He'd known he was going to die with the others, but he hadn't really believed it till now.

He'd hoped his father would come to rescue him, or Robin . . . but deep down he had no doubt they were both already dead. Maybe he'd meet them again, after he died, and they could live together in some forest in heaven. He was scared, but to his surprise he found he was mostly scared that he wouldn't have the strength to go to his death with dignity. He didn't want to break down in front of the crowds, and be dragged to the gallows screaming and crying. That was what the Sheriff expected, and Wulf was damned if he'd give the bastard that satisfaction. He was a woodsman, and proud of it. He clutched his wooden crucifix with bloody fingers, and wished he knew some proper prayers.

"Lord, this is Wulf. If it be your bidding that this be my last night of life, Lord, I pray you, give me the pluck to die proud. And . . . look kindly on my family, and the young ones."

He couldn't think of anything else. He watched the last of the light disappear from the narrow chink high up on the wall, and darkness closed slowly in around him.

The Sheriff strode happily about his private chambers, feasting his eyes on the recaptured gold that lay strewn in great treasure chests about his room. Every now and again he dipped a hand into the mass of gold coins and stirred it slowly, enjoying the feel of the heavy gold as it pressed against his fingers. A roomful of gold, ten woodsmen to hang, and Marian his promised bride. What more could life offer? Apart from the throne of England. And he'd get round to that, in time.

His chief scribe hurried around behind him, cowed and utterly subservient ever since the Sheriff had had his tongue out. He scribbled quickly on a writing slate, and tugged timidly at the Sheriff's sleeve. The Sheriff looked down, read what was on the slate, and smiled at the sweating scribe.

"My bride-to-be is overwhelmed with happiness. Thank you for asking. All is well. I have most of my wealth back, Robin Hood is defeated and almost certainly dead, and the barons have pledged me their support as King. All is well . . . just as predicted."

He leaned against the wall, looking with satisfaction at his riches, and hugged himself with barely contained delight. All his. Fine raiments, fine furniture, fine walls . . . The Sheriff grinned and ran his hand across the wall at his side. And then he looked down, puzzled, as his fingers stumbled over a small hole. He examined it closely, his puzzled frown deepening into a scowl as he realized the hole had been deliberately camouflaged as part of the wall's design. He spun round and glared at the scribe.

"Have you been spying on me, you little toad?"

The scribe shook his head vehemently and dropped to his knees before the Sheriff. He started to scrawl a denial on his slate, but the Sheriff had already forgotten him.

"Who would drill such a hole . . . ? Who would want to spy on me in my private counsels . . . ?" He broke off as the answer came to him. A boiling rage surged up in him till he thought he would explode, as many things suddenly became clear.

"*Mortianna!*"

He ran out of the room, and the scribe heaved a sigh of relief. He started to make an obscene gesture after the Sheriff, and then thought better of it. You never knew who might be watching.

The Sheriff fumed and muttered angrily under his breath as he made his way down the dimly lit corridors and stairs into the depths under Nottingham Castle, his rage growing hotter and more intense the nearer he got to Mortianna's domain. He finally burst into her chamber, and glared about him into the gloom.

"Mortianna! Where are you, damn your eyes!"

A familiar shuffling and hissing filled the room as the albino hag emerged from the shadows and fixed the Sheriff with her disquieting crimson eyes. "You come early. The signs have not aligned yet."

The Sheriff's rage boiled over and he stepped forward, his hands clenched into white-knuckled fists. "Stop it, you charlatan!"

Mortianna looked away from his blazing eyes and reached into the bag of runes at her wrist. "Since thou art so impatient, I shall try for thee anyway." She scattered the runes across the floor before her, dispensing with the usual gory ritual. She moaned softly at the pattern the runes made, and began to sway as her eyes rolled back in her head. "The union . . . the blood of the Lion and the house of Nottingham. New power, new souls . . ."

The Sheriff stepped forward and deliberately kicked the wooden dice away. "Enough! I found the hole! I found your stinking spy hole! You dared to spy on me! Tell me the truth for once in your life, you twisted crone!"

Mortianna straightened up, casually abandoning her act, and smiled almost condescendingly at the Sheriff. "Why this sudden interest in the truth? It has never served you before. Truth did not put Lord Nottingham where he is today. Mortianna did that."

The Sheriff raised a hand to strike her, but something in her calm gaze stopped him at the last moment. "You freakish hag! I despise you. After the wedding I'll have you thrown out into the streets! Without my protection, you won't live to see the morning. The people will tear out your black heart and burn it."

He broke off as Mortianna laughed harshly, and then backed away in spite of himself as she advanced on him, stabbing at him with a bony finger. She laughed in his face, and the ugly sound echoed back from the surrounding walls. "Without me, little Lord, you are nothing. You are straw, a flea bite, a speck. I birthed you from this body. I stole a babe in this very castle and killed it so that you might take its place. You are my son, Nottingham!"

The Sheriff stared at her speechlessly, and she laughed again. "You despise me? You *are* me! You know in your empty soul I speak the truth. All my life I've been a freak, but when you stud the Lady Marian and my grandchild sits on the throne of England, it is my blood, my twisted seed that will rule! Who shall be called freak then?"

The Sheriff turned away from her, thinking frantically. He held his position as Sheriff and Lord by right of blood.

His "father's" blood. If Mortianna spoke against him . . .
Even without proof, just the accusation would be enough to
bar him from the throne. And he couldn't risk killing her.
Mortianna would be bound to have taken precautions. . . .
The hag stepped forward suddenly and grabbed him by the
arm, and he winced at the unnatural strength in her bony
fingers.

"Now is not the time to doubt, little Lord! Together we
are strong. The bold will prevail."

The Sheriff nodded wordlessly, and she released him. He
backed away from her, out of the chamber, and carried
the sight of her triumphant smile all the way back up into
the part of the castle he ruled.

The woodsmen stood shivering together in the cold
morning as Azeem measured out a small amount of black
powder from a leather pouch. Scarlet leaned forward to
warm his hands at the campfire before them, and then
moved back again as Azeem gave him a hard look. The
Moor tossed the black powder into the fire, and a fireball
blasted ten feet into the sky as the fire exploded in a cloud
of acrid smoke. The woodsmen fell back, shouting and
cursing in surprise, and batted at the smoke with their
hands. They calmed down quickly once they realized they
weren't in any danger, and looked at each other sheepishly.
Azeem grinned.

"The mysteries of the Black Powder are many. My
people are still experimenting with it, since a trader brought
knowledge of it back from far Cathay."

Tuck took a pinch of the powder and sniffed at it
dubiously. "This smacks unnaturally of magic."

Robin turned away to study the crude map of Nottingham
he'd drawn in the dirt. "I'll use whatever I have to, to save
my people. Now pay attention." He waited while the others

199

crowded round the map. "Bull, you will position yourself by the gate to cut off reinforcements. John, you'll stay by this wall to cover our escape. I'll conceal myself here, below the scaffold, and cut our men free from the nooses when I hear the signal."

"No," said Scarlet quickly. "I'll do that. We'll need you to cover us with your bow."

Robin frowned slightly at his newfound brother. "It's dangerous, Will."

"So's your aim." Scarlet grinned.

Robin smiled and nodded, and then gestured at Tuck and Azeem. "Whatever Azeem is concocting, we must each be in place for it. Our success depends on all of us acting in total concert. We may be only six men, but—"

"Seven," said Fanny briskly.

She strode toward them out of the trees, a bow in her hand, her head held proudly erect. The woodsmen looked at each other, and then at Little John. He scowled at them all, and then turned the scowl on Fanny.

"What in blazes do you think you're doing, girl? And where are the children?"

"They're safe, with my mother. And I'm coming with you."

"Have you lost your senses? You're in no shape to be coming with us. Not after all you've been through. You've been hurt bad, girl. . . ."

Fanny sniffed. "You birth eight babies, and then you can talk to me about hurting. Our Wulf is due to be hanged, and you expect me to stay at home? To hell with that. I can use a bow, and that's all that matters."

Little John looked pleadingly at Robin to dissuade her. Robin looked thoughtfully at Fanny's determined chin, and nodded to her.

"All right, Fanny, you'll take position here. . . ."

Little John shook his head disgustedly.

12
THE RECKONING

The crowds came to Nottingham's main square, to celebrate the Sheriff's wedding and watch the woodsmen hang. None of them gave a damn about the wedding, and most had no wish to see good men die, but they came anyway. The Sheriff required it. His men had been out since dawn, spreading the word that not to attend would be regarded as an insult and a crime, and anyone caught not attending and applauding in the right places would wish they had. So the people came from all over the county, from every town and village and hamlet. And deep down in their hearts, they prayed for a miracle.

The crowds moved slowly through the main city gate, watched suspiciously by soldiers who methodically searched every man, woman, and child before letting them pass. A growing pile of knives and short swords grew beside the gate. A few tried to argue with the guards, but received only indifference or a casual blow to the head and an order to move on. The Sheriff was taking no chances. He had invited those barons supporting his claim to the throne to witness the executions and his marriage to a cousin of the King, and he was determined that nothing should go wrong.

An open cart trundled up to the gate, pulled by a bored-looking horse. Friar Tuck reined the beast to a halt at the soldiers' gesture, and smiled amiably upon them, positively radiating good will and reverence. One of the soldiers moved forward to give the barrels in the back of the cart a good looking over, and then stared hard at the man sitting next to the friar. The silent figure looked to be large and blocky under his cloak, but his face and hands were covered in bandages. The soldier decided very firmly that he wasn't going to search that one. Whatever the man had under his cloak, the soldier had no intention of catching it. He moved back a step, just in case, and turned his attention to Tuck.

"What have you got here, friar?"

"The Lord's finest brew," said Tuck expansively, "for the good Nottingham's fighting men. A special brew this; it has a mighty kick."

The soldier smiled for the first time, and waved them on. Tuck persuaded the horse into movement again, and the cart lurched and creaked into the main square before the castle. Back at the gate, Fanny smiled winningly at the soldiers. She was wearing her best dress and carrying a large woven basket. The soldiers ignored the smile, and gestured for her to open the basket. Fanny shrugged easily and did so.

"It's only rope, dearie. In case the Sheriff hasn't got enough to go round."

She cackled unpleasantly, and the soldiers waved her on, shaking their heads at each other. You get all sorts at a hanging. They turned back to the gate, and then fell back in a hurry as a gang of Celts swaggered past, comparing severed ears and pieces of jewelry they'd acquired at Robin's camp. They strode on into the square, laughing

202

harshly and knocking aside anyone who didn't get out of their way fast enough. No one was foolish enough to object, least of all the soldiers. They weren't being paid enough to mess with Celts. They looked determinedly the other way, and concentrated on the peasants still passing through the gate. So they never saw one of the Celts drop back from the group and disappear into the nearest concealing shadows.

He glanced about him to be sure no one was watching, then lifted his boar's head helmet to scratch desperately at an itchy nose. Bull sighed contentedly as the itch faded away. He didn't know how the Celts could stand wearing those bloody helmets. They were hot and sweaty and you couldn't see worth a damn anyway. He took the opportunity to carefully examine the gate and portcullis that led from the square into the castle, grinned briefly, and then quickly pulled his helm back into place as a soldier glanced in his direction. Bull swaggered on across the square, glaring about him as a good Celt should, and people hurried to get out of his way.

Outside the city wall, a very large peasant staggered along, bent almost double under a massive load of firewood sticks. The bundle wasn't actually all that heavy, but it gave him a good excuse to keep his head down and his face hidden, and helped disguise his height. He leaned against the wall as though resting for a moment, keeping his floppy hat pulled low to hide his face from passing strangers. A length of rope suddenly unfurled from over the wall and fell down beside him. Little John grabbed the end of the rope and tied his bundle to it, and then gave the rope two quick tugs to signal all was well.

On the other side of the wall, on a parapet near the top, Fanny took a firm hold of the rope and quickly hauled rope and bundle up over the wall and down onto the parapet. She untied the bundle, tied one end of the rope to a handy nearby post, and then tossed the other end back over the wall.

Little John was still standing by the wall, arms folded across his great chest, and whistling in what he fondly imagined to be a casual manner. A few people stared at him as they passed, but moved quickly on their way as John gave them his best *Who do you think you're looking at* glare. John had a lot of faith in that look. The rope slapped down beside him, and he grabbed it quickly and looped it round himself. He waited till all was clear, and then clambered up the high wall.

In the main square, Tuck and the man swaddled in bandages busied themselves lifting barrels off the cart and placing them carefully in various locations round the square. The swaddled man placed a barrel carefully on the edge of the scaffold's raised stage, against one of the gibbet uprights. He paused and stared at the gibbet for a long moment. Ten nooses hung from the lengthy overhead beam, like the rotten fruit of a decaying tree. A soldier walked over and glared officiously at the swaddled man before gesturing brusquely at the barrel before them, and others scattered across the square.

"What the hell do you think you're doing?"

"Distributing libations for the celebration of his lordship's nuptials," said Tuck, moving quickly over to bow and smile graciously at the soldier. "Why, good sir, is there something amiss?"

"Yeah," said the soldier. "You are." He grabbed the swaddled man by the arm and hauled him away from the scaffold. "Get that barrel out of here. Move!"

Tuck bowed, and turned to the swaddled man. "Caesar has spoken, my friend. Collect our offerings and we shall depart."

"What's the matter with him?" said the soldier suspiciously. "Doesn't he have a tongue in his head?"

"Unfortunately not," said Tuck. "My friend is a member of a most holy and reverent Order of Lepers."

The soldier recoiled so fast he nearly fell over his own feet. Tuck and the swaddled man left him staring in horror at the hand he'd used to haul the man away from the scaffold, and sweating furiously.

Fanny sat comfortably on the edge of the parapet, bundle and basket beside her. She pulled two swords from inside the bundle and dropped them nonchalantly over the edge of the parapet. They thudded into the ground below and stood upright, quivering slightly. A boar's-headed Celt and a man in a cloak passed by, casually grabbed the swords, hid them under their cloaks, and continued on their way. A soldier came walking along the parapet, glaring suspiciously at Fanny. She smiled innocently, and pulled back her skirt to show a little more leg.

"Ain't doing no harm here, love," she protested prettily. "Likes a good hanging I do, and there's a lovely view from up here, ain't there?"

The soldier automatically turned to look, and Little John reached up over the top of the wall and grabbed him by the collar. The soldier just had time for a very surprised expression before John hauled him over the wall and dropped him. A short scream was followed by a loud thud, and silence. Little John clambered over the wall and sat down on the parapet beside Fanny. He slipped his bow and some arrows from the bundle and stared sternly at his wife.

"See what happens when you flirt with strange men?"

Down by the scaffold, a grubby young pickpocket was quietly working the crowd with an innocent face and quick hands, but since they were mostly peasants, he had little enough to show for his efforts. He eased in behind a likely-looking prospect, deftly lifted the man's cloak, and reached for the purse at his belt. And then he froze as he saw a forbidden sword hanging hidden at the man's side. As he hesitated, a large hand clamped down on his. Will Scarlet smiled nastily at the pickpocket.

"Nothing there but trouble, lad. Now get lost, or I'll tie your fingers in a knot."

The pickpocket disappeared back into the crowd the moment Scarlet released him. Scarlet grinned, and pulled his hood farther forward to hide his face. A commotion began in the crowd around him, as people pointed up at a castle balcony overlooking the square. Scarlet looked up, and scowled as he saw the Sheriff present his bride-to-be to the crowd. Marian had never looked lovelier, dressed in opulent finery for her wedding, but her face was set and strained. The Sheriff was dressed just as grandly, and smiled and laughed expansively with the barons who had come to publicly show their support for his marriage to a cousin of the King. The Celtic Chief Ordred stood at the back of the balcony, grim and silent as ever in his burnished black armor. The crowd cheered them all, after a little encouragement from the surrounding soldiers.

Sometimes it seemed to Marian that it was all just a dream, a nightmare from which she might eventually awaken. But she never allowed herself to think that way for long. It would be only too easy just to let go, and retreat into a safe, cozy madness where nothing could touch her. It would be easy. The woodsmen were dead or captured. The dream of hope and justice was over. And Robin was dead. So easy. But Marian couldn't just run away and hide. It wasn't in her nature. She could still save some of the woodsmen, and Sarah. And as the Sheriff's wife she should at least be able to protect her people. And maybe one day, if she kept her wits about her, she might find a way to avenge her dead love.

The Sheriff was busy introducing her to the barons. She ignored them. She had no time for traitors. Her gaze fell upon the huge form of the Celtic chief, and a chill shuddered through her. In his black armor and dragon's helm he looked like a demon summoned up out of Hell. And if some of the rúmors she'd heard about her husband-to-be were true, perhaps that was exactly what Ordred, was.

She looked away, staring disinterestedly out over the crowded square, and her gaze stumbled to a halt on the oversized scaffold. Ten nooses hung limply from the gibbet crossbeam, swaying slightly now and again in the drifting breeze. She was going to have to watch the hangings. The Sheriff had insisted on it. The deaths were a symbol of his victory over the woodsmen, and an unmistakable sign to the watching crowd and the barons as to where the true power lay in Nottinghamshire. Marian squeezed her eyes shut and bowed her head, praying for the strength to see the horror through without breaking down. She didn't want to give the Sheriff that satisfaction. She opened her eyes and then fell back a step, startled to find the Sheriff standing right beside her. He looked meaningfully at the Locksley medallion she was wearing round her neck, and she raised one hand protectively to hold it.

"A little inappropriate for your wedding day, don't you think, my dear?" the Sheriff murmured, carefully keeping his voice low, so the barons wouldn't hear.

Marian looked out at the scaffold again. "No more so than your idea of a wedding gift." She didn't bother to lower her voice.

The Sheriff shrugged, and gestured to his men below. "It's time. Bring them out."

The officer in charge nodded quickly, and shouted a

series of orders. There was a hurried bustling of guards as they moved into position, and then the gate to the dungeons swung open, and the condemned men were led out into the courtyard. Black-costumed drummers led the way, beating out a slow funereal march. Then came the prisoners, eyes squeezed up against the painful light after so long in the dark. They still wore their chains and shackles, and there were two guards to every woodsman. The Sheriff was taking no chances. The guards hurried the half-blind prisoners along, pulling roughly at their chains. The watching soldiers and Celts laughed and hurled abuse at the woodsmen as they passed through the gate into the square, but most of the watching crowd was silent.

Marian watched it all with quiet dignity, though the sight tore at her heart, and then her breath caught in her throat as her gaze stumbled over a familiar face on the edge of the crowd. Tuck was parking a barrel-laden cart beside the inner city wall. He clambered down from the cart, glanced nervously at the barrels, and then he and a cloaked companion unhitched the horse and hurried away, losing themselves in the crowd that now filled most of the square. Marian looked quickly away, hoping the Sheriff hadn't noticed her reaction, and then looked casually about the square. It didn't take her long to spot Fanny sitting on a parapet at the far wall, with a cloaked man large enough to be Little John beside her, doing something surreptitious with a large bundle of firewood.

A sudden commotion close at hand brought her gaze back to the scaffold. A wounded soldier, his face half-hidden by a grubby, bloodstained bandage, was barging his way through the crowd, using his pole-like crutch as a weapon to clear him some space. He cursed the crowd vigorously in a harsh, cracked voice, and ploughed his way through them, heading toward the far wall. He passed by Tuck's cart without even glancing at it, and climbed up toward the parapet. Both the voice and the gait were disguised, but Marian would have known them anywhere. It was Robin. The Sheriff had lied. Robin was alive. . . .

Marian didn't know whether to laugh or cry or scream. She could feel a warm flush heating her cheeks, and turned a little away from the Sheriff so he wouldn't notice and grow suspicious. She watched Robin's progress as unobtrusively as she could, hardly breathing when guards or soldiers glanced in his direction, but no one challenged him as he settled himself comfortably on the parapet.

The last of the prisoners emerged into the square, screwing up his eyes against the light and stumbling over his unsteady feet. Wulf glared about him defiantly, a small figure weighed down by chains and exhaustion and hopelessness. But even so, a new strength ran through him as he saw a familiar face watching from the crowd. He screamed in blind rage and threw himself at Will Scarlet. He didn't manage half a dozen steps before the guards grabbed him and threw him to the ground, beating and kicking him as he struggled to get to his feet again. Several of the crowd cried out angrily, and one man stepped forward to intervene. Two soldiers clubbed him to the ground and beat him savagely.

The Sheriff watched the commotion from his balcony, and smiled coldly as he spotted the object of Wulf's rage. He gestured to one of his mounted guards, who urged his horse through the crowd, grabbed Scarlet by the collar before he could escape, and dragged him over to stand reluctantly below the balcony. The Sheriff smiled down at Scarlet, as soldiers dragged the semiconscious Wulf to the scaffold.

"Ah, my dear turncoat. I was wondering what had happened to you. Did you succeed?"

Scarlet swallowed hard, searching his mind frantically

for a way out, but everyone's eye was on him. The Sheriff and Marian in particular were studying him coldly. Neither of them looked particularly friendly to him.

"I found Locksley's lair," he said finally, thinking fast. "Alas, he was already dead."

"You're sure?" said the Sheriff sharply. "You saw his body?"

"Well, no," said Scarlet. "But there was a grave. . . ."

The Sheriff gestured to two soldiers, who searched Scarlet roughly and took away his sword. The Sheriff shook his head sadly.

"What is the world coming to, when you can't even trust a traitor to stay bought?" He nodded to the two soldiers. "Stretch his neck with the others."

The soldiers hauled Scarlet away to the scaffold, ignoring his struggles and protests. The Sheriff turned to Marian and raised an eyebrow at her hostile face.

"You swore to me that Robin was dead," said Marian. "You even swore you'd seen the body."

The Sheriff shrugged. "I lied."

Up on the parapet, Robin couldn't believe how quickly his plan had gone wrong. He looked across to a concealed niche farther down the parapet, where the swaddled man had pulled away his bandages to reveal Azeem's worried face. They shared a concerned look, and then both of them strung their bows and reached for their arrows.

At the scaffold, Scarlet was still kicking and struggling and cursing as he was dragged up onto the raised stage. The two soldiers held him firmly as the hooded executioner started to fling another noose over the center beam, only to pause as he realized there wasn't enough room. The ten woodsmen stood beneath the gibbet shoulder to shoulder, with no room for an eleventh man. The executioner looked

210

to the Sheriff for instructions, and Scarlet looked back at him reproachfully.

"Well, my Lord Sheriff, seeing as things are rather crowded here, it appears I'll have to respectfully decline your kind invitation."

The executioner glared at him, looked quickly about the scaffold, and then smiled unpleasantly as he spotted the barrel Tuck had earlier placed on the stage, by the gibbet's upright. He hauled Scarlet over to the barrel, forced him down on his knees, and tied him securely in place so that his head was positioned over the top of the barrel. He leaned a giant ax beside it, and patted Scarlet reassuringly on the head.

"Always room for one more, lad. But latecomers and smart arses go last."

Up on the parapet, Azeem studied the scene in disbelief. He'd already set light to a tar-tipped arrow, ready to fire at the barrel Scarlet was now draped over. The arrow would have set off the gunpowder in the barrel, wrecking the gibbet upright, and the rescue could have begun under cover of the smoke and confusion. Now he hadn't a clue what to do for the rest. There was no way they could get past so many soldiers without some kind of diversion. He looked across at Robin, who was scowling thoughtfully.

Robin watched helplessly as the executioner moved unhurriedly along the line of condemned men, making them step up onto stools and then slipping the nooses around their necks. Wulf was the first in line, the first to die. The executioner had a special high stool for him. Wulf was trembling slightly, but he kept his head erect and his mouth firm. Up on the parapet, Little John and Fanny looked on in horror, helpless to intervene. They looked across at Robin, who was still thinking desperately.

There was a sudden commotion in the crowd as Tuck

pushed his way through, heading for the scaffold. He crossed everyone and everything, calling loudly for everyone to make way for the Lord's work, and hoped he'd have thought of something useful to do by the time he reached the prisoners.

He'd almost made it when a drumroll began, and a sudden hush fell across the square. The executioner stepped forward and kicked the stool out from under Wulf's feet. Fanny screamed from the parapet, and Little John rose to his feet, bow in hand. Wulf dangled helplessly from the gibbet, twisting and kicking as the noose slowly strangled him. John threw aside his bow, drew his sword, and ran down from the parapet, screaming with rage. Soldiers moved to block his way and he crashed into them without slowing. His sword cut through them easily, backed by his strength and weight, but there were just too many of them, and his charge soon slowed to a halt, until it was all he could do to defend himself.

Robin stood, raised his bow, and took careful aim at the swinging rope of Wulf's noose. It was an impossible distance and a small, moving target, and from out of the corner of his eye he could see soldiers racing along the parapet toward him, swords in hand. Robin breathed deeply, calmly, refusing to allow himself to be hurried. He fired his arrow and immediately leapt from the parapet to avoid a wild swing from a soldier's blade. He never took his eyes off Wulf's rope as he fell to the ground, and he cursed disappointedly as the arrow struck the rope but only partially severed it. The rope started unraveling, but still held. Wulf's eyes bulged, his tongue protruding from his mouth as he fought for air.

Robin landed hard, but still held onto his bow and one remaining arrow. He scrambled to his feet, waited a second for his head to clear, and then nocked the arrow to his bow.

Last chance. Soldiers were running at him from every side. He breathed deeply, calmly. *Can you make the shot when it matters?* The world contracted to nothing but the half-unraveled strand of rope above Wulf's head. He aimed and fired in a single smooth movement, and the rope parted as the arrow hit it squarely. Wulf fell to the stage, gasping for breath as the noose loosened.

The crowd turned as one to see who could have made such a shot, and gasped as they recognized Robin Hood. Up on the balcony, the Sheriff gaped silently. And then the silence was broken as Marian whooped and cheered and called Robin's name. Azeem let fly with his fire-tipped arrow at Tuck's cart. Wagon and wall disappeared in a massive explosion. The ground shuddered as part of the wall collapsed, and thick black smoke billowed up into the sky. The soldiers heading for Robin stopped and stared wildly about them. The crowd panicked and ran in all directions. Little John fought on, hacking a bloody path through the soldiers and heading determinedly for the scaffold. The Sheriff leaned out over the balcony, his face purple with rage and frustration, and yelled to his soldiers.

"Get more troops in here! Executioner, hang them all! Now!"

The executioner moved quickly down the line of condemned men, kicking the stools out from under their feet. Choked cries issued from crushed throats as the woodsmen hung kicking at the ends of their ropes. Wulf rose shakily to his feet, and his eyes widened at the horror before him. He grabbed the legs of the man nearest him and tried to lift him so the noose would loosen. The man was heavy, and Wulf's strength had been all but beaten out of him, but he fought on grimly, straining to hold the man up.

Bull whipped out his sword and cut through the rope holding up the portcullis on the castle gate. The massive iron weight slammed down like a hammer on a company of soldiers rushing from the courtyard into the square, crushing them to the ground.

Tuck swung his cudgel about him in wide arcs, opening up a path through crowd and soldiers alike in his desperation to reach the men slowly strangling on the scaffold. He scrambled up onto the stage, grabbed one man by the legs, and lifted him up, but before he could reach up to remove the noose soldiers bore down on him from all sides. He lashed out savagely with his club to keep them at bay, still supporting the woodsman's weight as best he could.

Will Scarlet struggled frantically against the rope holding him to the barrel of gunpowder, but the executioner had done his job well. The ropes had no give in them, and he couldn't find a way to apply any leverage. All he could do was watch helplessly as the executioner stopped beside him and reached for the ax he'd left by the barrel.

Robin saw the executioner lift the ax and raced toward the scaffold. A soldier got in his way, and Robin cut him down without pausing. The ground shook again as Azeem set off another explosion, scattering soldiers like straws on the wind. Robin nodded his thanks, and gestured at his empty bow. The Moor put an arrow to his bow and fired it into a wooden post at Robin's side. Robin tugged the arrow loose, and nocked it to his bow.

The executioner looked back at Wulf and Tuck, still struggling to hold up two of the woodsmen, and laughed. Wulf called to the watching crowd to help, but though some stirred uneasily, none of them made any move to help or hinder. Bull fought his way toward the scaffold, but soldiers blocked his way, holding him back by sheer force of numbers.

The executioner looked calmly down at Scarlet, kneeling helplessly before him, and raised his ax, ignoring the noise and confusion around him. He had a job to do, and he took pride in doing his job well. Nothing else mattered. Across the square, Robin took aim with his single arrow. He'd already managed two excellent shots, and now he had to come up with a third. The executioner's ax rose, and hesitated at the top of its arc. Robin concentrated, and everything seemed to grow still and silent. The executioner's face grew to fill his vision. The ax started down toward Scarlet's neck. And Robin let the arrow go. The executioner staggered back from Scarlet, and the ax dropped from his hand as though it had suddenly grown too heavy to hold. The arrow had buried itself in his left eyeball. He raised a hesitant hand to his face, as though he couldn't quite believe what had happened to him, and then all the strength went out of him, and he crumpled limply to the stage and lay still. Will Scarlet let out his breath in a long, shuddering sigh, and started breathing again.

Little John burst out of a crowd of soldiers, wounded in many places but still swinging his sword viciously and roaring like a bull. He charged up onto the scaffold, scattering the soldiers attacking Wulf and Tuck, and slammed his great shoulder against the gibbet upright, the one Azeem had intended to blow apart with his black powder. The thick wooden upright splintered and fell apart under John's weight, and the whole gibbet collapsed, spilling the nine choking woodsmen onto the stage. Little John staggered to his feet, hugged Wulf quickly, and then he and his son set about removing the nooses from the woodsmen's necks. Tuck and Bull fought side by side to hold off the soldiers. Little John called to the crowd to help as he worked, cursing and pleading with them with equal vigor, but still they stood undecided, moved by his words but cowed by the soldiers and the habit of long subservience.

On the balcony overlooking the chaos, the barons looked at each other, and then at the Sheriff. Baron Forrester stepped forward as their spokesman and coughed meaningfully to get the Sheriff's attention. He ignored the barons, watching the battle below with a desperate, lost expression. The Baron coughed again, louder. The Sheriff turned slowly to look at him. Baron Forrester tried to fix him with an icy stare.

"You gave us your word you now controlled this county, Nottingham. Is this your idea of control?"

The Sheriff drew his sword and studied the Baron with a thoughtful, speculative look. Forrester's blood turned to ice. He could see his death in the Sheriff's dark, indifferent eyes. And then the moment passed, and the Sheriff's gaze moved on to the Celtic Chief Ordred, still standing patiently at the back of the balcony.

"Ordred, there seems to be some trouble in the square. Take care of it for me, would you?"

The Celt nodded, and moved forward to the edge of the balcony. The barons fell back to give him plenty of room. Ordred looked out over the chaos and smiled slowly at the prospect of battle and bloodshed. And then he saw Bull, in his Celt's disguise, fighting with the woodsmen against the soldiers, and he roared a furious challenge at the Celt who'd apparently turned traitor. He drew his great longsword and jumped from the balcony. It was a long drop, and the weight of his armor pulled him down, but his massive legs absorbed most of the shock, and he walked away from the fall unmoved, striding toward Bull with his sword in his hand and murder in his heart.

Marian saw a chance to escape, and lunged for the edge of the balcony to jump for her freedom. The Sheriff grabbed her at the last moment and pulled her back. She threw a punch at him, and the wind of its passing ruffled his hair as he ducked under it. He took a firm hold on Marian's arm and dragged her through the door at the back of the balcony, ignoring her frantic struggles. His face was calm and relaxed, as though he'd finally found the answer to a problem that had been puzzling him.

Robin yelled for the woodsmen on the scaffold to escape through the hole in the outer wall that Azeem had made with his black powder, and they hurried in that direction, led by Bull and Little John, who cut a bloody path through any soldiers foolish enough to get in their way. Azeem and Fanny covered them from the parapet with deadly fire from their bows. Robin cut down a soldier with one merciless sweep of his sword, and risked a quick glance at the balcony to make sure Marian was safe. He was just in time to see the Sheriff drag her back into the castle. Robin's heart missed a beat, and then rage and fear for Marian drove him forward through the soldiers toward the castle. He pulled two arrows from their unmoving targets and looked up to see two mounted guards bearing down on him. They were almost upon him and there was nowhere to run, but Robin didn't feel like running anyway. He fitted the two arrows to his bowstring, aimed, and fired. The two soldiers were thrown back out of their saddles as though an invisible hand had swept them away. Robin hurried on. Marian needed him; nothing else mattered.

Up on his parapet, Azeem looked incredulously at Robin running alone toward the castle, while everyone else was running the other way, and rose quickly to his feet. He threw back his cloak to reveal his dark skin and foreign face and called out to the woodsmen. They looked up and stumbled to a halt at the sight of him. He started to speak, and a sudden hush fell across the square, as soldiers, woodsmen, and the watching crowd all quieted. His great

217

voice boomed out across the square, and none of them could look away.

"Englishmen! I am not one of you, but I fight for you. I fight against the tyrant who holds your lives in his hand, and knows nothing of pity or justice. If one such as I dares rise up against your lord and master, will you not dare as much? Join us now. Join Robin Hood, and your names will live forever!"

The crowd looked at Robin, taking on what looked like the whole of the Sheriff's forces single-handedly, and a mounting roar swept through them as they turned on the soldiers and guards and Celts, and pulled them down by sheer weight of numbers. The scent of revolution was in the air, rich and heady, and the crowd and the woodsmen surged toward the castle. Most headed for the courtyard gate, after Robin, but a large number clambered up the wall and onto the balcony, to get at the barons. They turned to flee, only to find that the Sheriff had locked the door behind him when he left with Marian. The barons tried to draw their swords, and then fell screaming beneath a remorseless hail of swords and cudgels and fists.

The Celt chief cut and hacked his way through the crowd, not caring whom he killed if they stood between him and Bull. He finally caught up with him not far from the wrecked scaffold, and lashed out viciously with his sword. The woodsman ducked at the last moment, and the heavy sword crashed into the upright behind him and broke in two. Ordred snarled and threw the useless hilt aside. He looked quickly about him for another weapon, and his gaze fell on the barrel that Scarlet had been tied to. He grabbed it and raised it easily above his head. Bull flinched back, anticipating only too easily what such a weight would do to him. Ordred laughed, and Will Scarlet let fly with a fire arrow. It hit the barrel squarely and the black powder exploded, tearing the huge Celt apart. The dragon helm rolled across the ground toward Scarlet, and he grinned nastily at it.

"Never did like that hat."

Robin dodged arrows fired at him from behind the lowered portcullis that blocked the only entrance to the courtyard, and howled with rage and frustration as he caught a glimpse of the Sheriff dragging Marian deeper into the castle. The crowd arrived and surged around him, trying to lift the portcullis by sheer strength. The Sheriff paused briefly to look back at the mob baying for his blood and turned calmly to the nearest guard, ignoring Marian's struggles.

"Seal that entrance, and guard it with your lives. And bring the Bishop to my private chapel. Immediately."

The guard nodded quickly and turned away, shouting orders to his men. The Sheriff smiled at Marian, and hauled her off into the castle.

Robin watched impatiently as the crowd struggled with the portcullis. He looked around him for a better way. His gaze fell upon a giant catapult close by, obviously a brother to the ones used against his camp. It had been cocked but not loaded, and was currently aimed over the wall that separated the courtyard from the square. Robin smiled tightly. Not a way he would have chosen, but since there was no choice . . . He ran over to the catapult and climbed into the bucket that would normally have held the projectiles. Azeem suddenly appeared on the other side of the catapult and climbed in beside him. They looked at the wall looming up before them, and then at each other.

"Is she worth it?" asked Azeem.

Robin grinned. "Worth dying for."

Azeem grinned back at him, and nodded sharply. Robin hit the trigger with his sword. The catapult shuddered as the pent-up energy was suddenly released, and launched the two men in a long, smooth arc over the wall and into the courtyard beyond. Robin lost his breath as his stomach dropped away, but for a moment, at the height of the arc, he knew what it felt like to fly. He just had time to grasp the idea, and then the courtyard was rising up toward him at a dizzying speed. He braced himself, and then he and Azeem crashed into a wooden lean-to next to the castle wall. It collapsed under their weight, but broke enough of their fall to enable them to walk away from it more or less intact. Robin headed for the main door with Azeem at his side, their faces set and grim. Two soldiers made the mistake of trying to stop them. Robin and Azeem cut them down and hurried on without even slowing their pace. Marian needed them. Nothing else mattered.

From her high window in the Sheriff's private chapel Mortianna watched the Sheriff's men battling the peasants. They looked like ants, battling mindlessly for things that didn't really matter, but then, men had always seemed that way to her. Though she'd never made the mistake of underestimating the harm those ants could do, if they got angry and determined enough. And these ants were very angry.

She heard hurried footsteps approaching the chapel, and turned away from the window. Her son was coming, with his reluctant bride. He was right to hurry. Mortianna understood what the raving mob at his gates meant, even if he didn't. She didn't need to cast her runes to see his future. Or hers. She smiled slightly at the Bishop as he stalked nervously up and down before the altar. He was sweating, and his hands were shaking. Anyone would think he had something to be worried about. He glanced in her direction, and she smiled at him.

"We are doomed," she said calmly.

The Bishop snarled at her and looked away, for once his fear for himself greater than his fear of her. He'd known something was badly wrong when the Sheriff's men had dragged him unceremoniously from his chambers and brought him to this terrible place. What had once been a pleasant little room set aside for worship and contemplation had been savagely transformed. The floor and walls had been splashed with the blood of dead animals, and their small bodies stood impaled on spikes before the altar. A severed goat's head glared balefully from the altar, and beside it stood a gold chalice full of blood. The crucifix on the wall above had been turned upside down. The Bishop's hands clenched into fists, but there was no release from the fear and frustration building inside him. He was trapped in this awful place, face-to-face with all the things he'd turned a blind eye to for so long.

The door burst open and the Sheriff strode in, still holding Marian firmly by the arm. The Bishop whirled to face him, wringing his hands together desperately.

" 'Tis rebellion, my Lord! We must escape now, while there is still time!"

The Sheriff shook his head briefly. "Marry us."

"What?" The Bishop looked at him blankly. "Marry you?"

"Marian and I. Now."

Marian twisted round against the Sheriff's grip and spat in his face, struggling fiercely. "I'll never marry you! Never!"

Mortianna stepped forward and calmly slapped Marian across the face. There was unexpected strength in the blow, and Marian sagged back against the Sheriff, her head swimming. The Sheriff wiped Marian's spittle from his face and looked disapprovingly at the albino crone.

"This woman is to be my wife, Mother. You're going to have to learn to get along."

Mortianna sniffed and placed the flat of her hand against Marian's belly. "All may not be lost. She is ripe. You must take her, now. She will give us a son."

The Sheriff grabbed the front of Mortianna's robe, lifted her off the ground, and shook her like a rag doll, before throwing her away in rage and disgust. "That's all you care about, isn't it? Your precious grandson on the throne of England! I've never mattered to you, save as a means to that end. Well to hell with that and to hell with you. I'll take her, but not until we are properly wed. For once in my life, I will have something pure!"

The Bishop looked anxiously out the window, and the blood drained from his face as he saw the mob swarming past the raised portcullis and across the courtyard. They swept aside the few remaining soldiers and poured into the castle. He staggered back from the window and turned in horror to the Sheriff.

"We must leave now, dammit! It's madness to delay!"

Mortianna lashed out at him, and the long talons on her clawlike hand raised bloody wheals across his face. He cried out and fell back, tears of shock and pain running down his face to mix with the blood. Mortianna smiled at him and patted him gently on his unmarked cheek.

"Marry them now, or face me."

Robin and Azeem raced through the castle, plunging down corridor after corridor, fighting off increasingly desperate soldiers and searching for some sign of Marian and the Sheriff. More and more soldiers and armed servants appeared to block their way, but Robin and Azeem fought on, refusing to be slowed or sidetracked. Blood dripped from their blades as they ran, and they left a trail of blood and bodies behind them. Finally, they ran out of opponents, and Robin had to admit he was lost. He grabbed a wounded soldier and set the edge of his blade against the man's throat.

"Where is she? Where's the Lady Marian?"

The soldier took one look at Robin's face and decided this was no time to play the hero. Not on what the Sheriff was paying him.

"She's in the chapel. Down there."

Robin threw the man aside, and he and Azeem raced down the corridor the soldier had indicated.

In the chapel, before the bloody altar, the Bishop stumbled nervously through the Latin phrases of the marriage ceremony. He picked up the chalice from the altar with trembling hands and passed it to the Sheriff, who sipped at it impatiently. The Bishop offered it to Marian, and she slapped it away. The Bishop shrank back as some of the blood within spattered across his sleeve.

Something heavy crashed against the chapel door, shaking it in its frame. Mortianna glanced at it thoughtfully. She'd already locked and bolted the door, and pushed the heavy crossbar into place. The door was secure. It could hold off an army. The Sheriff gestured impatiently for the Bishop to continue with the ceremony. He was still holding Marian by the arm, the knuckles of his hand showing white with the pressure. The Bishop reluctantly continued, shouting to be heard over the relentless crashing against the door from outside.

"Do you, Cedric, Lord Nottingham, take this woman as your wedded wife. . . ."

"Yes, yes," snapped the Sheriff. "Get on with it."

Mortianna moved in behind Marian and pinned her arms to her sides, glancing uncertainly at the door. The crossbeam was holding, but cracks were appearing in the door itself. "Make haste!" she hissed. "It will mean our deaths if we are caught here!"

The Bishop swallowed hard. "Do you, Marian Dubois . . ."

The Sheriff clapped a hand across her mouth before she could answer. "Yes, of course she does. Right, that's it. We're married. Nice service, Bishop. Now get the hell out of my way."

He turned smiling to face Marian, still held firmly by Mortianna, and began unbuttoning his tunic.

Robin and Azeem panted heavily as they slammed the statue they'd found against the door, again and again. It was a life-sized statue of the Sheriff, which seemed only appropriate. The door shuddered and cracked, but still it held. The statue's head broke off suddenly, and rolled away. Robin let go of the statue and looked desperately about him. The Sheriff was in there. He could hear his voice through the door. There had to be another way in. There had to be.

The Sheriff tore Marian away from Mortianna, and threw her to the floor. He dropped on top of her, pinning her easily with his weight, his hands at her wrists. She fought him furiously, heaving and struggling beneath him, but she couldn't even get a hand free to hit him. The Sheriff studied her silently, and there was a frightening blankness in his eyes that was somehow more terrible than any lust or anger. He forced her hands down and knelt on her arms, pinning them as he tore at the front of her dress. Mortianna watched, smiling. The Bishop faltered his way through the remains of the marriage ceremony, with rolling, panicked eyes. The Sheriff suddenly stopped his assault, looked at the shuddering door and glared at Mortianna.

Mortianna nodded, and disappeared through the side door.

Out in the corridor, Azeem leaned exhaustedly against the wall and snarled something uncomplimentary about English oaken doors. Robin dropped his end of the statue and looked desperately about him for inspiration. An idea came to him, something so desperate he wouldn't even have considered it under normal circumstances. But as things were . . . Robin yelled to Azeem to keep trying with the statue, and ran off up the nearby stairs.

It had been a long time since he guested at Nottingham Castle, and he was relieved to find the stairs led where he thought they would. They brought him to a door that opened out onto the roof, a wide expanse of rough stone and slates overlooking the chapel's only window. He looked down and immediately wished he hadn't. It was a hell of a way to the ground below. Fortunately, the distance down to the chapel window didn't seem nearly as far, in comparison. A yards-long pennant was flapping in the wind, conveniently close to hand. He ripped it free and tied one end to a solid-looking gargoyle.

Azeem beat against the unyielding chapel door with the head from the Sheriff's statue. The door groaned and shuddered under his blows, but still held firm. A sudden shriek of rage brought Azeem spinning round as Mortianna appeared out of nowhere, running toward him with a long pike in her hands. Azeem threw himself to one side, but the steel head of the pike buried itself in his thigh, slamming him back against the chapel door. He gasped once as blinding agony flared in his leg, and then he grabbed the shaft of the pike with both hands, to prevent her from pulling it free and coming at him again. For a moment they stood there, face-to-face, both panting fiercely from their exertions, and then a slow horror filled Mortianna's face as she took in the Moor's dark, decorated skin. When she spoke, the words were a bare whisper.

"The painted man . . ."

She raked at his face with a clawed hand. Azeem pulled his head back, grabbed the statue's head, and struck at her with it. Mortianna recoiled in shock at the sight of her son's severed head cast in stone, and Azeem pulled the pike from his thigh, gritting his teeth against a fresh wave of pain and weakness as blood coursed down his leg. Mortianna threw herself at the Moor, her clawed hands reaching for his eyes. He lifted the pike to meet her, bracing it against the door behind him, and she impaled herself on it in her blind rage.

Once again they stood face-to-face, breathing harshly. Their blood spilled onto the floor between them. Mortianna looked down at the pike piercing her just below the heart, and then she looked at Azeem with her cold crimson eyes. And slowly, terribly, she pulled herself along the pike toward him, forcing the shaft through her body so that she could get her hands on the man who'd killed her. Blood spattered onto the floor, and she grunted once as the pike head burst from her back, slick with blood. She smiled at Azeem, inching forward, refusing to die.

He pushed her away from him with the pike, and then released it, backing away from the uncanny hag as quickly as his injured leg would allow. Mortianna reached down and pulled the pike out of her body. She stood there for a moment, the weapon in her hand, watching blood flow thickly from the wound the pike had made. And then the unnatural strength seemed to flow out of her along with the blood, and she turned slowly away from Azeem, her eyes dull and unfocused. She staggered off down the corridor, leaving a trail of blood behind her. Azeem shook his head slowly, and tied a length of cloth tightly round his thigh. Questions could wait. He picked up the stone head and resumed pounding on the chapel door.

Inside the chapel, the Sheriff lay on top of Marian, pinning her to the floor with the weight of his body. He smiled down at her furious face and waited for the last words of the marriage ceremony from the Bishop. The Sheriff had lost all sense of time and place. The world had narrowed to this place, this moment, and this woman, and nothing else mattered. He would have Marian as his wife, and no one would stop him, and the pulse pounding in his head was louder than any pounding on the door. Marian struggled fiercely and wept tears of helpless rage, but he did not see them.

Robin looked out over the long drop to the courtyard below, took a firm hold on his end of the pennant, and then launched himself into space. He sailed out over the court-yard as the pennant unfurled, and then it reached the end of its length and snapped him round in a long arc, back toward the castle wall. The chapel window loomed up before him with heart-stopping speed, and he quickly changed his grip on the pennant to ensure he hit the window squarely. He crashed through the stained glass feet first, let go of the pennant, and hit the floor rolling.

The impact knocked the breath out of him, but he was still back on his feet in a moment, glaring about him, sword in hand. The Bishop gaped at him and then turned and bolted out the side door. Robin didn't notice. Like the Sheriff, his world had narrowed to the only things that mattered: Marian and the Sheriff. Robin moved slowly toward them. The Sheriff released Marian and rose unhurriedly to his feet. Marian seized the opportunity to roll away, pulling her clothes about her.

"Do you mind, Locksley?" said the Sheriff calmly. "Marian and I wish to be alone. We've just been married."

Robin lifted his sword. "Then prepare yourself for divorce, and your soul for Hell."

The Sheriff pulled his clothing straight and drew his sword. "Rushing to your death for the sake of a woman? Lust has made a fool of you. I want the bitch too, but I'm not foolish enough to die for her. Do you by any chance recognize this blade, Locksley?"

He showed Robin the hilt of his sword. It only took Robin a moment to recognize the crucifix sculpted into the hilt. It was his father's sword.

"That's right," said the Sheriff. "I killed your father, with his own sword. Appropriate, don't you think, that I should use it again to send you to meet him?"

Robin met his gaze steadily. "I have nothing to fear from my father's sword."

The two men moved toward each other, their swords reaching out to touch lightly.

The Bishop frantically scooped offerings from the church's coffers into the pocket of his traveling cloak and looked quickly round his chambers to see if there was anything else he might be able to take with him. He had to get out of Nottingham while he had the chance, but there was no point in leaving as a pauper. The door behind him swung open with a crash, and the Bishop whirled guiltily to see Friar Tuck standing in the doorway, his face set and grim and unforgiving. The Bishop looked at the cudgel in Tuck's hand and smiled at him uncertainly. Tuck did not smile.

"So," he said flatly. "It is true. You sold your soul to Satan. For rather more than thirty pieces of silver."

The Bishop drew himself up and glared at Tuck defiantly. "The Lord said 'Render unto Caesar what is Caesar's.' That's all I did. I swear it."

Tuck advanced slowly on the Bishop. "That is not all. You accused innocent men of Devil worship and let them be executed, knowing that black arts were being practiced here, in what should have been the center of faith and justice."

The Bishop smiled and shook his head, as at a pupil who had made a simple and understandable mistake. "This is all a terrible misunderstanding. Come, brother friar, I am sure you would not strike a fellow man of the cloth."

"Think again," said Tuck.

The Bishop shrugged, and then lashed out with the knife he'd surreptitiously drawn from his sleeve. Tuck side-stepped the blow with a speed surprising in a man of his girth, and swung his cudgel with all his weight behind it. The force of the blow caught the Bishop off balance and launched him backward. He crashed through the window behind him and disappeared from sight. It was a long drop, and he screamed all the way down.

Tuck looked out the window, and made the sign of the cross over the body lying still and broken on the ground below. He turned away, put down his cudgel, and helped himself to a generous glass of the late Bishop's wine.

"The Lord's will be done," he said solemnly. "With a little assistance."

Robin and the Sheriff dueled each other across the chapel and back, their swords coming together and flying apart too quickly for the watching eye to follow. Sparks flew on the air as the blades crashed together, but the only sounds in the chapel were the ring of steel on steel, the slap and slide of boots on the floor, and the harsh grunting and strained breathing of the two men as they strove to force themselves beyond their limits. This was their time, and they knew it; they would never fight again with such pure hate and fury, would never fight again with so much at stake.

Marian huddled under the blasphemous altar, out of the way, and looked frantically around for something she could use as a weapon. The main door shook and shuddered under Azeem's assault, but still it held, and she couldn't get past the two fighters to remove the crossbeam.

Robin blinked sweat out of his eyes and backed cautiously away as the Sheriff pressed home a new attack. Robin had always been better with a bow than a sword, and the Sheriff's skill more than equaled his. He pushed the thought aside angrily. He was good enough. He had to be. He and the Sheriff stamped and lunged, cut and thrust, back and forth across the chamber, neither able to gain the upper hand for long. Robin's breathing came fast and hurried, and his back and sword arm ached from constantly blocking the Sheriff's blows, but still he fought on, long after any other man would have weakened. He couldn't give up. He wasn't just fighting for himself. He was fighting for Marian, the woodsmen, and England itself.

Robin blocked a vicious cut from the Sheriff, but the force of the blow sent him staggering backward. The Sheriff laughed at him breathlessly, his eyes hot and wild.

"You're as weak as your God, Locksley."

He swung his blade in a long, low arc, and Robin gathered his failing strength and leapt above it. He landed well, and cut at the Sheriff while his opponent was still off balance. The Sheriff ducked, but Robin's sword still cut away a thick swath of his hair. Robin grinned wolfishly.

"If I have to, I'll take you a piece at a time, Nottingham."

He gestured mockingly at his cheek, reminding the Sheriff of where he'd marked him before. The Sheriff snarled at him like an animal.

"I will do the only taking today, dead man."

He whirled round suddenly, grabbed Marian by the arm, and dragged her out from under the altar. He pulled her into a savage kiss and then threw her away, laughing. Robin howled with rage and threw himself at the Sheriff. The two swords crashed together and Robin's blade shattered, broken in two by the superior weight and craftsmanship of the sword that had once been his father's. Robin backed quickly away, and tripped over the end of a shattered pew. He fell sprawling, and the hilt of his broken sword flew from his hand. The Sheriff loomed over him, the point of his sword reaching for Robin's throat. Robin looked despairingly at Marian, but she still lay where she'd been thrown, dazed by the force of her fall. The Sheriff glanced briefly at Marian and laughed softly.

"She's mine now!"

He drew back his sword for the killing thrust, drawing out the moment so he could savor it, and Robin snatched a dagger from inside his tunic and slammed it between the Sheriff's ribs. For a moment the tableau held, neither man moving, and then the Sheriff slowly lowered his sword and looked down at the knife hilt protruding from his ribs. He frowned slightly as he recognized the jeweled hilt of the dagger he'd given Marian as a present, and then nodded wearily, as though it were only to be expected. The weight of his sword pulled it out of his hand as his strength faded. The Sheriff bared his teeth in a humorless grin, pulled the dagger from his ribs in one quick movement, and advanced slowly on Marian.

Robin struggled to his feet and snatched up his father's sword. Marian got her feet under her and backed unsteadily away from the Sheriff, her blood running cold. The Sheriff sneered at her, dropped the dagger, and moved past her to collapse into the alcove by the shattered window. He stared out at the scene below, as his life's blood ran out of him. The woodsmen and the mob had routed his men, and were pouring into the castle. He looked back, at Robin and Marian standing together, and then down, at the growing bloodstain over his ribs.

"I wonder," he said hoarsely. "Who was Dad?" His face twisted as the pain wracked him, and he glared at Robin. The Sheriff swayed and fell, dead.

The chapel door finally flew open, and Azeem, Bull, and Little John burst in, ready for battle. They stopped as they saw the Sheriff's unmoving body, and lowered their weapons. Robin, relieved and exhausted, dropped his blade and moved toward Marian.

But from a tapestry behind him, a dark form appeared—it was Mortianna! She raised her knife and hissed with evil menace, poised to strike Robin. But Azeem was quicker. He picked up a nearby sword and let it fly. His aim was good.

With the sword in her chest, Mortianna fell. She writhed on the ground, clawing for the body of the Sheriff, trying to control him, even in death. Shuddering horribly, Mortianna gave one last death rattle and lay still.

Azeem turned to Robin. "I have fulfilled my vow, Christian."

Robin nodded with a tired grin. He took Marian into his arms, and for a long moment they stood together, losing themselves in each other. Marian raised a trembling hand to Robin's face, as though half-afraid he might disappear like a dream.

232

"You came for me! You are alive!"

Robin held her eyes with his. "I would die, before I let another man have you."

They kissed as if they were never going to stop. After a while, Azeem and Little John looked at each other and left the chapel, dragging the fascinated Bull with them.

It was a simple wedding, held in the heart of Sherwood, with Tuck as the priest and the woodsmen as congregation. Sunlight poured in golden shafts through a cathedral arch of forest green. Tuck's voice echoed richly on the quiet afternoon as he bound Robin and Marian to each other, and he smiled slightly as he came to the question that had to be asked, no matter how ridiculous it was.

"If any man know any reason why these two should not be joined together . . ."

"Hold!" The sudden voice was loud and authoritative. "I know a reason."

The stunned congregation whirled round to find themselves facing a huge mounted man in full armor. A ring of mounted soldiers surrounded him. There was a sudden rasp of steel on leather as the woodsmen drew their swords. Some nocked arrows to their bows and picked targets with cold calculation. Tuck reached out and seized his club. Little John and Will Scarlet moved forward to protect Robin, but he waved them back. There was something about the mounted man. . . . Robin watched narrowly as the huge figure dismounted and strode forward alone, to stand before Robin and Marian.

"Who interrupts my wedding?" said Robin.

The armored man pulled off his helmet to reveal a familiar face. "Your King, Robin of Locksley."

"Richard!" said Marian.

Robin and Marian and all the congregation dropped to one knee before him, and bowed their heads to King

Richard, the Lion-hearted. But none of them put away their weapons. King Richard noted this, and smiled slightly.

"You realize, I cannot allow this wedding to go forward . . ." he began, and then paused as Robin lifted his head and fixed the King with a cold, speculative gaze. The King smiled. ". . . without giving away the bride." His smile widened as he looked down at Marian. "You look radiant, cousin."

"We are deeply honored, Your Majesty," said Robin.

"It is I who am honored, Lord Locksley," said the King. "Thanks to you, I still have a throne. Proceed with the ceremony, good friar."

Tuck put aside his club and quickly finished the ceremony before any other interruptions could take place. Robin and Marian kissed, and everyone cheered.

"Save that," said Tuck, after a while. "We're wasting good drinking time."

They broke apart, laughing. Fanny and Wulf brought in a marvelous wedding cake, so huge it had to be carried in on its own trolley. Azeem presented Robin with a knife to cut it.

"I wish you many sons, my friend," he said solemnly. "And many daughters."

Hundreds of doves were released to mark the moment, and the sound of their wings filled the forest. And Robin and Marian and the woodsmen and King Richard celebrated together all through that day and long into the night, in the great green dream of Sherwood.